Lady Emily ; bk. 14

S0-ARO-849

IN THE SHADOW
OF VESUVIUS

IN THE SHADOW
OF VESUVIUS

TASHA ALEXANDER

WHEELER PUBLISHING
A part of Gale, a Cengage Company

Henderson County Public Library

Copyright © 2019 by Tasha Alexander.
A Lady Emily Mystery.
Wheeler Publishing, a part of Gale, a Cengage Company.

ALL RIGHTS RESERVED
This is a work of fiction. All of the characters, organizations, and events portrayed in this novel are either products of the author's imagination or are used fictitiously.
Wheeler Publishing Large Print Hardcover.
The text of this Large Print edition is unabridged.
Other aspects of the book may vary from the original edition.
Set in 16 pt. Plantin.

**LIBRARY OF CONGRESS CIP DATA ON FILE.
CATALOGUING IN PUBLICATION FOR THIS BOOK
IS AVAILABLE FROM THE LIBRARY OF CONGRESS**

ISBN-13: 978-1-4328-7652-4 (hardcover alk. paper)

Published in 2020 by arrangement with Macmillan Publishing Group, LLC/St. Martin's Press

Printed in Mexico
Print Number: 01   Print Year: 2020

For Erica, Gunther, and Xander.
I loved Menandering with you.

Pub

ACKNOWLEDGMENTS

Myriad thanks to . . .

Charlie Spicer, my fabulous editor, who loves Pompeii almost as much as I do.

My team at Minotaur: Sarah Grill, Andy Martin, Sarah Melnyk, Danielle Prielipp, David Rostein, and David Stanford Burr.

Anne Hawkins, Tom Robinson, and Annie Kronenberg: always the best.

Jonathan Santlofer, my dear friend who explained just how important the choice of pencil is to an artist.

Chiara Comegna, the erudite archaeologist and guide who shared invaluable insights during my exploration of the excavations at Pompeii, Herculaneum, and Oplontis.

My son, Alexander Tyska, for his moving

7

and precise translation of Virgil's words.

Brett Battles, Rob Browne, Bill Cameron, Christina Chen, Jon Clinch, Jamie Freveletti, Chris Gortner, Jane Grant, Nick Hawkins, Robert Hicks, Elizabeth Letts, Carrie Medders, Erica Ruth Neubauer, Missy Rightley, Renee Rosen, and Lauren Willig. Love you all.

My elegant and amazing stepdaughters Katie and Jess.

My parents. How I wish my dad could have read this book.

Andrew, my touchable dream.

Of the many misfortunes that have occurred in this world, no others have given posterity such joy.
— JOHANN WOLFGANG VON GOETHE,
WRITING ABOUT POMPEII

1
1902

Some corpses lie undisturbed longer than others. We expect that our own mortal remains, shrouded in silk, buried in mahogany coffins, and marked by granite stones, will be left untouched for eternity. So, too, did the Egyptians, whose mummified bodies now entertain the ghoulish among us at unwrapping parties. Their elaborate tombs offered no protection. Why should our fate be any different? Even the victims of the unexpected eruption of Mount Vesuvius nearly two thousand years ago, blanketed by impossibly deep layers of ash and pumice, have reemerged. Plaster casts, formed by archaeologists, allow tourists in Pompeii a glimpse of the terror and heartache of their final moments. None of us is safe from exposure after death.

Standing in the ruins of an ancient dining room, a triclinium, as the Romans called it, we — my husband, Colin Hargreaves, Ivy

Brandon, and I — had gathered around a group of these casts. Three walls remained, each covered with bright frescoes. The fourth side of the room, marked with columns, opened into a charming garden, in the center of which stood a fountain.

"They would have dined here in the summer," I said. "The chamber is positioned to take advantage of the angle of the sun at that time of year, flooding it with natural light. The columns frame the outdoor features beautifully, and —"

"I never would've thought the Romans wore sideburns," Ivy said, crouching next to one of the casts. "This gentleman looks as if he stepped off the streets of London last week."

Ivy, who since we were children had tried to provide a tempering influence on my more outrageous iconoclastic impulses, was not prone to interrupting anyone. From the earliest days of our acquaintance, I had observed her effortlessly perfect manners, but had never managed to emulate them. Her patience was unmatched. Once — from a safe distance — I watched her listen for more than half an hour, an expression of rapt attention on her face, to a dull MP drone on about some speech he had given in the Commons that afternoon. She never tried to get in a single word.

My husband struggled not to laugh. "Emily, you'd best stop lecturing," he said. "No detail about ancient dining rooms can compete with the gruesome pleasure of the mortal remains they contain." I turned back to the casts. Two of them, a woman and a male slave, identifiable by her hairstyle and his thick belt, curled in fetal positions, she covering her face with her arms, he frozen for eternity with one hand stretched toward the sky. The third, which Ivy was examining, lay with his arms at his sides, one knee bent, the other straight.

"Did you say sideburns, Ivy?" I asked. "The Romans didn't wear them. Not like that." I forced myself to kneel beside my friend. I like to believe that, after more than a decade spent investigating heinous murders, I am capable of remaining undaunted in the face of violent death. I have observed a multitude of bodies in a variety of hideous states and, while always grieved that any human should suffer such an end, I can compartmentalize these emotions in order to pursue justice for the dead. Yet almost from the moment I stepped into the ruins at Pompeii, the tragedy of the site overwhelmed me. I could hardly bear to look at the casts, let alone scrutinize them. Their humanity was all too palpable.

Colin squatted on the other side of the man. "This doesn't look right." He pulled a penknife from his pocket and began to dig into the plaster.

"Don't!" I reached to stop him. "This is an archaeological site. You can't —"

"This man is no Roman, at least not an ancient one," he said, his deep voice calm as he continued to remove bits of the cast from the man's arm. Chalky flakes fell away under his blade, revealing a patch of grayish-blue skin. "I shan't go any further. If he were a victim of Vesuvius, we would find hollow space beneath the plaster, not flesh. Our friend here has not been buried long enough to decay. I'd wager he hasn't been dead more than a few weeks."

Ivy's brown eyes widened and the color drained from her rosy cheeks. She turned away from the cast, struggled to her feet, and was sick behind a convenient cypress tree.

We had arrived in Pompeii four days earlier, traveling at Ivy's invitation. She had recently made the acquaintance of two Americans, a brother and sister, Benjamin and Calliope Carter. He, a moody painter, and she, an enthusiastic archaeologist, were preparing to leave London to work for an American called Balthazar Taylor at what many consider the world's greatest ancient site. My friend's gentle kindness endeared her to everyone she encountered, and soon after meeting the siblings, she hatched a scheme to follow them to Italy. Knowing of my passion for the ancient world, she invited me to join her.

Inseparable in our youth, Ivy and I had not seen much of each other of late. My work and her devotion to motherhood — at last count, she had a brood of six — meant that our paths no longer crossed with regularity, but this was not indicative of a loss of affection between us. When she asked me to accompany her on her excursion abroad, I rejoiced at the chance to rekindle our friendship. Colin, whose discreet work for the Palace now included special attention to King Edward VII's personal protection, was harder to bring around, but was at last convinced by a sly move on the part of Ivy's husband, who could not abide the idea of his wife traveling with only a solitary female companion. I adore Robert, but his views can be rather old-fashioned.

On this occasion, I was profoundly grateful for his outdated morals. When Colin hesitated, Robert went straight to the king, who went straight to my husband, bursting into our library in Park Lane before our butler could announce him. *Hargreaves, old chap, you can't let the ladies down. They need a chaperone, and there's none better than you,* His Majesty had said. Colin knew the futility of arguing with Bertie (I would never be able to think of him as Edward, the Seventh or otherwise), but that was not what persuaded him. Robert — and the king — had appealed to his sense of duty, something Colin would never shirk. And so, by the next morning, my husband was organizing the details of our trip. I suspect he took no small measure of delight in leaving London. A gentleman driven by honor and principle, he had never held the king in high regard. Bertie, during his tenure as Prince of Wales, had proven more interested in gambling, mistresses, and cruel pranks than in useful occupation, and as a result, Colin had nothing but scorn for him.

The only disappointment that stemmed from our trip was the knowledge that another mutual friend, Margaret Michaels, was unable to join us. After a decade of marriage to an extremely even-tempered Oxford don, she was not-so-eagerly awaiting the arrival of her first child and had expressed in no uncertain terms how unfair

16

it was that she be excluded from the adventure. The baby, she said, was sure to be a delight, but if she could have hired a servant to give birth in her place, no sum would have been too great to pay.

Colin found for us a charming villa south of modern Pompeii, only a few miles from the excavations with sweeping vistas of the Bay of Naples in one direction and of Mount Vesuvius in the other. After an uneventful journey, we were soon comfortably settled and ready to tour the ruins. The Carter siblings proved able guides, giving us a splendid overview of the site.

"You must call me Callie," Miss Carter said, when we first met her under the brick arch of Pompeii's Marina Gate. "Calliope is such a mouthful, ironic for the muse of epic poetry and eloquence, don't you think? Dear old papa loved the classics. I'm fortunate he didn't decide to call me Polyhymnia or Euterpe." She was considerably shorter than I, but gave the impression she could command an army battalion without visible effort. With Titian hair and a voice so melodious she would have sounded as if she were singing if she didn't speak with such an assertive rhythm, the name suited her. Her alluring figure was more like that found on an ancient depiction of Aphrodite than the pigeon breast silhouette favored by the current crop of fashionists, and although her face, with a spattering of freckles across her nose, could not be described as beautiful or even pretty, it was undeniably intriguing. Her eyes, hazel, with flecks of green that would perfectly suit some legendary Irish queen, flashed with intelligence.

Her brother, Benjamin, bore almost no resemblance to her, at least not physically. His features were as unremarkable as hers were beguiling, but his fiery temperament mirrored Callie's. He explained that his expertise was not in archaeology, but as an artist. He had exhibited his work at two small shows in New York before they came abroad and now hoped the Italian landscape would inspire him to the greatness that, so far, had eluded him.

"Callie insisted I take this position so she might have access to Mr. Taylor," he said. "She was convinced — rightly so — that, faced with the force of her personality, he would take her on as well." His sister's tenacity impressed me; it was not so easy in those days for a woman to earn a place in an archaeological expedition.

The excavations at Pompeii go back hundreds of years. We have records of accidental finds from as early as the late fifteen hundreds, but it was not until the eighteenth century that digging began in earnest. The Kings of Naples, especially Ferdinand IV, who had the questionable taste to commission a sculpture of himself as Minerva (still on display at the museum in Naples; you may judge for yourself the value of this work), were responsible for the first large-scale exploration of the site. They were motivated not by the quest for knowledge, but for treasure, and were little better than the charlatans who pillaged Egypt in the early part of the nineteenth century. Desirous of acquiring personal collections that could rival those of other European monarchs, they ordered their minions to ruthlessly cut paintings from walls, destroyed items they deemed not valuable enough, and, when faced with a group of sculptures of similar subjects, would keep the one in the finest condition and smash the others. All responsible scholars shudder at their methods.

Fortunately, after the unification of Italy in the 1860s, a man called Giuseppe Fiorelli took charge of the site. A remarkable individual and an archaeologist beyond reproach, Fiorelli grasped the importance of his role. He mapped the city, numbering every block, building, and door, and insisted that private residences and shops, as well as the spectacular public structures, be excavated. He sought information, not merely art, and cunningly began to create narratives about the lost city and its inhabitants that resonated with the public, ensuring widespread support for his work. He founded a national school for archaeology, and his perfection of the system used for creating the plaster casts of the volcano's victims forever preserved the memory of the city's ancient citizens, drawing droves of tourists to the site. I cannot condemn them as I do those who unwrap mummies in their parlors. Humans have an infinite capacity for morbid curiosity, but Fiorelli's casts give us something more: a glimpse into individual personalities that we rarely see in the ancient world.

Even so, they troubled me. Looking at those faces, frozen at the moment of their deaths, engulfed me in a deluge of emotion through which I could not wade. But now, faced with a fresh corpse instead of one two thousand years old, I found myself once again able to compartmentalize.

"I'll send for the police," Colin said, handing Ivy a clean handkerchief after she'd finished being sick. He turned away while she cleaned herself up and ran a hand through his tousled curls. "Perhaps you, Emily, would be so good as to inform the archaeologists of our find?"

2
AD 79

These dark days, engulfing me with gloom
and hopelessness, have inspired me to write
my story, the narrative of a woman silenced
while simultaneously being one of the best-
known poets of her time. In Pompeii, at
least. But that is the fate of slaves, is it not?
Even after they purchase their freedom. I
must go back in time now, and explain how
all this came to be.

I am officially Quinta Flavia Kassandra,
my first two names taken from the man who
owned me, Quintus Flavius Plautus, but I
have always been known only as Kassandra.
My father, Aristeides, named me for the
doomed princess of Troy. Apollo gave her
the gift of prophecy, but when she refused
to become his lover, he cursed her, con-
demning her to a fate in which no one
would ever believe her predictions. Hence
my father's choice. I was born a slave,
destined to have a voice that would never

be heard.

He was a scholar and philosopher, born in Athens, the most glorious city in the world. At least to hear him tell it. My mother hailed from Macedonia, the land of the great Alexander, and gave me her golden hair and lapis blue eyes. Pirates attacked the ship meant to carry them to Ephesus, and they soon found themselves in Pompeii's slave market, my mother heavy with the child they had years ago given up hope of ever having. Plautus's steward, a man of uncommon kindness, bought both my parents. They might have had a happy life in their master's house, if she had not died bringing me into the world during our city's last great earthquake.

Greek to the core, Father railed against all things Roman, but even he could not deny we had landed in circumstances not altogether horrendous. Well educated and wealthy beyond measure, Plautus installed my father as the tutor of his children and gave him charge of the family's substantial library. I grew up alongside my master's daughter, Octavia Lepida, born on the same day as me, and although my station required that I do whatever she asked, we were more like friends than mistress and slave. Her mother, Claudia, the quintessential Roman

23

matron — noble, capable, loyal, and beautiful — never allowed her children to treat their inferiors badly. I was educated with Lepida and her brothers until the boys went off to school. After that, Lepida focused on the skills essential to a good wife, spending hours at her loom and assisting her mother with the household accounts and management. My duties expanded to include dressing Lepida's silky raven hair and learning how to artfully apply cosmetics to her smooth face, but I always preferred reading aloud to her, from the enormous collection of scrolls in the library.

The habit had started when we were quite young. Lepida plagued me with questions about Greece, a place I had never been and of which I had no real knowledge. All I could do was recount for her the myths my father had told me, charming her with my use of the gods' Greek names. As a Roman, she was taken with all things Greek, confident in her belief that, while there was no place better than Rome, there was no culture superior to the Greeks'. We would sit in the peristyle garden, doric columns around its perimeter, our bare feet in the fountain, the flowers of *Citrus medica* trees fluttering above us as we lamented the tragic fate of Orpheus and Eurydice, Hero and

Leander, Pyramus and Thisbe.

I adored all things Roman and argued frequently with my father about the merits of the empire. He admonished me to remember my heritage; I was a Greek. But how could this be, when I had been born under Roman rule and had never set foot in the land of my ancestors?

By the summer of my fifteenth year, Lepida and I had grown out of telling myths, replacing them with poetry. I read Homer to her — she insisted — and then Virgil. We would hide from her mother and exclaim over Ovid's *Amores* and *Ars Amatoria,* half-delighted, half-horrified. *We take no pleasure in permitted joys. / But what's forbidden is more keenly sought.* We wondered if we would ever fall in love. Lepida wanted a soldier, because the great poet wrote *lovers are soldiers,* but I was more taken with another of his lines: *Let love be introduced in friendship's dress.*

We stretched out on couches at the family's villa beyond the city walls, our eyes drawn to the endless blue of the Bay of Naples below us and speculated about the men we would love. Lepida would have a husband, but I, a slave, could not officially marry. Not until my father had saved enough money to buy our freedom. I knew he would, eventually, and then I would be on my way to becoming a Roman matron in my own right.

Obsessed with our visions of strong men who would love us in all the ways Ovid promised, it was natural that we both noticed a new-comer to the house. Plautus, one of the top men in Pompeii, had many powerful friends, but until Titus Livius Silvanus appeared, we paid no attention to any of them. Tall, bronzed from the sun, broad shouldered, with dark hair cropped close, he carried himself with an impressive air of confidence, his wool toga draped over his left arm. Lepida spotted him first and pulled me through the atrium to the doorway of her father's tablinium, where he met with his clients. The two men were engaged in conversation about a business concern of some sort. We had no interest in their words.

"I'm certain he was a soldier," Lepida said, whispering as we peeked into the room, not wanting to draw their attention. "Look how he holds himself."

"His voice sounds kind," I replied. "And I like his eyes."

"What are you girls doing?" Plautus said. "Mean you to interrupt us?"

We giggled. We were young.

He waved for us to come into the room

and introduced us to the visitor. Two weeks later, we both considered Silvanus a friend. Three weeks after that, Lepida was engaged to him. The following week, when he returned his fiancée to the house after a banquet, he asked to see me alone. I was a slave; I knew what that meant. My life would never be the same.

3
1902

I left Ivy in Callie's capable hands after informing Augustus Mau, an exceptional German archaeologist, whose work at Pompeii will always be held in the highest regard, about our discovery and then made my way back to the house containing the modern corpse. The building, only partially excavated, was out of the way of the better-known stops in the city. Whoever had placed his victim there had chosen wisely; not many tourists would bother to make the trek to such an isolated location when there were so many other splendid places to explore. Here, instead of ancient façades, embankments of earth rose from the street on either side of me, waiting for archaeologists to uncover their hidden secrets.

I picked my way through stones and bricks, thankful for my sturdy boots. Returning to the triclinium filled me with solemn sorrow, and I said a quick prayer for all three sets of mortal remains in front of me. Then, I turned my attention to the one that did not belong. The man's clothes must have been removed, as there was no sign of them in the plaster covering him. If it were not for his facial hair, no one would have ever questioned his presence. Sideburns of that sort — thick and long — had gone out of fashion ages ago, but there were still some men who wore them. Perhaps our victim was older, clinging to the style of his youth, or perhaps he was an eccentric, who cared not for the opinions of others.

There was no sign of fresh plaster anywhere in the house, and an exhaustive search of the premises revealed nothing I could tie to the crime. I heard the crunch of footsteps behind me and turned to see Colin, Benjamin Carter, and another gentleman, whom my husband introduced as Mr. Taylor.

"It is an absolute pleasure to meet you, Lady Emily." He spoke with the brash confidence so often found in Americans and swept up my hand to kiss it. "I apologize for the circumstances, but Hargreaves here tells me you're no stranger to death. If there is anything at all I can provide to make the situation more bearable, do not hesitate to ask." Thunder sounded, and a soft rain began to fall. A shiver ran through me. No one can feel entirely at ease hearing any sort of rumble so near a volcano.

"You look anxious, Lady Emily, but fear not. It won't erupt." Mr. Taylor smiled — revealing an astonishing set of large white teeth — but then his face fell and he turned to his employee. "I wish I hadn't agreed to let you work here, Carter. There's something unsettling about thinking of you painting so close to a fresh corpse."

"Your dig is beyond the city walls," I said. "Why was Benjamin working here?"

"Carter is an artist of astonishing technical skill. There's not much for him yet at our site — we're still in early days — and knowing watercolors are his preferred medium, I had a word with Ettore Pais, the director of the excavations. He agreed to let the boy do a series of paintings and put together a list of the places and objects he wants included," Mr. Taylor said. "Various expeditions have done engravings and taken photographs of the buildings in the city, but I prefer paintings. They better capture the essence of the originals."

"You're quite right on that count," Benjamin said. "Photographs are at once perfect and a cold, soulless disaster. I'm fortunate to have an employer who recognizes this."

He glanced at the casts and then quickly looked away. "I was hoping to see the body before the police arrive. Does that make me sound morbid?"

It did, but I refrained from answering his question. I was accustomed to this sort of creepy curiosity and categorized the young man as someone likely to attend mummy unwrapping parties. "Were all three here when you were working?"

Benjamin cocked his head as he studied the casts on the ground before us. "I can't say with any certainty. You begin to get inured to them. If you didn't, it would be impossible to get anything done."

"True words, Carter," Mr. Taylor said. "I like to believe such things don't bother me, but I can hardly bring myself to look at them. Their faces . . . seeing them haunts me."

This, I could understand. Pompeii overwhelmed, not simply due to its scope, but because of the constant reminders of what Vesuvius did to the people in the city. The casts forced us to face mortality, that of those already dead, and our own, as well. "You made no mention of them in your notes?" I asked.

"I have no need for notes. I'd come only to copy the frescoes — they're in extraordi-

31

nary shape, which is why this house was partially excavated when nothing else around it was. I'm told some treasure hunters found it first and were frightened off by the Germans."

"When was this?" Colin asked.

Benjamin frowned and squirmed, shaking his head. "A year or two ago, maybe? I'm not certain."

"There's no reason you should know, Carter. This is only your first season and you're an artist, not an archaeologist," Mr. Taylor said, his attitude toward his employee magnanimous. "I've funded digs in Pompeii for more than a decade, and have studied the site extensively. Mau excavated here three years ago and no one — aside from Carter doing his paintings — is currently working in this part of the city."

"Secluded and abandoned," Benjamin said. "The perfect place to stash a body. Who would notice another lost soul in a city of the dead?" He had circled the casts, but did not look closely at any of them, keeping a careful distance, as if their presence disturbed him, his actions at odds with his earlier eagerness to see the body.

"Is there anything we can do to help, Hargreaves?" Mr. Taylor asked.

"No, thank you," Colin said. "There's

nothing to be done until the police arrive."

"You know where to find me if you require assistance." Mr. Taylor adjusted his hat and took his leave, Benjamin following close behind. The police did not arrive for hours, and it took them an inordinately long time to remove the body. The chief inspector, prone to frequent sighs, inspired no confidence, and I insisted that we accompany them back to the coroner's office in Naples.

By the time we returned to the villa, it was after midnight, but Ivy was still awake, a piece of embroidery she'd been working on the previous day untouched in her lap. "It's so odd," she said, scrunching her perfect brow and twisting a handkerchief in her hands. "I find myself unaccountably captivated by the ancient dead. I want to sketch all of them and imagine the stories of their lives. I'm drawn to them, not out of morbid curiosity, but by something else, as if their mortal remains can somehow reveal their whole history as individuals. Yet this new death . . . that cast was identical to the rest on the surface, but knowing that his whole body was inside, intact, not just a skeleton . . . his family not yet aware of his fate. It . . ." She swallowed hard.

"It is a wholly different thing," Colin said,

his deep voice reassuring. "You need not explain."

"What did you learn from the coroner?" she asked.

"Very little," I said. "Our victim was strangled and has been dead for approximately a month. The plaster slowed decomposition to some degree. The police, who are singularly unhelpful, haven't the slightest idea who he might be. I made a rough sketch of his face, but I haven't half your talent as an artist."

Ivy, who breathed life into everything she drew, reached out and gently touched the paper I held in front of her. "He could be anyone. What a tragic end to a life." She sighed and then started to laugh, softly at first, then more loudly, until it consumed her.

"Are you quite well?" Colin asked. "Shall I fetch you something to drink? Some brandy, perhaps?"

"No, forgive me," she said. "I assure you I'm not descending into hysteria, only thinking of my dear Robert. He wanted you, Colin, to provide Emily and me with a respectable chaperone on this trip, and here we are, embroiled in intrigue and investigating a murder. Not what he had in mind for our holiday."

The next morning, Colin received word that the police were not planning to return to Pompeii, instead asking him to see if any of the archaeologists at the site recognized the man in my sketch. Ivy, fully recovered from her shock, accompanied us, and, before long, we had learned the dead man's name. Karl Richter, one of Herr Mau's workers, identified him as a journalist who, a few years earlier, had visited the site while researching an article.

"There can be no doubt. It is Walker, Clarence Walker," Herr Richter said. "He's a man of impeccable integrity. Works for *The Times* in New York. I was the one tasked with giving him an overview of how we approach a dig —" his voice faltered. "He had a guide called Mario Sorrentino, but Walker wanted to understand something about the method of archaeology and asked me to school him in the basics."

"Do you know where we might find this Sorrentino?" Colin asked.

"I couldn't say. Assuming he still works here, you could try early or late in the day at the ticket booth. All the guides loiter around there. You say that Walker returned to Pompeii and was killed then? I can't imagine that he would have come back."

"It's not unusual for a person to want to revisit such a spectacular place," Ivy said.

"Quite right," he said. "But the ruins didn't captivate Walker the way they do so many others. He appreciated them, understood their significance, but in an academic way. They did not tug at his soul. I do not mean this as criticism. He was attentive and asked probing questions — he wanted to do his job well. He had that uncanny ability to make you feel, when he talked to you, as if there was no one in the world more interesting or important, and he showed genuine enthusiasm for the excitement and pleasure I take from my work. I enjoyed my time with him, brief though it was."

"Did anything odd or unexpected happen when you were with him?" Colin asked.

"Not that I can recall," Herr Richter said.

"The piece he was working on, was it published?" I asked.

"Yes, I still have a copy at my home in Berlin. He sent it to me, thanking me for my assistance, such as it was."

"Did you see him when he returned to the site?" I asked. "It wouldn't have been much more than a month ago."

"No. I would have thought he'd get in

36

touch, even if only to say hello. I had no idea he came back."

"Hallo! I was hoping I might find you, Mr. Hargreaves, around here somewhere. It's always good to see you, Richter." A lanky gentleman approached, the fine layer of dust coating his clothes identifying him as an archaeologist, his brash accent American to its core. "I'm James Stirling, director of Taylor's dig. Apologies for not waiting for a formal introduction, but I understand you're hoping to identify the unfortunate fellow you found yesterday. I wonder if I could see the sketch?"

My husband extended his hand to the man before introducing Ivy and me. "You weren't at the dig this morning when we came by."

"No, Taylor and I had a meeting with Pais to go over some details of our plans," Mr. Stirling said. I handed him the drawing. "I don't know him, I'm afraid, but how terribly sad that he's dead." His voice grew quieter, hardly above a whisper. "*Manibus date lilia plenis.* Give lilies with full hands."

"What a lovely phrase," Ivy said.

"It's Virgil, from the *Aeneid,*" the American replied.

"Walker was a journalist," Herr Richter said, "but visited before you came to work

37

for Taylor."

"This is only my second season at Pompeii. Taylor didn't bring me on board until he decided to embark on a bigger project than the ones he'd funded in the past," Mr. Stirling explained. "Does Walker's family know yet? They must be devastated."

"No doubt they will be," Colin said. "They have not yet been notified."

The color drained from Mr. Stirling's face. "Forgive me. I am a coward in the face of death. The thought of receiving such news — particularly given the violent circumstances of the poor man's demise — is so very troubling."

"Mr. Walker returned to Pompeii about a month ago," I said. "You might have seen him then."

"No . . . no, I didn't." He sighed. "I wish I could offer more than condolences. *Mors ultima linea rerum est.* Death is everything's final limit. The poet Horace." He turned and walked away without another word, Ivy staring at him as he went.

Colin frowned. "Strange bloke."

"Yes, perhaps," Herr Richter said. "But kind to a fault."

"Kind or not, there's something odd about him," my husband said as we left Herr Richter to his work. "Emily, if you

38

don't object to finishing these interviews on your own — you're more than capable — I could inform the police of our victim's identity. I don't like keeping this sort of news from a family longer than necessary. I'll plan to rendezvous with you later. Let's meet at the ancient amphitheater."

After he took his leave, Ivy and I spoke to every person working in the *scavi* — excavations — but learned little more about Mr. Walker. A few of the Germans recognized him, but could offer no insight into his character beyond that which Herr Richter had already shared. One of the Italians lauded his generosity, explaining that the journalist had brought a bag of oranges for them to share after he and his guide had visited them. Beyond that, those who recalled him described him as sincere and earnest, but not all that interested in Pompeii itself. None of them admitted to having seen him when he returned to the city.

It had rained throughout the night, but the morning sun had dried all but the most stubborn puddles in the city. A little after noon, we stopped for luncheon in front of the ruins of a thermopolium, a casual sort of restaurant common in Roman cities. On the wall above where tables would have stood, there was a glorious fresco showing two gladiators engaged in combat. Tempting though it was to place on the ancient countertop — covered with colorful pieces of marble — the basket packed for us by the cook at our villa, we didn't want to damage the site, and instead sat on the curb in front of the shop.

"A well-chosen location," Callie called to us, her voice like a song. "Although when the place was teeming with people, you never would've wanted to sit there. Your feet would be dangling into the filthy water constantly flowing through the streets carrying the city's refuse with it. I've been looking for you all morning. I hear you've got a picture of the dead man. Will you think me morbid if I want to see it?"

"Not in the least," I said. "I was surprised not to see you at Mr. Taylor's site when we were there earlier."

"Apologies for that. I got a rather late start after a diabolical night. Argument with my brother. I adore the boy, but he can be a trial." I passed her my sketch. The color drained from her face, she tilted her head, blinked twice, and then threw her hands in the air. "I know him. Well, I don't *know* him, but I recognize his face. We were never introduced. He was on our ship from New York. I saw him on deck nearly every day when I was taking my morning constitutional."

"You never spoke to him?" I asked.

"No, I don't engage strange men in conversation unless they are intriguing in some irresistible way. This one was rather ordinary and old-fashioned. The sideburns were a dreadful mistake. Terrible to speak ill of the dead and all that, but there it is. There was another man, one of the crew, whom I found rather fascinating. Spent more than a few evenings with him. A sailor of exquisite skill."

"Exquisite skill at reciting poetry, I assume?" I was annoyed to feel hot color on my cheeks.

Callie flashed a wicked smile. "Quite, Emily. Reciting poetry. What a delicious man he was. Very strong. I do hope he's on board during my return voyage. But, to the matter at hand. What do you know about Mr. Walker?"

Ivy, who had sat as still as a statue while Callie spoke, stirred now. "Not much beyond his name. It's dreadfully sad."

"Actually, we hadn't mentioned his name," I said. "How did you know it?"

"Gossip flies faster than Mercury's winged slippers. Every archaeologist in Pompeii is talking about the murdered journalist."

41

"Did you recognize his name when you heard it?" I asked.

"No. I wasn't here when he was researching his piece for the newspaper."

"But you were here when he returned," I said. "You arrived on the same ship. Did you see him after you disembarked?"

"No, but I'd have taken notice if I had. The coincidence of running into him would've been quite a surprise. It's rather unnerving, all of it." She drew a deep breath and paused before she started speaking again. "I'd better get back to work. I do hope we can speak more about this. Not that I can contribute anything, but I admit to being hideously fascinated by the man. He's the only victim of murder I've ever known."

"You said you didn't know him," Ivy said.

"Correct, but I saw him when he was alive, and that's enough to give me chills."

"Why don't you and your brother join us for dinner this evening?" Ivy asked. "Although I'd prefer we talk about archaeology rather than murder."

"Thank you. I accept for us both. Benjamin will be eternally grateful," Callie said. "He complains constantly about the quality of our meals." We watched as she walked away, her flaming hair barely contained under a pith helmet, and the neat suit she wore flattering her curvy figure.

"An interesting lady," I said. "I suspect she knew Mr. Walker better than she admitted. Did you see her face when she looked at the picture? If she got a late start in the morning, why would she be wandering around Pompeii instead of getting straight to work?"

"What do you think she meant by that story, about the sailor?" Ivy asked. "Surely she didn't — she wouldn't —"

"I'm quite certain she would and she did. We aren't in the nineteenth century any longer. Morals are changing with shocking speed."

"Not that radically, I hope. I'm terribly fond of Callie, yet . . . well. You've always been more of a New Woman than I, but surely this shocks even you?"

"Yes, a bit, although it would be naïve to believe this sort of thing doesn't happen. That she would be so free about referring to it, in the presence of new acquaintances, is what surprises me. It's one thing to do it, quite another to speak about it."

"Dear me, aren't we a couple of dowdy matrons?"

"We might be matrons, technically speaking, but we are not dowdy in the least," I

43

said. "I commend Callie, who, I'm quite certain can't be more than five years younger than us. She is living life on her own terms, and that's to be much admired. Even if I would choose a slightly different path."

"Slightly different?"

"Colin was awfully tempting before we were married."

"Emily! You didn't?"

"Of course not." I paused for a moment, basking in the memory of my husband's courtship: the way his dark eyes seemed to see through me, the rich, undeniably sensual tone of his baritone voice, and the ever-so-pleasant feelings that consumed me when we used to waltz in my library at Berkeley Square. "Perhaps it was a lost opportunity. There's always a special thrill to the forbidden, or so they say."

4
AD 79

That fateful night, when I followed Silvanus into a small room off the peristyle of Lepida's father's house, I was convinced I knew what to expect. Plautus did not allow anyone in his family to use slaves in this way; he considered it weak and unbecoming, but I had heard stories about what went on in other households. Nerves consumed me — delicious, tantalizing nerves — as he closed the door behind us and turned to face me. I could not imagine a man more handsome. His noble features were perfectly Roman. He ought to hold a high-ranking position in the government, be a tribune, a consul. Poets should write epics about him. I held my breath as he stepped toward me. I wanted to close my eyes and lose myself in the moment, but at the same time, I could not bear to look away from his face.

"You are a fascinating girl, Kassandra," he said, turning from me and lowering himself onto a chair. "I hear you are a poet. Is this true?"

This question came wholly unexpected, and I hardly knew how to respond. I was a slave, he a patrician. He need not waste time seducing me with words. "It is true, yes, but my skills are not well developed. Not yet."

"You speak freely."

"You asked me a direct question. I gave you a direct answer."

"Plautus is impressed with your talent. You recited for him a poem you wrote about Aeneas. I would like to hear it."

"My poem about Aeneas?" My brow crinkled. "It is of little consequence, I assure you. I only meant it as an homage to Virgil. You might prefer that I recite some of the *Aeneid* instead."

"I know Virgil as well as I know my own thoughts," he said, leaning forward and resting his elbows on his knees. "Give me your poetry."

I stood in front of him, but said nothing.

"You are shy now?" Was he flirting? I couldn't tell. "I beg you to bring back your earlier confidence. A poem. One of your own. Now."

I drew a deep breath, closed my eyes, and began to recite, no longer wanting to look at him, terrified to see his reaction to my immature, derivative work. I gave him only a few lines.

"Look at me, Kassandra." His voice, commanding and deep, must be obeyed. So I obeyed. A slave has no choice. He was staring at me, his dark eyes full of question, but I saw no criticism in them. "You do have talent, my little Greek girl. A flair for language. I will come again and expect to hear more. I won't be satisfied with only a handful of lines next time." He rose from the chair and stepped forward, standing so close I could feel his breath on my lips, but he did not touch me. Without another word, he turned and left the room. I felt more vulnerable than if he had taken me. Words, I learned that evening, can have more power than anything physical.

5
1902

As the afternoon faded, and Ivy and I finished our interviews — Mr. Taylor and a number of others remembered meeting Mr. Walker, but no one was able to give us much that illuminated the dead man's character — the time came to meet Colin at the amphitheater. Questions about Callie and Mr. Stirling swirled in my head as we walked, but our surroundings distracted me from adequately contemplating them. Pompeii mesmerized me. It was impossible not to catch glimpses of the past, standing in the exact spot ancient people had so long ago, feeling the acute pain of the heartbreak of their final moments. It was intoxicating and frightening, a lure I couldn't resist.

The sun having grown quite hot, Ivy snapped open her parasol and admonished me to do the same, but I liked the feeling of the heat on my face. "Your mother would be horrified and warn you of freckles," my friend said.

"Despite having spent most of my youth avoiding parasols, the promised freckles have not yet developed. At any rate, I welcome the ruin of my complexion. It will add character to my face." The clusters of tourists around us were all heading in the direction of the Teatro Scoperto, the Great Theater, where the German archaeologists were currently at work, but we followed the Via dell'Abbondanza past the Stabian Baths, to where it turned into the Strada dei Diadumeni. Much of this area was unexcavated, and we paused as we crossed the hill to look down on the ruined city beneath us. "How can destruction be so beautiful?"

"It's a conundrum," Ivy said, slipping her arm through mine. "I wonder if, before the city was razed, there were ladies like us, best of friends for ages, then not so close after their families married them off to stern Roman politicians. Perhaps they found each other again, as Vesuvius started to rain fire down on their city, and they escaped, together."

"Fire did not rain down on the city. More like pumice and ash."

"Don't spoil my romantic picture. Would our wretched stern politician husbands have saved us, do you think?"

"No, we would have saved them. Unless we were escaping from them as much as from the eruption."

"Perhaps we would have been in love with gladiators. They could've saved us."

"We wouldn't need saving, Ivy, in this time or any other," I said. "But surely you don't find gladiators appealing? They were brutal killers."

"Handsome, strong, brutal killers, forced to do their evil work," Ivy said, her soft brown eyes glowing. "I would've bought them all and freed them if I were alive then."

"I don't think it was quite so simple."

"That, my dear friend, is the beauty of fantasizing about the past," she said. "We can make it anything we like."

"I shall evermore think of you as She Who Frees Gladiators," I said.

We had reached the amphitheater, where the Pompeiians would have watched Ivy's gladiators in *spectacula*. Built in the early days after the Romans colonized Campania, the structure was vastly older than Rome's famous Coliseum. When first excavated, its frescoes were nearly intact, but, like so much else, they were destroyed or stolen in our supposedly enlightened modern age, and now all that remains are copies of the originals. We entered, not through the vomitorium, as the ancients would have, but through the tunnels used by Ivy's gladiators, and saw Colin sitting high in the seats of the *summa cavea,* where the members of the lowest classes would have been relegated. He stood and hailed us as we climbed to meet him.

"I assume you chose this spot because you object to the senatorial class and the wealthy being the only ones allowed in the best seats?" I asked after giving him what could be considered a rather scandalous kiss of greeting.

"You know me too well, my dear." His dark eyes sparkled in a way that made me wish we were alone, but his countenance grew serious. "Sit. We have much to discuss. A telegram is en route to Mr. Walker's family to notify them of his death, and arrangements for formal identification and the return of his remains to the States organized. The police consider the case closed."

"Closed?" I had far too much experience with the incompetence of official investigations for this to surprise me, but felt outraged nonetheless. "They know who killed him? Already?"

"I said they *consider* the case closed, not that they've actually solved it. I suspected we'd run into something like this. This part

51

of Italy is a nest of corruption and crime. The Camorra, a criminal organization, control much of the area, although their power has lately waned. Apparently, Mr. Walker penned an article about their failure to get their preferred candidate elected in Naples last year, and the police are satisfied that his death was retribution for what the Camorra view as an insult from the journalist."

"Retribution isn't effective if one disguises and hides the victim," I said. "Have they made an arrest?" I asked.

"They don't often arrest members of the Camorra."

"How convenient. Should I ever decide to join the criminal underground, Naples shall be my first stop." I frowned. "Do you think the Camorra are responsible?"

"It's possible, but we have no evidence to support the theory beyond a piece in a New York newspaper that unlikely anyone here would have seen."

"There are loads of immigrants in New York, aren't there?" Ivy asked. "Perhaps one of them read it and sent it to family here."

Colin nodded. "Possible, but unsatisfying. We have the murder of a foreigner, no immediate clues, no idea as to where the killing occurred, and only a vague notion as to its timing. Easier for the police to pin the crime on the Camorra and move on to cases they have a better chance of solving."

"What would this criminal society think of being blamed?" Ivy asked. "Would they take it lying down?"

"An insightful question, Mrs. Brandon," Colin said, smiling at her. "Most likely, they would view it as a sign that city officials weren't interested in interfering with them. It could be a subtle move to placate the Camorra without actually giving anything up to them."

"Surely you, Mr. Hargreaves, shall not stand by and let justice be perverted? I expect better things of you."

"It's not my place to interfere," he said. "However, if we were to quietly investigate and managed to solve the crime, I doubt the police would object to us handing them the evidence necessary to convict a murderer."

"What if the Camorra are responsible?" I asked. "They won't look kindly on our actions."

"I wouldn't expect even the Camorra to frighten you off, my dear."

"Quite right. If anything, it spurs me on." I was less than best pleased with the police in Naples. How could they be so quick to abandon the search for Mr. Walker's murderer? Why would a man with no apparent interest in Pompeii return to the site, only to be killed before any of the people who had earlier made his acquaintance knew of his arrival? What had motivated him to make this second trip?

As we left the ruins, we stopped at the ticket booths and inquired after Mario Sorrentino. Neither the clerks nor his fellow guides had seen him recently, but one of his colleagues told us where he lived. Colin, insisting that Ivy and I return to the villa to dress for dinner, attempted to call on him, but there was no answer at his rooms, so he left a note requesting an interview. The guide didn't send a response.

The murder dominated our conversation that evening when Callie and Benjamin came to dine. Callie considered it something of a lark — not the death itself, but the idea of our investigating it — but her brother was much more serious.

"If you insist on pursuing the case, I shouldn't let the police know," Benjamin said to my husband after we had finished eating and retired to the terrace. "They won't look kindly on foreign interference."

"There's no cause for worry on that

count," I said. "Mr. Hargreaves specializes in situations that require discretion. The police won't have an inkling of what he's doing until he's proved the murderer's guilt beyond all doubt."

"It's just that . . . well, these locals can be a bit hotheaded." Benjamin scowled. "Violent, even. You don't want to anger the Camorra."

"They won't object if we prove someone outside their organization guilty," Colin said. "If they give the matter any attention at all."

A maid approached with a tray of glass goblets, fashioned in ancient style, filled with honeyed wine; Ivy wanted it served as a nod to the ancient residents of Campania. Colin grimaced when he tasted it and poured himself a whisky instead, from the bottle he had brought with him from England. For too much of his life, his time abroad was spent taking covert action for the Crown, and part of his ritual was to bring a piece of home with him, generally in the form of a fine single malt.

"What about you, Emily?" Callie asked. "Our acquaintance may only be brief, but I feel confident in predicting you will not leave this to your husband. You'll investigate as well."

I liked Callie. She was sharp, insightful, and pert, unbound by the mores that governed polite society, but not so radical as to be tedious. I found myself surprised that Ivy had taken such a shine to her. From childhood, Ivy had always been a tempering influence on me, pulling me back from my most outrageous schemes, gently persuading me that I ought not reject everything I disliked about society all at once. She had enjoyed our debut Season more than I, quickly found a husband, and adapted readily to the role of dutiful wife. Through all of this, she never lost herself, because there was no hidden part of her longing for more, chafing against the chains that prevented women from voting or getting the educations they deserved. She was content, happy even, with the world the way it was.

"Perhaps I should start by asking you a few more questions," I said, careful to modulate my tone so that it sounded neither threatening nor judgmental. "Now that you've had the day to think about it, can you recall anything else about Mr. Walker from your time on the ship? An overheard conversation, perhaps, that might offer insight as to his reasons for returning to Pompeii?"

"I'm afraid not," Callie said. "As I told

56

you, I noticed him while I was walking on the deck, but did not form an acquaintance with him. His sideburns put me off."

Benjamin was leaning against one of the columns on the terrace, turning his wine-glass in his hand. Small lights from boats dotted the dark expanse of the bay below. The villa was not electrified, but Ivy had placed oil lamps of the ancient style on tables and around the fountain. Their flames flickered bravely in the salty breeze, casting a soft glow over the scene and lending a certain nobility to the American's profile. One could almost picture him in a toga. Until he spoke, of course. His accent shattered the illusion.

"I didn't see Walker when we were on the ship," he said. "I'm quite certain of it. But, then, I don't have an eye for the gentlemen like my sister does." The venom in his tone took me aback, but Callie's response came equally sharp.

"My brother likes to flatter himself by thinking he can protect me from cads. I try not to let it irritate me too much. I didn't have an eye for Mr. Walker. If he noticed me, that's hardly my fault."

"Did he notice you?" I asked.

"Not so far as I know, but Benjamin judges harshly anyone he views as a potential suitor. Why he would've considered Mr. Walker as such is beyond me."

"I never said I did!" Benjamin's glass was in danger of shattering as he tightened his grip on it. Ivy stepped forward, ready to soothe him, but he got control of his anger and sighed. "I didn't see him on the ship and I didn't see him in Pompeii."

Commotion from the front of the villa and a booming voice prevented further discussion.

"No, no, don't announce me. I object to being announced. It quite ruins the surprise." Jeremy Sheffield, Duke of Bainbridge, companion of my childhood, whose oft-stated goal was to be the most useless man in Britain, marched past a maid. She muttered something in Italian, but did nothing to stop the advance of our visitor.

"Ivy Brandon, passion of my youth, perfect English rose, quintessential example of all the best Britain has to offer, I throw myself on your mercy and beg you to give me sanctuary." He bowed low in front of her as he spoke.

"Passion of your youth?" Ivy's laugh rang loud. "I've never heard you utter something so ridiculous, and I've heard more than my share of the absurd coming from you. Why on earth do you require sanctuary? And what are you doing here?"

"I've been in Rome. It was quite dreadful, if you must know. I had the misfortune of inflaming the interest of a young lady there, who took my attentions rather more seriously than she ought. I've had to flee. Her mother was beginning to terrify me. I heard you were visiting Pompeii and could think of nowhere I'd rather be. You will take me in, won't you? I'm desperate."

"Bainbridge, when will you learn?" Colin asked. "Toying with the ladies always gets you in trouble."

"So it does, Hargreaves, so it does. But it's so bloody much fun. Pardon my language. I didn't realize you had other guests." He flung his hat onto a nearby table and grinned.

Ivy, rising to her duties as hostess, introduced our American friends. The good duke, as was his habit when he met a potential new conquest, lingered over Callie's hand, but she pulled it away before he could kiss it.

"You shan't tempt me with any aristocratic charms, Mr. Sheffield."

"It would be *your grace,* actually," Jeremy said. "But you'll wound me if you refuse to call me by my given name."

Callie beetled her brows. "Then prepare

to be wounded. I despise the aristocracy."
Her words were harsh, but her dancing
hazel eyes cast a different tone.

"I shall make it my life's work to convince
you to admit that at least one among us is
undeserving of your scorn." Jeremy was
standing dangerously close to her now, but
I was happy to see it. It had been too long
since I'd seen him flirt so outrageously.
Heartbreak has a tendency to remove the
joy from a great many things. Heartbreak
that comes from a once-beloved fiancée trying to murder one is even more unpleasant.
Four years had passed since Jeremy had suffered these horrors, and his recovery from
the blow had come slow. A grin spread
across his face as he bantered with the
American. "None of which is to say I don't
deserve a great deal of scorn, but all of it
derives from my actions, not my birth."

"Is that so?" Callie asked, making no attempt to hide the fact she was taking measure of his appearance and feeling great
satisfaction with what she found. "Perhaps,
then, I shan't consider you entirely beneath
my notice."

"Callie, dear, what were you working on
today?" Benjamin asked, his attempt to
disrupt his sister's flirtation clumsy and
obvious. "We've been so distracted with this

other business that we haven't spoken of anything else all evening. Did you finish with the trench you were digging?"

"My dear brother, don't bother," she said, a wicked grin on her face. "I'm certain *his grace* is even less interested in trenches than you are."

The veins in Benjamin's neck bulged. "Callie, I only —"

Ivy stepped forward, her voice soft. "Jeremy, of course you're welcome here and may stay as long as you want. I'll have a room made ready. Are you hungry? We've eaten, but I can have Cook put together a cold plate for you." She crossed to him and expertly drew him away from Callie without ruffling any feathers. I wouldn't have been able to do it so well. Perhaps I ought to have paid better attention to some — if only a very few — of my mother's lessons. "We must bring you up to date on everything happening here. Colin, naturally, is investigating a mysterious crime. Callie is an archaeologist and, if you are very well behaved, I'll persuade her to take you on a tour of the ruins. Benjamin, her brother, is an artist, and though he doesn't yet know it, I'm counting on him to help me stage a Roman banquet in the ancient style. He'll be able to paint frescoes that would have delighted Nero himself. But before anything else, do tell me about the girl you abandoned in Rome. Is she English? I can only assume her mother's dearest hope is to see her married to a duke."

"Too right, Ivy, too right. It's a blasted curse, this title."

Callie all but howled. "Marriage is bad enough in and of itself. Add a title to the mix, and it goes beyond unpalatable."

"You object to marriage?" I asked.

"Absolutely. It's nothing more than a glittering jail, minded by men who think all women care about are baubles and babies. No one could tempt me down such a ludicrous path."

"Is that so?" Jeremy asked, scrutinizing Callie, albeit more subtly than she had him. "How very interesting."

I knew then we were in for a great deal of trouble.

6

AD 79

Even now, as I look back on the past with the benefit of age and wisdom (admittedly, more wisdom than age, as only two years have elapsed since the events at the beginning of my story), I cannot quite understand how Silvanus misled me. Perhaps it was not his intention, but a man of his experience knew what a slave girl would expect from someone like him, and I can assure you it was not poetry.

My father had a tiny cubiculum of his own in the back of the house, near the small secondary kitchen, but I slept on the floor of Lepida's room, which opened onto a narrow corridor leading to the open court of the atrium. Frequently, as my mistress slumbered, I lay awake, but after that first private meeting with her betrothed, I developed the habit of slipping out of the chamber and sitting in the atrium, staring at the stars above me. Soon I began taking a wax

63

tablet and stylus and wrote poetry inspired by the heavens, complicated tales of impossible love. For I had convinced myself that I loved Silvanus.

He had asked for me the next time he visited Lepida. We retired to the same room as before, and again he did not touch me, only demanded more poetry. I tried Virgil on him, but he objected, insisting on something written by my humble self. I refused and gave him Ovid, but nothing too amorous.

"You would do well to obey me, Kassandra," he said, standing intoxicatingly close. "A poem, one of your own."

I stared into his dark eyes as I recited one that had come to me a few nights earlier on a moonlit excursion to the atrium. He listened intently and nodded when I had finished.

"Good girl," he said. "Will you write it down for me? Then I'll be able to read it whenever I want." He lifted his hand to my cheek, stopping before he touched it. I ached to feel his skin against mine and knew then that I could refuse him nothing.

The following morning, when Lepida was off somewhere with her mother, I went to the library and asked my father for blank papyrus. He gave it to me almost without noticing, so absorbed was he in his own work, repairing a damaged scroll from Livy's monumental history of Rome, *Ab Urbe Condita Libri*. With great care, I sat down and copied out the words of my poem from the tablet upon which I'd originally scrawled them. I rolled up the papyrus, tied it with a piece of twine, and, unsure what to do with it — I had no private space of my own — hid it in the library's Latin room, in the back of a box that contained volumes of Seneca's philosophical writings. Plautus kept a complete library and, hence, included the works of the Stoics, but, as an Epicurean, was unlikely to come looking for them. My little scroll would be safe there until Silvanus fetched it.

For that was my oh-so-clever idea. I would not give it to him, but tell him where to find it, hoping that by making it a game, a hunt, he would find me more alluring.

As I left the library I was fairly floating, lost in my fantasies. Lost, that is, until I saw Lepida, who was sitting on a bench in the peristyle, swathed in a red silk tunic fastened at the shoulders with gold brooches. She called to me, asking that I join her.

"Look what Silvanus has sent," she said, holding out her hand to show me a pair of pearl earrings. "He is the best among men, is he not? I will be fortunate to have him as a husband."

A sickening feeling crept through me. Until that moment, I had not thought Lepida had given Silvanus much consideration. Oh, I knew she believed him handsome; that was clear from the first day we saw him. But she had never expressed any particular interest in him. Girls like her did not expect much out of marriage, at least not in terms of affection. A husband would provide for her. He would respect her, trust her to manage his household and bear him children. But he would not love her, not with the sort of passion to be found in the myths of old. Marriage was about duty and loyalty. Love was something else altogether.

Or so I had believed. But I knew Lepida as well as I knew myself, and I recognized the look in her eyes as she fingered the dangling pearls in her hand. She was in love with Silvanus. As a slave in her household — for I assumed her father would let me go with her when she was married — she could not object to her husband taking a physical interest in me, but as her friend, I could not welcome the attention. Not in my heart. Not anywhere. I must do what he wanted, but I would have to learn to guard my emotions. I could not let myself crave and

66

nurture a passion for the man who had won her love.

7
1902

Before I got out of bed the following morning, my husband brought me the longest telegram I had ever seen. I cringed at the thought of what it must have cost, knowing that we would be footing the bill.

"I asked *The New York Times* to send the full text of the Walker's articles about Pompeii and the election. Unless I'm missing something, I can't see anything that might catalyze a murder."

"Nor do I," I said after reading the first. "This is well written and engaging, certain to inspire tourists to visit the ruins, but there is nothing else to it. What about his piece on the Camorra?"

"It's no more enlightening. He was writing in general about elections abroad and only makes the barest reference to the results in Naples."

"So we're nowhere."

"More or less. No clues, no hint of motive, looks from every angle to be a hopeless business. A perfect challenge." His eyes brightened. He'd devoted his life to serving crown and country and was always happiest when his missions proved intellectually stimulating. As was I. But that was not all the job entailed. The physical effects of his work troubled me as much as they thrilled him. I wished he'd never had cause to learn how to treat bullet wounds and that I'd never again find a new scar on his skin. He'd had a brief respite from danger, serving the king at home rather than running about the Continent in pursuit of unnamed threats to the empire, but it would not last. Protection duty did not suit him. For now, though, I rejoiced at us being able to work side by side, reasonably confident that he would come to no harm.

After dressing, we made our way to the terrace, having settled into a routine of taking breakfast there. Why spend time anywhere else when one had such a view? Looking at the Bay of Naples, deep blue with diamonds of sunlight dancing upon it, it was easy to see why the ancients had built their villas here. Ivy poured us tea while Jeremy, kitted out in an elegantly tailored linen suit and slouching with his usual air of studied ennui, filled a plate with cheese and olives.

"I've decided to entirely embrace Italian culture at the exclusion of all others," he said. "I shall fire my cook, replace her with one from here, cancel my account with Fortnum's and insist that every morsel of food that comes into the house is directly imported. I never knew olives could taste like this. And the coffee. Oh, the coffee! What is wrong with the English? I shall never take tea again."

"And next month, when you go to France, you'll claim a lifelong devotion to their cuisine," I said. "You'll never fire your cook, she's the only one who looked after you when you were a child."

"Nanny was horrid. You know that." He pulled a face and glowered at me. "I admit to a certain tendency toward getting carried away when I travel, but don't you think it a rather charming eccentricity? I've devoted years to cultivating it."

"You're an inspiration to us all," Ivy said, her voice dripping with sarcasm.

Ah, the mundane ways in which we occupy ourselves in the moments before something — or someone — crashes in and unalterably changes our lives! No morning could have been more ordinary, no conversation more banal. And then, the maid announced a visitor; innocuous enough. But when she spoke the person's name, I was so taken aback that I, who refuse on principle to faint, grew lightheaded. *Katharina* von Lange? Surely I had heard her wrong. I remembered — all too well — *Kristiana* von Lange, but she'd been dead for a decade. My confusion only increased when a young lady, dressed in a smart walking suit, stepped onto the terrace.

Years before we met, Colin had forged a close working relationship with Kristiana, the Countess von Lange, one of his counterparts in Vienna. She was more than a colleague, however. They had shared a long and passionate affection for each other that was severed after she refused Colin's proposal of marriage. She went on to wed a count, and, so far as I knew, that was the end of their personal connection.

I became acquainted with her ten years ago, a few months before Colin and I married, when I found myself embroiled in a case that took me to Vienna, and though my then-fiancé never gave me the slightest cause to doubt his fidelity, in the shadow of the countess, I always felt unsophisticated and awkward. She was stunningly beautiful, with dark hair and glittering emerald eyes, elegant, intelligent, capable, and cosmopolitan, while I was an extremely young lady of extremely limited experience.

During the investigation, I uncovered a political intrigue of great import to the Austrian government. As one of their most trusted agents, the countess's expertise was required, and, in the course of her successful efforts to rectify a situation that could have had a catastrophic effect on her entire country and beyond, she was killed.

The news of her death affected Colin like nothing I had seen before. Gone were his stiff upper lip and stoic reserve. He mourned her, the woman he had loved, and I understood his grief. We all carry our pasts with us, and his relationship with the countess had helped form him into the gentleman I adored above all others. Still, one cannot help but wish one's husband's former lover was more unattractive crone and less enchanting goddess.

Regardless, I had not thought about Kristiana in years. Yet now, standing on the terrace of our villa, was a young lady who looked the very picture of the Countess von Lange, with one exception. She had the same dark, shining hair, the same refined features, the same elegant figure. But instead of the countess's striking green eyes, the girl's dark orbs were a perfect match for my husband's. She held out her hand to shake Colin's.

"Mr. Hargreaves, I am Katharina von Lange," she said, her manner cordial and casual. "Everyone calls me Kat, so you may as well do the same. I thought I ought to come meet you. It turns out you're my father." Her voice had an exotic lilt to it, and there was a slight accent to her English. "I understand how you must be feeling in the face of this revelation, as I, too, was unaware of it until recently. My mother —"

"Your mother? Kristiana?" Colin, steady on his feet and showing no sign either of shock or dismay, stood in front of her. She nodded. His voice, low and calm, revealed to no one but me that he was choking back emotion. I searched for a hint of doubt in his eyes and was stunned to find none.

Ivy and Jeremy stared, silent.

The girl continued. "I can't say we were close. She died when I was eight. I knew nothing about you until her solicitor came to me last week and delivered the news."

"Please, sit," Colin said, offering her a chair. "You'll forgive me if I find myself at a loss for words. This is wholly unexpected."

"I would imagine so, *Father.*" She grinned and laughed. "Forgive me, I couldn't resist. The countess liked her secrets, didn't she?

It's what made her so good at her job. Not that I knew about any of that until last week, either. After her death, Herr Gruber — the solicitor — informed me of the news and brought me a letter from her. I was away at school in France, in the care of Ursuline nuns. Lovely education, rotten social life, but I'm getting ahead of myself. Apparently, she penned a letter every time she was about to set off on a mission, so that if she was killed, she could explain things to me in her own way. As I was so young, it was rather short on detail, but I understood that she served Austria and lost her life as a result. From then on, Herr Gruber has forwarded to me a letter from her annually on my birthday. He tells me she left one for every year until I reach the age she was when she died."

The maths were simple enough; the countess's messages from beyond the grave would go on for close to another twenty years. The thought did not sit well with me. I hoped she hadn't left any missives for my husband.

"Were you led to believe the Count von Lange was your father?" Colin asked.

"No, no, the count knows nothing about me either," she said. "I've never met him. This year, Herr Gruber brought my birthday letter in person. In it, my mother explained why she kept me a secret. She had refused to marry you because she worried that a man of your occupation — if I may be so crass as to call it that — would be made vulnerable should he choose to have a family. When she found herself with child, she didn't tell you for the same reason: to protect you. I'm here now because she had instructed her solicitor to reveal your name when I completed my education — including a minimum of two terms at university in Vienna — but only if you already had other children, which, evidently, you do. Not everyone is so concerned with your safety as the countess was."

She looked directly at me for the first time since she'd entered the room. I blanched at her words and opened my mouth to speak, but could find no appropriate words.

"Truth be told, I find the entire subterfuge rather absurd, but I accept that she thought she was doing what was best for us all," she continued. "I prefer a more direct approach and would never let myself succumb to such ridiculous fear, but she was of another generation, wasn't she?" She scowled at me. "I suppose you are, too, but I understand you are considerably younger than she. Well played, Father, well played."

"I assure you —" Colin started.

"I'm teasing. You'll learn soon enough that I have a terrible aversion to propriety. It's what comes from too many years in a convent school. At any rate, here I am, desperate to know you all — you must introduce me to your friends — I observe that I've shocked them horribly — but if you don't offer me some breakfast soon, I may collapse. I'm utterly famished. And then, perhaps, we could all go to the ruins. We can begin to forge a familial bond while looking at the wreckage of other families."

The only wreckage I was considering was that she could cause my own family. We gave her breakfast, of course, but I can recall no details of what transpired while she ate other than that she presented Colin with a letter written by her mother, this one addressed to him. The world no longer made sense to me, and I sat watching everything around me turn blurry and strange. Did I believe her claim? In that moment, I couldn't believe or disbelieve anything; confusion consumed me. I must have taken some tea, for I was holding an empty cup. My throat went dry and my eyes smarted. I wanted to flee, desperate for a little privacy so that I might compose myself, but I didn't want the girl to judge me as weak and flighty, the way her mother had done before.

"Emily, darling, would you be so kind as to come assist me before we set off?" Ivy asked. "You remember I bought that new camera, the Brownie? The clerk who sold it to me promised I need only press the button and that the machine will do the rest, but I can't make it work. You're better with this sort of thing than I, and I'm relying on you to take a look at it and help me learn how to use it. It's in my room."

"Of course," I murmured, hardly aware of what I was saying. She looped her arm through mine and maneuvered me off the terrace, but before we reached the wing that housed our bedrooms, Colin caught up with us and pulled me away.

"A moment, please, Ivy, if I may?" he asked.

"Bring her to my room when you've finished," she said, her voice strong and sharp, as it was only when she was defending someone she loved. She gave my arm a little squeeze before disappearing into the corridor.

"My dear girl, please tell me you believe I knew nothing about this," he said. "I am —" He pressed a palm to his forehead. "Shocked. Speechless. Cowed. Terrified. Do you believe me? I had no indication that . . . Kristiana never uttered a word . . . I . . . ."

I saw no need to let him continue when he was so visibly upset, but I hated how easily her name formed on his lips. "I do."

"You must despise me, but I swear this happened long before I knew you, long before —"

"It is of no consequence," I said, the words a lie. The fact was, I wanted a great deal more information. I'd always believed their affair had ended after she turned down his proposal, or, if not then, certainly by the time she had married the Count von Lange. But I couldn't remember when they had wed. "Are you certain she's telling the truth?"

"I have no reason to doubt her. I read the letter Kristiana left for me. It confirms her story with more than enough detail to satisfy me. It is, perhaps, best not to discuss that further."

I waited for him to offer to show it to me, but he did not. A searing heat flooded through me. I hated that there was something new and private between him and the countess. "She has your eyes. That, and your own belief, will have to suffice." He took me in his arms. I gave into his strong warmth, melting against him, willing myself not to cry as I breathed in his scent, cinnamon and tobacco. What right did I have to judge him for actions that took place so long ago? Actions that had nothing to do with me? "What are you going to do?" I asked.

"I've not the slightest idea, but I won't leave her alone and unprotected. She'll remain here with us for now, so that we can become better acquainted. The rest we will have to figure out later. If, that is, you don't object?"

"No, of course not. If she really is your child, how could I keep you from her?" I tried to smile. He would never shirk his duty to look after his daughter. His eyes brightened and his features softened. I knew I had said the right thing, even if it made me feel as if I were being consumed by flames.

He kissed the top of my head. "I can only endeavor to deserve you."

"You're certain — beyond doubt — that you're her father?"

"Yes." I knew his tone well enough. He would say nothing more about it.

"Go back to her," I said, uncertain of how much longer I could hold my emotions in check. I wanted to scream and rail and cry. And I wanted him to see none of it. He kissed me again, this time on the lips, and started back down the corridor. Once he was out of sight, I raced to Ivy's bedroom, flung open the door without knocking, and

79

threw myself onto the bed, where I lay, facedown, sobbing.

"There, there, it will all be fine in the end." She was rubbing my back and speaking in the voice she must use with her children when they were in need of reassurance.

"I don't know why I'm so upset," I said, sitting up and accepting the lacy handkerchief Ivy handed to me. "This all happened so long ago it shouldn't matter."

"What an inane thing to say, Emily. Of course it matters. Beyond having just found out you're the stepmother to a nearly grown girl — whose mother, if memory serves, made you feel inadequate in every regard — you're being forced — again — to face the uncomfortable truth that your husband loved someone before he met you. But you know Colin adores you. He threw her over the instant he fell for you. Surely you don't doubt that now?"

"No, no I don't." I frowned. "I trust him absolutely. It's just that —" I stopped. "Everything inside me is a jumble. I'm afraid this girl — *her* daughter — will remind him of that old love and lead him to regret his choice to marry me. She gives him a glimpse into another life he might have led."

"It most certainly does not. To start, the countess turned down his proposal. Presumably he was disappointed at the time, but he has given no indication since that he cares any longer."

"She turned him down in order to keep him safe," I said. "I was not so considerate."

"It's all well and good for her to have said that, but it may have been nothing more than an excuse. Maybe she didn't love him enough to want to marry him."

"I appreciate your support, Ivy, truly, I do, but she hid her own child away — so that even she couldn't see the girl often — to achieve the same end. You cannot tell me it's anything but self-sacrifice for a mother to have done such a thing."

"Well . . ." Ivy pursed her rosy lips. "I must say that, in the course of my admittedly limited acquaintance with the countess, *motherly* was not an adjective I would ever have chosen to describe her. She was dedicated to her work and likely sent the baby away as much for her own safety — and convenience — as for Colin's. It wasn't an entirely noble gesture."

"If he had no other children, the solicitor would never have revealed Colin's identity," I said. "The countess died a decade ago.

Does that not prove she was concerned with keeping him from vulnerability? More concerned than I."

"Colin wanted to marry you — quite desperately. How many times did he propose before you accepted him? I lost count. He only asked the dreadful countess once. Clearly, she didn't have the effect on him that you do. The poor man couldn't have made his adoration of you clearer. Did he not, after all, deed you all the books in his library?"

"And all the port in his cellar." The memory felt so far away, almost like it belonged to someone else.

"Colin Hargreaves is a man who knows his own mind. You respected him enough not to second-guess him or to decide for him how best to conduct his life. The countess refused to give him the same courtesy."

I took her hand. "Thank you, Ivy, you have offered supreme consolation. I believe I can bear to face the others now."

"I'm pleased to hear that. But now I do need you to help me with my camera. You know me better than to have thought I would outright lie to get you away from them. Robert purchased it for me, and I despise it. Drawing is much more to my taste. If we could somehow jam the wretched thing, I'd have an excuse for coming home with not one single photograph."

In the end, I convinced her to leave the Brownie unmolested and present it to Kat, who was delighted with the gift. I stood apart from the others with Jeremy, who was leaning elegantly against a column on the terrace. "This is quite the development," he said. "Interesting times, these, eh, Em? Will you have her presented at court? Host a debutante ball?"

"Don't be impertinent." I whacked him on the arm. "I have no idea what we shall do. I'm leaving that entirely up to my husband." We both stared as Kat pointed the camera at her father.

"You're too good for him, my dear girl, far too good for him."

8
AD 79

As I write these words, I am struck by how young I was back then, convinced I had full control of my heart and confident I could read Lepida's thoughts. I saw Silvanus in private six more times before his wedding, and on each occasion, he extracted from me another of my poems. After the first that I hid in the library, I no longer bothered with subterfuge. My cunning had no visible effect on him beyond a slight annoyance, but it had stirred the embers of my affection, and I no longer wanted the flame to grow.

But grow it did, despite my good intentions. No longer did I hesitate to share with him my work. Instead, I wrote for him, not that I expected he would notice. I did not compose love poems; that would have been coarse and obvious. Instead, I embarked on a great epic, recounting the tale of a hero invented by myself, modeled on Silvanus. I would praise the man I loved without ever naming him and make him the greatest warrior Rome had ever known. Hector and Achilles were weaklings compared to him, Aeneas a mere child. The muse Calliope sat by my side, the verses coming almost without effort. I prayed to Mars and Minerva for an understanding of war, but it was to Diana that I made my most frequent offerings. Like her, I would never marry, and I would scorn any attention from men. Poetry would be my only love.

The first lines of my epic delighted Silvanus. He demanded more, desperate for the rest of the story, never realizing he was the inspiration for it all. Before Lepida left her father's house, I had completed the first book of my great work and gave it to her betrothed.

When the auspicious day chosen for the wedding arrived, I helped my friend prepare, even fixing in place the flammeum that would veil her head. I stood near her when she uttered the required words to Silvanus: *Ubi tu Gaius, ego Gaia.* I followed the torchlight procession from Plautus's house to the groom's, but did not have the heart to join the others in their exuberant songs. I hung back as Lepida applied oil to the door of her new home, tears smarting in my eyes as her husband lifted her over the threshold. Try though I might, I could not hold my feelings in check. I envied Lepida for the attentions she would receive from her husband that night.

At last, mired in unhappiness, I returned to the only home I had ever known. Plautus had not given me to his daughter, despite Lepida's pleas. Neither of us wanted to be separated and couldn't imagine him refusing such a simple request. But in the end, he did, not because of his own feelings or inclinations. What did he care for one Greek slave, more or less?

The source of my anguish came not from my master, but from someone else altogether. My father, who, since my mother's death, had never cared for anything beyond his books and ideas, held all the blame for my misery.

9
1902

I'm not entirely certain what motivated me to suggest that Ivy give her camera to Kat, but I suspect it was an effort to disguise my unease with the situation. The earth beneath me no longer felt reliable, all the stability upon which I counted erased in an instant. The girl exclaimed over the gift, and Colin, who deduced that the idea was mine, whispered thanks.

"I know incorporating her into our lives won't be easy," he said, "but I'm most appreciative of your support." I smiled, all the while knowing I was a fraud. How could he accept so readily that she was his daughter? The answer was simple. Unlike me, he wanted to believe her, and, unlike me, he was privy to whatever intimate details the countess had written in her letter. I was an outsider, alone.

Kat had showered the warmest thanks on Ivy for the gift and started taking pictures of everyone but me, instructing them to pose. Before long, she announced that she preferred candid shots and started circling the terrace like a lion in search of prey, peering through the camera as she went.

"How did you know to find us here?" I had decided I ought to try to engage her in conversation.

"After Herr Gruber departed, I contacted Buckingham Palace," she said, not looking at me. "My mother's letter suggested that you, Father, were an agent of some sort, so I thought I'd go straight to the top, but my telegram did not lead to a helpful reply. I sent two more: one to the Foreign Office and one to the Department of Defense. Then I learned that you English are more reticent than I expected, so I did the only other thing I could think of."

"I'm almost afraid to ask," Colin said.

"I found a clerk at one of the Fleet Street papers much more willing to be of assistance. He gave me your London address. The skeleton staff you keep there when not in residence forwarded my telegram to your house in Derbyshire. Your butler — Davis, I believe he is called? — replied, saying you were in Pompeii."

"Did you tell him who you are?" I asked.

"Oh, heavens, no! That's best left to my

father," she said. "I presented myself as an old family friend whose parents had recently died and was in need of consolation."

"Well done," Colin said.

"Thank you." She grinned. "So! We've all breakfasted and you lot look dressed for exploration. Can I persuade you to take me to the ruins?"

"While we were about to set off for the archaeological park, I'm afraid our plans for the day aren't quite so straightforward," Colin said, and explained, without going into particulars, our role in investigating the murder.

Kat expressed neither horror nor shock, only clapped her hands. "This is better than I could have imagined. I can move right into the family business."

Family business? Yes, her mother was a spy, and her father an agent of incomparable talents, but there was no family business.

"I don't want you to become embroiled —" Colin started, but she interrupted, sliding her arm through his and pulling him toward the door.

"You'll learn soon enough there's no point arguing with me. I'm coming with you and expect to have heard a complete account of every gritty detail of the case by the time we reach the excavations."

89

I caught a glimpse of pride in Colin's dark eyes as he let her lead him to our waiting carriage. Ivy looked worried and Jeremy huffed. I did not feel it was my place to interfere. If my husband wanted the girl to accompany us, that was his decision. Our plan was innocuous enough: to examine each of the plaster casts in the city to make sure there were no other modern victims hidden among the ancient dead. Nothing sensitive or delicate in that; bringing her along would not hinder our work.

Most of the casts were housed in the museum near the ancient Porta Marina, but once that space had been filled, the general consensus was that any more would be better displayed where the remains had been found. The emotional impact of seeing them in situ was far more powerful than viewing them in a gallery. We quickly determined that nothing had been added to the museum's collection — we had expected as much, but had to be thorough — and then commenced taking an inventory of the rest, armed with maps of the site.

The task was daunting. Pompeii is unlike other ancient sites, in that it is an entire city, not simply a temple, a marketplace, or even an acropolis. Only three-fifths of it have been excavated thus far, but those three-fifths are comprised of acres and acres of houses, shops, taverns, temples, baths, and every other sort of building found in a Roman provincial city. We had to scour its entirety, not simply check each place marked on the map as containing casts. Our murderer could have hidden another one anywhere, in the backroom of a bakery, perhaps, or a cubiculum in the remains of a modest dwelling overlooked by casual tourists. While the most celebrated houses, those containing the finest paintings, the best-preserved peristyles and atria, could be locked, the rest of the site was accessible without a set of keys.

Knowing the scale of the work before us, we decided to separate. Colin announced his intention of taking Kat with him, leaving Ivy, Jeremy, and me together. Father and daughter would scour Regions I, VII, and VIII, while we started with Region VI. I watched as they walked away. Her raven hair was darker than his rich brown, and she had none of his curls, but there was something in her posture that mirrored the confident manner in which he always carried himself. Much though I despised myself for feeling so, I couldn't help but wish there was some way to deny the relationship between them. What would our lives be like now, with her in them? How often would I be left behind as they went off together?

"Don't wallow, Em," Jeremy said. "It's beneath you."

"There's no need to scold her." Ivy poked him with the tip of her parasol. "She's every right to be unsettled by this development."

"Thank you, Ivy," I said.

"You're welcome, but don't think I shall let you sink into melancholy, even if Miss von Lange is an unwelcome disruption."

"You're a master of understatement, Ivy," Jeremy said. "She's like one of those storms in the ocean — what are they called? Typhoons? — that barrels down and capsizes your ship."

"You're such a comfort, Jeremy," I said. "Whatever would I do without you?"

"If you'd let me finish, you would have heard the part when I mention your extremely sturdy lifeboat: Ivy and me. We'll make sure you skate through with grace."

"You're mixing metaphors," Ivy said, "and I'm not certain I like being compared to anything extremely sturdy. But he's correct, Emily, you do have us, and we'll do all we can to help you — if I may, Jeremy, correct you — sail through."

"I was picturing a steamship, not a sailboat," Jeremy said, "but I won't argue the point. All that matters, Em, is that you've got plenty of other things to occupy your mind. Like murderers, for example. And if that's not enough, I'm prepared to whisk you away to whatever romantic location you choose and show you once and for all that I'm twice the man Hargreaves is."

This made me laugh. I was grateful for the distraction and ready to get down to work. From the Herculaneum Gate in the northwest corner of the city, we made our way through structure after structure. The homes of the wealthy proved the simplest to search; there was an obvious path through most of them. The labyrinth of what tourists dismiss as insignificant was more difficult, with countless rooms and storage spaces, stairways and alcoves, and claustrophobic corridors that appeared to lead nowhere.

While the main streets of the city were relatively wide, the rest were narrow and close, with no space between the façades of the buildings lining them. There was no distinction between residential and commercial areas. Even the largest homes owned by the wealthiest families were surrounded by shops and taverns. Vesuvius loomed over it all, a constant reminder of its destructive force. Our exhaustive exploration gave me an entirely different perspective on the place than I had gained from casually wandering through it as a tourist. Now, I could imagine what it must have been like to live there — constant bustle — and could almost hear the clatter of donkey carts in the streets, the splashing of water, the sound of shopkeepers hawking their goods. What it didn't do, however, was reveal a single cast of a body that shouldn't have been there.

I consulted my map. "We've only a small bit of Region IX left to cover. The Central Baths should be straightforward. We've finished with the dyehouse and the inn, but there are still two more houses."

"More like mazes. I'm beginning to have a deep appreciation for what Theseus suffered in his search for the Minotaur," Jeremy said.

"I'm shocked to find you so well versed in mythology," I said. "Surely you haven't been reading Bulfinch?"

"Of course not, but I have paid a certain amount of attention when Miss Carter talks about it. Ladies do like a gent who can listen, and you know I make a habit of hoarding quotes and little bits of useless information that give one the appearance of being educated."

"Naturally," I said. "Heaven forbid anyone realize you actually are educated."

"My time at Harrow is eclipsed only by that I spent at Oxford in total hours dedicated to making sure I learned absolutely nothing."

"Yet you spent so many more years at Harrow," I said.

"My efforts — or lack thereof — were more concentrated at university. I had matured."

He wanted us to believe that, and may even have believed it himself, but I remembered his marks at school were never all that bad. He didn't want to disappoint his father, not that he ever would admit such a thing. After the old duke died during his son's second year at university, Jeremy did not step up to his new responsibilities, instead making a point of behaving even more outrageously. He took great pride in having come down from Oxford with a degree he claimed would disgrace every Bainbridge ancestor, but at the same time, his refusal to move his mother into the dowager house at Farringdon, the family estate in Kent, offered a glimpse into the gentleman he truly was. He wouldn't allow her to lose both her husband and her home in one fell blow, regardless of what tradition dictated.

"The awful truth about you, my friend, is that you aren't nearly so blackhearted as you'd like everyone to believe," I said.

"Don't ever say such a thing in public, Em. I may have loved you madly since you were ten years old, but I will never forgive you if you destroy my reputation."

"I can't decide which of you is more ridiculous," Ivy said, dropping onto a stone block in the middle of a bakery. Its large oven, fashioned from brick and shaped like a low beehive (I borrow the description from Herr Mau), looked strikingly similar to its modern counterparts, and three large mills that would have been turned by donkeys, dominated the room next to it. "I'm convinced my heels are bruised. How far do you think we've walked today? And how much further do we have to go?"

Pulling my friend to her feet, I all but dragged her through the Central Baths and the House of Marcus Lucretius. She rallied a bit in the expansive garden at the House of Epidius Rufus, rhapsodizing as to how it must have looked filled with flowers and a tinkling fountain. Jeremy, apparently unmoved, lit a cigarette and paid more attention to its smoke streaming into the sky than to anything else around him. Then, in a room — numbered 20 by Fiorelli — off the atrium, probably used as a triclinium, I noticed something that did not belong.

The room was decorated with paintings showing the musical contest between Apollo, playing his lyre, and the Phrygian satyr, Marsyas, the first to master the double flute, which Athena had invented and then discarded, not liking the unattractive way the instrument made her cheeks puff. The satyr believed himself in possession of a talent greater than Apollo's, and the Muses judged the ensuing competition. Needless to say, Apollo won, for he could play the lyre upside down, a feat nigh-impossible with a flute. Four of the room's panels depicted the Muses, and directly beneath the center of each of them, on the floor, was a single clay disc, similar to those used as voting ostraca in ancient Athens. Once a year, the citizens would vote, yes or no, on a simple question: Is anyone a threat to our democracy? If the majority said yes, they would reconvene a few months later, each person bringing with him an ostracon upon which he had written the name of the man he considered a potential tyrant. (I need hardly mention the Athenian ladies were entirely excluded from this process.) Whoever got the most votes was exiled. Like those used in Athens, the ostraca I found were painted black, with a small hole in the middle. Scratched into the surface of each, revealing the red pottery beneath, was a single word: *Hargreaves.*

"This does not bode well for Colin," Ivy said. "It's obviously meant as a threat."

"Let's not leave him to have all the fun. My surname is Hargreaves as well," I said, gathering the discs and wrapping them carefully before putting them into my bag. "Someone doesn't like us investigating, but that doesn't necessarily constitute a threat to our safety. It may be nothing more than a message to say we should stop what we're doing."

"Is it too much to hope you will heed the advice?" Jeremy asked. "If you are in danger, I could whisk you off to Rome — no, Florence. I can't go back to Rome until I'm certain that wretched mother of that wretched girl isn't still there."

"Don't bother making any travel plans," I said. "If anything, this encourages me as it suggests the murderer is still in Pompeii, and further, that he isn't a student of ancient history, given that he chose an anachronistic vehicle for his message. The Romans didn't use ostraca, only the Greeks."

"So not an archaeologist, then?" Ivy asked.

"Who else but an archaeologist would wrap the body in plaster?" Jeremy asked.

"The method is not the same as that used by the archaeologists," I said.

Ivy pressed her lips together. "Perhaps the difference is meant to deliberately deceive."

"A definite possibility," I admitted. "Regardless, if the murderer is still here, he must either be local or have some connection to the excavations. There's not much else in the city. Let's finish our search for casts and then visit the stands outside the ruins to see if any of them sell souvenirs of this sort." We made our way through the remaining structures in our section of the map, careful not to sacrifice thoroughness to speed, but found nothing else. Our survey of the merchants beyond the ancient walls was only slightly more fruitful. Three of them carried discs of the type we had found. They had Roman names scratched on them, compounding the historical error of their presence. True, the Greeks had colonized southern Italy, but, even so, ostraca did not make sense as a souvenir of Pompeii. When I inquired about this, the merchants all shrugged, unconcerned. How many people would notice, let alone care? Tourists wanted anything that looked ancient. As for who had bought them? No one remembered anything about the customers in question.

Fatigued, we returned to the villa, where Colin and his daughter were sipping whisky on the terrace with Callie. Kat shot a look that dared me to comment, so I ignored her. She then convinced Jeremy to join them. So much for his adoption of all things Italian at the exclusion of everything else. I pulled my husband aside, wanting to show him the ostraca privately.

"You can see that someone painted over the Roman name, let it dry, and then scratched *Hargreaves* into it," I said as he examined one of the discs.

"Ten years of exile, wasn't it?" Colin asked. "Do you think we'd be allowed to choose the location? I could do with ten years alone with you on Santorini."

"Don't joke," I said. "You know this is serious. I found them under a group of paintings of the Muses Calliope included."

"You suspect Miss Carter might be responsible?" he asked. "Surely she wouldn't be so clumsy. Drawing deliberate attention to the Muses would be akin to signing her work."

"I don't have any reason to think she's guilty, but she did admit to seeing Mr. Walker on the boat. Can we take her at her word when she claims not to have an acquaintance with him? If they were involved, he might have followed her to Pompeii. I know it's absurd, but I can't help wanting to protect Jeremy. He's already fallen in love with one murderer and seems rather taken with Callie."

"Bainbridge is most decidedly not in love with Miss Carter," Colin said. "I can promise you other emotions are governing him. He's a grown man, perfectly capable of protecting himself should it become necessary. You, my dear, are not responsible for him."

"I take it you didn't find anything unusual in your half of the city?" I asked.

"Nothing to speak of, but I will say that Kat has an uncanny ability to hone in on a person's character with astonishing speed, a talent her mother possessed as well."

I didn't much relish considering any talent the countess possessed. "Do you think she would be an asset to the *family business,* as she called it?"

"I don't want her to continue her mother's work, if that's what you mean," he said. "I'm well aware of how dangerous that would be. She's far too young to take on such responsibility."

"I may not share the talent that she and

her mother do, but am confident I'm on safe ground saying you won't be able to stop her should she decide to pursue such a course."

Colin shook his head and sighed. "Strong-headed ladies are my blessing and my curse. And you, my dear, are without question the most talented lady of my acquaintance, not only when it comes to investigation."

I appreciated the compliment but took little pleasure in being part of any group that included the countess. "We must return to the matter at hand. As our search turned up no additional modern casts, it appears our villain has only killed one person. What does that suggest to you? A crime of passion?"

"Possibly, although he chose a time-consuming method of disposing the body," Colin said. "Making the cast would've involved a not insignificant amount of plaster, and he wouldn't have been able to move it — a harrowing task, given its weight — until it had dried."

"So not Callie, then?" I asked. "Unless someone — her brother, for example — helped her."

"We'd need a great deal more evidence before we could support such a claim. Tomorrow we'll return to the excavations and take a closer look at the shed where supplies are stored. The modern town is too small to have a shop that would sell plaster in that quantity. If he didn't use what is on hand at the site, he would have had to go to Naples."

"Which seems unnecessarily complicated," I said. "Particularly if he had access to and familiarity with the ruins. How well secured is the site at night?"

"The gates are locked, but they are hardly impenetrable."

"I suspect our villain killed Mr. Walker in the ruins. He could have hidden the body, stayed inside until the site closed, and then applied the plaster under cover of night. The process would not have been nearly so delicate as the casts done by the archaeologists. He wasn't filling a hollow made by hardened ash, after all, only applying fabric strips coated in plaster to the body. He would've had ready access to water. The fountains throughout the city have working taps."

"It would have been a messy project," Colin said. "We should take a walk through the unexcavated areas of the city in the morning. They're covered by vegetation, but we might be able to identify a clearing he could've used as a makeshift workshop."

"Have you had any response to the message you sent Mario Sorrentino?"

"Not yet, but I will keep trying." He touched my cheek. "It's good to have a few moments alone with you. I know things are difficult with Kat, and I must apologize again for my choices that led us to this outcome."

"There's no need for you to —"

"There is, Emily." He took my hand in his and raised it to his lips. "I am fortunate to have such an understanding wife."

Understanding was not a word I would apply to myself. I was still reeling, half-angry, half-stunned, all the way hurt. But how could I admit that to him, when I knew how unreasonable it was? I could not bear to be candid, not when doing so would reveal this unwelcome side of myself. I forced a smile and kissed him on the cheek.

"We should return to our friends before Jeremy gets himself in too much trouble."

Whatever he was up to, we were too late to find out. Ivy and Kat were cozied up on the terrace — the girl made no attempt at concealing her preference for my friend over me — but he and Callie were nowhere to be found.

"They left together," Kat said, grinning. "Something about a moonlit stroll, although I wonder how they'll fill the time before the

104

moon rises. His grace is quite a romantic, isn't he?"

10
AD 79

Most would judge me harshly for the criticism I hurled at my father. I hadn't been foolish enough to speak it aloud while we were in Plautus's presence, but I was no silly child, even then. I awoke long before dawn on the morning after Lepida's wedding and lingered on my bedroll, wondering what the day would bring. My duties would change now that Lepida was gone, and I considered what this might mean for my future. Claudia, her mother, was a generous mistress. With luck, I would find myself assigned to her, or perhaps I'd assist my father in the library. I was an excellent copyist, receiving frequent compliments on my penmanship, knew how to repair scrolls, and was as familiar with the contents of the library as anyone. I could place my hands on any scroll in an instant and would have no trouble maintaining the collection list.

So when, after I had pulled on a simple

wool tunic and grabbed a hunk of bread from the kitchen, my father summoned me to come to Plautus with him, I had already half convinced myself that I was about to be made his assistant.

In this, I was both absolutely correct and entirely in error.

Plautus was in his tablinum, finishing up with some clients. I stood next to my father in the doorway, studying the mosaic on the floor, a jumble of fanciful sea creatures. The octopus was especially fine. The clients left and Plautus waved for us to come forward.

"I will always be grateful for the care you gave my daughter," he said, smiling at me. "She would not have taken to her education so well without your encouragement and is now poised to be one of the most influential women in Pompeii, an excellent partner for her excellent husband. All great men know the importance of having a wife upon whom they can rely, and Titus Livius Silvanus will value her."

"It was my pleasure, dominus," I said, my head bowed. "I love Lepida like a sister."

"Which no doubt has made you wonder why I did not allow you to accompany her to her new home," Plautus said. "That, my child, is due to your father. He has purchased both his own freedom and yours. As of today, you are no longer slaves. Lepida will now be your friend rather than your mistress."

I remember that moment, and the sharp burning in my gut that accompanied it, as if it had happened today. I was elated and terrified, taken totally aback. My father had never hinted we were so close to manumission. So why the burning pain, you ask? Why the need to heap blame on my father? Not for buying our freedom — that took me a step closer to becoming a Roman citizen — but for removing us from Plautus's house. I had grown accustomed not only to the luxury of it, but to its society, its library, the music and poetry that filled its halls. The sculptures in the garden, the exquisite frescoes covering every wall and ceiling. And now, it would never again be my home. Never again would my work be so free from strife, for the job of body slave and companion to Lepida had never been onerous.

Quite unlike my new life.

11
1902

To remark, casually, that vegetation covered
the vast unexcavated sections of Pompeii
grossly underestimates the jungle that
Colin, Kat (who insisted on accompanying
us, but avoided looking at or speaking to
me unless absolutely necessary), and I faced
the next day. We slogged through it, but
found no sign of where the murderer had
covered Mr. Walker's body with plaster.

Ivy had stayed at the villa, occupied with
her embroidery. Jeremy did not appear at
breakfast, and when we ran into him that
afternoon, he was still wearing yesterday's
suit, which no longer looked quite so fresh
as it had. Kat muttered a few comments
under her breath about men who stay out
all night, but I did not feel it my place to
criticize her for speaking about so inappropriate a subject. Jeremy was in right high
spirits and accompanied us on our search
of the supply shed in which the archaeolo-

gists kept their stash of plaster. Comparing the inventory records with what was actually on hand told us that two large sacks were missing. We uncovered not a single clue as to who might have taken them or when, but at least we knew where the murderer had got his plaster, and his familiarity with the archaeologists' supplies — not to mention his access to them, for there was no sign of forced entry into the shed — suggested that he had some affiliation to the site.

For the next three days, Colin and I conducted a new series of interviews with every single person employed in the excavations. Any of them might have committed the crime, but very few raised in us suspicion. I did not give full credence to Callie's continued insistence that she never spoke to Mr. Walker on the ship, and her brother's disproportionate anger when he talked about her potential suitors tugged at me. Mr. Stirling's behavior, when he sought us out to see my sketch, struck me as odd, but, so far, we could not identify any connection to link him with the dead man.

Kat elected to make plans of her own rather than accompany us during this time. She wanted a darkroom of her own, and had arranged for Benjamin to take her to

110

Naples to help her procure supplies. Colin balked at her going alone with a young man, and his daughter, all charm, begged Ivy to play chaperone. I didn't regret not being asked. I should have liked Kat — she was spirited and smart and reminded me more than a little of myself at her age — but every time I laid eyes on her black hair and beautiful face, I saw her mother. That she spoke to me only when it was categorically unavoidable and, even then, refused to make eye contact, didn't help. Someday, perhaps, we could be friends, but it felt as if that wouldn't happen until another geological era.

Once our interrogations were complete, Colin and I turned to the hotels in Pompeii, and scoured their registers (the Italian hoteliers were far more accommodating than others I have dealt with elsewhere) until we identified the place Mr. Walker booked to stay upon his return to the city. Arriving before his room was ready, he had left his luggage — a single small bag — at the desk, but never returned to collect it.

"Is the case still here?" Colin asked.

"Of course, sir," the clerk said. "We assumed Signore Walker had a change of plans, but that, eventually, he would come for it."

111

"I'm afraid that won't be possible. Mr. Walker was murdered. We'll need to take possession of his luggage immediately." Colin's voice, strong and low, could persuade nearly anyone to do nearly anything.

"I will get it for you without delay." He disappeared into a small room behind the desk and returned a few minutes later. "You are his family?"

"No," Colin said. "We're the people who will bring his murderer to justice. I assure you, however, that his possessions will be returned to his next of kin."

We did not open the bag until we were back at the villa. Its modest contents did little to illuminate its owner. Inside, we found a change of clothing, a nightshirt, a copy of *National Geographic* that included an article about Pompeii, a book — *Red Men and White,* a collection of stories set in the American West by Owen Wister — and a return ticket for passage back to New York on a ship sailing only a week after he had arrived.

"He must have left the rest of his things at the dock," Colin said. "Probably with the shipping company. He would have needed more clothing for a transatlantic crossing. I'll send a telegram to them."

In an effort to learn more about our

victim, he also contacted the American Embassy in Rome, but, when they replied the next day, provided only scant information. Beyond his two trips to Pompeii, Mr. Walker had never traveled outside the United States. He had left a steamer trunk with the shipping company, but it contained nothing of note. Neither his family nor his employer could offer the slightest insight as to who might have wanted him dead or why he had returned to Pompeii. His editor at *The New York Times* assured us that the reporter had not penned controversial stories, but focused more on culture and the arts. His election piece was originally assigned to someone who had fallen ill before completing it. Mr. Walker had not done the research, but had finished it on behalf of his colleague.

"As if we needed more confirmation that the Camorra has nothing to do with this," I said, flinging down the folder the embassy had sent us. "So far as we can tell, Mr. Walker led a wholly unremarkable life until the moment of his death. Or at least until several moments before his death. Half an hour, perhaps." Colin and I were alone on the terrace. Callie, naturally, was working, but Jeremy and Ivy had abandoned us to spend the day at the seaside. Kat was with

Benjamin, setting up her darkroom in a small chamber off the sitting room. "Why did he revisit a place he supposedly found uninteresting? And how is it that no one saw him when he did? We know that he arrived in Europe on the same boat as Callie and Benjamin, but we have no way of accounting for his movements between the time the ship landed and when he was killed."

"What about the ship?" Colin asked. "It's quite the coincidence that he was on the same vessel as the Carters. Perhaps they knew him better than they are willing to admit?"

"Callie was adamant in her dismissal of him, but I suspect you're right," I said. "Mr. Walker wasn't the sort of individual who would catch the attention of a woman of her tastes. Benjamin, however . . . remember how they argued on the terrace when they came for dinner? There's something more there. Perhaps Mr. Walker had attempted a flirtation, angering Benjamin. Could he be a dangerously overprotective brother?"

"Who went so far as to murder a man in whom his sister expressed no romantic interest?"

"No, that's ridiculous." I frowned. "Why don't we invite Mr. Taylor for tea and see

114

what he can tell us about his industrious employees, the Carter siblings?"

Mr. Taylor arrived at the villa a few hours later in a motorcar, dust swirling around him. He peeled off his goggles, hat, driving coat, and gloves, thanking the maid as she took them from him. "I can't say how delighted I was to receive your invitation. I'm passionate about archaeology, but am no scientist. I prefer the results to the act of digging, and so far this season things have been slow going. I'm more than willing to wield a spade and do my part. Heaven knows I'm better at unskilled labor than anything requiring a delicate hand, but confound it, I do look forward to what will eventually come. Frescoes, Hargreaves, that's what I'm after. I'm convinced we've found ourselves a villa, and an enormous one at that, but it will be a long time before we get through the layers that have buried it."

We took tea on the terrace, although both gentlemen refused the genial beverage in favor of Colin's whisky and cigars. Mr. Taylor was a cheerful guest, quick to smile and eager to regale us with stories about his previous seasons in Pompeii.

"As I said, I'm nothing more than an

enthusiast, but an enthusiast with a great deal of money. I first saw Pompeii years ago, when I made my Grand Tour of the Continent, but only later had the idea of digging here myself. Mau agreed to have his men train me, and they are taskmasters. I can't say I precisely enjoyed the work, but I'm not the sort of man who wants to be a mere dilettante. Yes, I could throw my money around, hire experts, and swan in and out like so many do in Egypt, but I find that distasteful. I won't waste my time on something for which I have no aptitude — you should see the disastrous results of my attempt to learn how to draw — but archaeology is something I can do. I'd rather lend a hand than sit back and play benevolent patron, but I've always hired experts. I know I'm not knowledgeable enough to direct a dig."

"How did you settle on the site you now occupy?" I asked.

"In the past, I'd funded projects already in progress, but decided I wanted a dig of my own. We know that there were many villas beyond the city walls. The area offered more space to build and gave the wealthy more privacy than in town," he replied. "The literature — Pliny and so forth — tells us as much. I polled every archaeologist I could find who has worked in the region and then bought the land the majority of them recommended as the most promising."

"Did you bring Mr. Stirling on board before or after you'd chosen a location?" I asked.

"Before. He was with me last season. We did a great deal of preliminary work before I could come to a decision — digging test trenches, evaluating the merits of various options."

"Did you hire the rest of your staff or did he?" Colin asked.

"I left most of it to him. He is, after all, director," Mr. Taylor said. "He chose to consult me when it came to evaluating candidates."

"You did handpick a few of your workers," I said. "Benjamin Carter, for example."

"Yes, and I suppose there were a few more. Perhaps I'm more of a tyrant than I'd like to believe."

"Tell us about the Carters," Colin said, watching the smoke streaming from his cigar.

"An enterprising pair, aren't they?" Mr. Taylor bared his teeth with a broad smile, his eyes crinkling in his tanned face. "I met Benjamin in New York last autumn. He was in the Metropolitan Museum, drawing in one of the Egyptian galleries. I recognized his talent at once, assumed he was interested in archaeology, and offered him a position on my staff. He refused, explaining his focus was landscape painting, and that he was sketching ancient artifacts only as an academic exercise. A month or so later, he wrote to me at the insistence of his sister. Miss Carter is a force of nature, as I'm sure you've noticed. She studied at Radcliffe and, after finishing there, took it upon herself to learn everything she could about archaeological method. That girl's going to be a real lally-cooler. Spent a season in Egypt with Flinders Petrie, one of the best-respected archaeologists in the world. His wife took her under her wing and would have happily kept her on staff, but Miss Carter prefers the Romans to the Egyptians. She did mention that she'd hoped to work with someone else, another Englishwoman married to an Egyptologist even more famous than Petrie. Unfortunately that lady was unwilling to take her on."

"But you were," I said.

"I told her so long as her brother came, too, I'd be happy to have her. I don't care much about social niceties, but one can't entirely ignore the problems that would arise from having an unescorted female working on the site."

He would believe what he wanted. Until men stopped viewing unescorted females as problematic, we would continue to struggle for our rightful place in the world. "How is her work?" I asked.

"Flawless. She has endless patience, and, so far as I can tell, that is the most valuable quality an archaeologist can possess. She loves nothing better than digging a trench with painstaking care, keeps meticulous records, and is more comfortable in mud up to her ankles than in a ballroom."

"And her brother?" Colin refilled Mr. Taylor's whisky.

"He's an artist of astonishing technical skill and is good with a camera. There's not much for him to do yet for me, but, as you know, he's doing a series of paintings for Pais."

What a far cry from the early days of excavation at Pompeii! The Kings of Naples had refused to let anyone visit the site without a permit. Even with one, tourists were required to always be accompanied by an approved guide, and all drawings and notes were strictly forbidden. They did arrange, in the mid-eighteenth century, to have a book of engravings produced, but it was not made available to the public, only given by the king as gifts to select individuals. These policies led to outrage by many visitors, Goethe included, and to the production of illegal books based on the memories of artists lucky enough to have been granted access to the site. How fortunate we are to live in more enlightened times, when archaeology has become a science and Pompeii is open to all!

The conversation veered to Greek literature, and Mr. Taylor and I had a lively debate about the depiction of women in the *Iliad* and the *Odyssey*. His opinions were what I would expect of any ordinary man. He carelessly tossed off the contributions of the goddesses and hardly noticed the mortal females, assuming them all to be slaves and seductresses. Most disappointing, however, was that it had never before occurred to him to consider the topic.

"The scathing look on your face tells me I've made a grave mistake in my analysis of the works of Homer," he said.

"I don't mean to offend," I said, "but so long as you gentlemen consider the female of the species as only slightly more useful than decorative furniture, we all lose out. Think of the contributions women could make, if only we were allowed a seat at the proverbial table. The ancients had better sense than we in this regard. Compare Ares and Athena. He is all blood and brutality, but she, equally talented on the field, brings an added dimension to war, concerned with the nuances of justice and a more intellectual approach to strategy."

"They provide an interesting contrast, and Athena's more feminine characteristics suggest we should value these things more, but you can't claim the ancients were more enlightened than us. Women in Pericles's Athens were little better than prisoners in their homes, kept out of view in the gynaikonitis. They had no public role."

"Most did not, that is true, but it's significant that the goddesses were equally respected as the gods. Our culture and our religion don't give females so much. And as for us mortals, women have long been skilled at using backstage manipulations to achieve political ends. I've no doubt that was true, even in fifth century Athens. Consider Aspasia, Pericles's mistress. Plato tells us she trained Socrates in rhetoric and wrote her lover's funeral oration."

"And Pliny tells us she was a woman of ill repute," Mr. Taylor said.

"As men often do when faced with women of uncommon wit and education," Colin said.

"Hence, centuries of being forced into the background," I said. "I should like to see that change in my lifetime."

"I can see why you and the intrepid Miss Carter get along so well. I'm impressed with your knowledge of the ancient world, Lady Emily. Should you and your husband ever wish to see Herculaneum, I'd be delighted to play guide. The ruins there are even better preserved than those at Pompeii. We take one day off a week, so consider this a standing offer for a picnic and tour on the Sunday of your choice."

"That would be delightful," I said. "But don't think you've distracted me from my defense of lady archaeologists."

He grinned. "Callie is one of the best in the field, yet, as things stand, she would never be able to get permission to lead a dig, and, even if she could, I don't think many of her male colleagues would take direction from her. Perhaps there's something in the nature of men that prevents us from giving you ladies your full due."

"Nature is nothing but a convenient excuse," I said. "We're quick to blame our shortcomings on it, when instead we should be working to overcome those faults. Had you been born in a society that treated women as the equals of men, it would never

122

occur to you that Miss Carter shouldn't lead a dig or that men would balk at her orders."

"We have free will, but we are not free from original sin," Mr. Taylor said.

"Before this conversation descends into a pit of religious mire, I should like to circle back to another topic, that of Clarence Walker," Colin said. "Other than his piece on Pompeii, are you familiar with his work, Mr. Taylor? You live in New York, so it's not unlikely that you've read him."

"I have a house there, but spend very little time at it. Mrs. Astor and her Four Hundred bored me to tears. I prefer European society; it's far less prudish than its American equivalent. I don't know Walker beyond the article you mentioned. I read it, but it didn't make much of an impression on me. I certainly never ran into him in Manhattan."

"It is probable that whoever killed him was connected to the excavations," I said, "but that doesn't preclude someone he could have met in New York. There are a considerable number of Americans working at Pompeii."

"Most of them at my dig," Mr. Taylor said. "I don't make a practice of hiring violent criminals, at least not so far as I know."

"How long have you known Stirling?"

Colin asked. "He's a bit of an odd fish."

"That may be, but he's a fine fellow. Met him a few years ago and took to him at once. Might be too obsessed with poetry for his own good, but I can't imagine he'd hurt any living creature, even if provoked. He's soft."

"Unlike Benjamin Carter," I said.

"Carter? Another decent man. Sure, his temper flares on occasion, but he's never given me cause for worry. And on that note, I'm afraid I must take my leave. I've a dinner engagement with a delightful young lady in Naples this evening. Her mother is chaperoning us, wholly unaware that I find her more charming than her daughter. I do hope I can avoid making a mess of the whole thing."

12
AD 79

The argument that ensued after my father and I left Plautus was one for the ages. I can admit now that my fury over losing every familiar part of my life was not merited, but at the time, it consumed me. My father let me shout and rail against him, not commenting until I had finished, and then only to say something about Achilles and rage. This only further fueled my anger.

I stormed out of the house — something I couldn't have done without permission while still a slave — and stalked through the streets, so furious that all coherent thought was impossible. And then, as I turned a corner, I noticed a graffito on the wall of a thermopolium that so shocked me I could not breathe. It was two lines from one of the poems I had given Silvanus. Below them, a second person (the handwriting markedly different from that of whoever had scrawled the verse) had commented that

125

truer words had never been so beautifully expressed.

This improved my mood, slightly.

I kept walking and then I saw them again: the same lines of my poem, this time scratched into the wall of a house. No one had responded, but I couldn't help feeling bolstered. Had Silvanus liked my poems enough to share them with someone else? Someone inspired to share them with the rest of the city? Or had he, himself, hired someone to do it?

By the time I returned to Plautus's house, I was no longer filled with ire. My mistress, Claudia, sent for me soon thereafter and presented me with a wooden box. Inside, were two heavy gold bracelets, formed as snakes that would curve up the wrists when worn, their eyes bright emeralds.

"I'm grateful to know you, Kassandra," she said. "You've worked hard and have always been a wonderful companion to my daughter. You'll always be welcome in this house. I'll miss not seeing you every day."

I could hardly speak, taken aback by her generous gift. I'd never owned something so valuable or so beautiful. I thanked her, again and again, and clutched the box to my chest, determined not to let it out of my sight until it was safe in our new home.

My father did not seek me out that evening, but I would see him on the morrow. No doubt he would chastise me for my behavior, but I hoped that the chaos of relocating would mitigate his words. Regardless, I was not looking forward to any of it.

13
1902

Mr. Taylor's acknowledgment of Benjamin's
temper, coupled with my own observations,
prompted me to invite the young man to
accompany Ivy and me to Naples, ostensibly
to help us procure supplies for her Roman
banquet. Admittedly, his artist's eye would
be useful when searching for period appropriate decorative objects, but I was more
interested in getting him away from Pompeii and from his sister so that I might
further question him about Mr. Walker. But
no matter how I approached the subject, he
revealed nothing.

Naples was not the city I expected it to
be. Teeming with people, dirty, and chaotic,
it felt — though didn't look — more like
some Eastern marketplace than part of Italy.
There were beautiful bits, to be sure, but
Benjamin's constant reminders that we
must remain vigilant to avoid pickpockets
and, then, nearly getting run down by three

separate people on bicycles did not endear the place to me. The sun beat down relentlessly, making us unbearably hot.

Our first official task was to scour antique shops for couches that Benjamin could transform into reasonable facsimiles of their ancient counterparts. This took nearly half the day, but was worth the effort. Although the wood on the ones we found was shabby, their dimensions were perfect, and our friend was confident he could dress them up enough that they would've been welcome in any ancient villa.

"A wealthy family would've had them made from solid silver," he said, after we'd entered an art store to buy supplies to decorate them, "but metallic paint will do the job for us."

"Solid silver is far too soft to be used in furniture construction," the clerk behind the counter said. "Bronze, maybe. If you're set on silver, the Romans sometimes covered wood with foil, but elaborate inlays were more fashionable. I'd suggest —"

"I don't appreciate your interference," Benjamin snapped, "and would thank you for leaving us alone."

"Forgive me," the man said. "I meant no —"

"Perhaps we'll take our business elsewhere." He stormed out of the shop, leaving Ivy and me to apologize for his ludicrous behavior.

"I didn't realize paint was such a volatile subject," Ivy said when we came out.

"Forgive me," he said. "I have a tendency to overreact, particularly when my expertise is questioned. It's a disgraceful failing. Let me make it right." He went back inside, emerging a quarter of an hour later with a large parcel.

As quick as he was to anger, he was equally fast to return to high spirits, apologizing again and again and thanking us for our understanding. I couldn't riddle out his character. It was as if he was trying to adopt what he believed was an artistic temperament, but not doing a very good job of it. For the rest of the afternoon, he was a perfect companion, helping us select silk for tunics and convincing Ivy to have a wig made in appropriate Roman style. He'd gleaned an impressive amount of information about trends in fashion and hair from wall paintings and done an admirable job of internalizing the sensibilities of the city's ancient residents.

Once we'd found every item on Ivy's exhaustive list, we stopped at a café, where Benjamin pulled out a notebook and started making sketches of his ideas for how to decorate for her soirée. Seeing a bookshop across the piazza, I excused myself, wanting to find copies of Dante's *Divine Comedy* and Virgil's *Aeneid*. When I returned, with those and many more — it is impossible to leave a bookshop with only what one planned to purchase — my friends were still engrossed in their plans. I had to tear them away so that we didn't miss our train.

Back in Pompeii, Ivy and I planned to hire a cab to take us home, but the young American refused our offer to drop him at his hotel. "Look, there! I see Stirling at the far end of the platform," he said. He shouted to his colleague, who turned and gave a halfhearted wave, but did not come over to greet us. Instead, he increased his pace and rushed away. "I'll catch up with him and we can walk together — we're both at the same hotel. Hope to see you both soon at the dig."

"Mr. Taylor doesn't seem too concerned with his employees being on site," Ivy said after Benjamin had rushed off. "Do any of them work when they're supposed to?"

"He might have sent Mr. Stirling to Naples. The museum is there, after all. He might have needed to consult with a colleague. Or he could have been collecting supplies."

131

"I suppose," Ivy said, wrinkling her nose, unconvinced. "More likely he was off in search of books of poetry. But it's wrong of me to think uncharitably of him. He's never anything but kind to us."

When we reached the villa, the sun had started to sink into the sea, splashing gold and pink into the water below, and the air had grown chilly. Ivy retreated to freshen up and dress for dinner, while I opened my parcels from the bookshop.

"Books, Em?" Jeremy asked. "You brought half your library with you. Surely you can't need more?"

"All thinking people are in constant need of more books. Where are you off to?" He was wearing evening kit.

"A midnight excursion through the ruins."

"I'm not sure that's the best choice of dress," I said. "I presume you're going with Callie?"

"I am," he said, a shocking tone of mischief in his voice.

"Would I also be correct to presume that, when you stayed out all night, you were with her as well?"

He grinned. "Your intuition is at once appalling and a wonder."

"But with her *all night*? Where were you?"

"A gentleman never kisses and tells."

132

"I'm not asking for details," I said, "and would sooner push you off a cliff than listen if you tried to share them. But *all night?*"

"Too scandalous for you?" His eyes danced. "It wasn't quite that bad, Em, so you needn't fear for my reputation. We sat in a tavern until it closed and then walked around town talking until the sun rose. I escorted her back to her digs, where she assured me she would be able to slip inside and change her clothes without disturbing her brother. She came back down, we took breakfast at the perfectly respectable Hôtel Suisse, and she went to work. Soon thereafter I stumbled upon you, Hargreaves, and his abominable daughter in the ruins, where I believe my contribution to the investigation of the plaster shed was critical to the enterprise."

"Callie changed her clothes but you didn't."

"A lady has to be more careful with her reputation."

"I wouldn't have expected her to care about that," I said.

"She doesn't, but she does care about her job, very much. Taylor might not look kindly on her having stayed out all night. A duke, on the other hand, can come and go as he pleases."

I studied his face. There was a certain glow about him, a brightness in his complexion that suggested he was falling in love, and while the logistics of their relationship might prove daunting, I liked Callie for him. More than that, I rejoiced at seeing him happy and was about to say so when I noticed something I hadn't purchased mixed in with my packages of books: a small wooden case. Inside was a thin sheet of soft metal — lead — rolled into a tube, a single nail stuck all the way through. I carefully pulled out the nail and started to unroll it. The metal was in dire condition. It looked as if someone had attacked it before impaling the cylinder with the nail. Visible beneath these marks of violence was a short passage of text:

I curse Lady Emily Hargreaves and her life and mind and memory and liver and lungs mixed up together, and her words, thoughts and memory; thus may she be unable to speak what things are concealed, nor be able to communicate anything she finds. I bind her tongue, so that it will be twisted and devoid of success.

"Blimey, Em, bringing down the wrath of the gods, are you?"

"What's the commotion?" Colin asked, entering the room, dressed for dinner, his tousled curls still damp from the bath. "You're not trying to get Bainbridge to read, are you?"

"This is far more interesting than any old book, Hargreaves," Jeremy said. "Emily's been cursed."

My husband did not look surprised; he was used to me attracting unusual attention. I handed him the message. "Lead, fashioned in the style of a Roman *defixio*," he said. "A curse tablet. They were quite common in the ancient world. The nail pushed through was meant to strengthen the potency of the words. Most of these other marks were made by a jab of the nail, but some are symbols."

"Magic symbols, I presume," I said. "This is quite encouraging."

"Encouraging?" Jeremy pulled a face.

"If I've managed to inspire someone to put a curse on me in an effort to stop my tongue, I must be doing something right."

"What's this about a curse?" Ivy, in a divine dinner gown of crimson silk, entered the room, Colin's daughter following. My friend gasped when she read the tablet; Jeremy took her arm to steady her. Kat, on the other hand, whooped. I can only conclude the idea of my being cursed delighted her.

"This is brilliant, Lady Emily, and if you don't mind my saying, I agree that it's a positive sign. Maybe the questions you've asked the archaeologists have set someone on edge."

Perhaps I had misjudged the girl.

"This is very serious, Kat," Ivy said.

"No, no, it really isn't," I said. "First off, I don't believe in whatever pagan god is being appealed to. Second, curses do not work. The tablet, like the ostraca, may be a sign we've caught the attention of our murderer, but surely that's a good thing. It tells us he's worried we may be onto him."

"Whoever penned this — scratched it, I should say — has a fair knowledge of both the cultures of ancient Greece and Rome," Colin said. "I believe I'm on safe ground suggesting that this delicate attention comes from the same person who put our surname on the ostraca."

"And I believe I'm on safe ground suggesting that we are looking for someone who prefers scratching to writing," Jeremy said. "Must be an eccentric bloke."

"Must be a murderer, Jeremy," Ivy said, concern writ on her pretty face.

"Possibly," Colin said. "The text doesn't

136

threaten physical harm, only that Emily will be silenced. Similarly, being ostracized meant exile, not injury. Perhaps it's not the murderer sending these messages, but an associate. Someone who knows what the villain is capable of and wishes to advise us to stop searching for him."

"He's cursing her organs, Hargreaves," Jeremy said. "How is that not a physical threat?"

"There are many examples of ancient curses that specifically call for bodily harm. The falling off of limbs, the shriveling of . . . never mind," Colin said. "It's most likely nothing more than an attempt to warn us off the investigation."

"I like your idea of two villains," I said. "One, the master, the other a mere accomplice, someone who is not altogether comfortable with what has occurred. Feeling guilty about Mr. Walker's death and terrified that we may bring violence upon ourselves if we cross his colleague, he is trying to stop our pursuit of justice."

"An excellent fiction, my dear, and also a theory worth consideration. Either way, I agree it's encouraging."

Ivy regarded him with astonishment as he went off to collect the ostraca so we could compare the handwriting with that on the *defixio*. When he returned, we could see at a glance they were both penned — scratched — by the same individual.

"Are you going to stand by and let them go on like this?" Ivy asked, turning to Jeremy.

"Nothing else to do," he replied. "Can't stop them. As you see, they're excited by curses and threats and all sorts of other untoward things. Part and parcel of the work, or so I'm told. Don't try to dissuade them. They won't be distracted by anything else."

He wasn't entirely correct in this observation. I was distracted by Kat staring at her father and me, her eyes narrowed.

"Who knew you were going to be in Naples today?" she asked.

"All of you," I said, "and Benjamin, obviously. He could've told any number of people."

"He would have had to ask for time off work, so Mr. Taylor would know, too," Kat said. "Unless the request would have gone through Mr. Stirling. I've spent a great deal of time with Mr. Carter, working on photography, and know him well enough to say he doesn't have sufficient knowledge of ancient history to have made this."

"I can't share your opinion," I said. "He's

demonstrated a decent grasp of ancient culture." She glared at me.

"He did have ample opportunity to slip the tablet in with the books," Colin said.

"He wasn't with me in the shop," I said, "but he could've done it on the train."

"Did you not hear me, Lady Emily?" Kat scowled. "He couldn't have made it."

"Making it and delivering it are two separate things," Ivy said.

"Quite," Colin said. "Did you notice anyone following you today, Emily?"

"No, and I was careful to keep an eye out," I said. "I'm not infallible, though."

My husband nodded. "No one is. Where were your parcels on the train?"

"On the luggage rack across from our seats," I said. "The one directly above was already full when we boarded. The car was horrendously crowded. People were standing in the aisle. It wouldn't have been difficult to insert something into our things without us noticing. We saw Mr. Stirling at the station in Pompeii. Benjamin rushed off to catch up with him so they could walk back to their digs together. He must have been on the train, as well."

"He certainly would be aware of *defixiones,*" my husband said.

"Wouldn't all of the archaeologists?" Ivy

asked. "We're surrounded by classically educated individuals who possess the knowledge, background, and means to commit the murder as well as to send these messages of warning. How do we begin eliminating suspects?"

"You can start with Callie," Jeremy said. "Walker was strangled, correct? She wouldn't have had the strength to do that. She's little more than five feet tall. Would have had trouble even reaching his neck."

Kat, to no one in particular, muttered something about men in love.

"I'm inclined to agree with you, Bainbridge," Colin said.

Jeremy grinned. "Glad to hear that, Hargreaves. Wouldn't want to make the mistake of falling in love with a second murderess."

"Love, did you say?" I asked.

"I only suggest it as a possibility," Jeremy replied. "Stay focused on the crime, please, not my romantic life."

"With pleasure, my dear boy," I said. "It will be a relief not having to worry about you anymore."

"You worry about me, Em, do you? How very sweet. I shall have to bring you flowers tomorrow. For now, though, it doesn't appear there's anything left for me to do here.

I'm off. See you in the morning."

"Planning to be out all night?" Colin asked.

Jeremy grinned. "Of course not. But I do expect you all to be snug in your beds by the time I come home. You, especially, Miss von Lange. You're far too young to be embroiled in any of this nonsense."

14
AD 79

Arguing with my father always proved futile. I had expected him to chastise me in the morning, but he did not so much as mention the furious abuse I had hurled at him the previous day, leaving me feeling worse than if he had criticized my behavior. I stayed silent for the duration of our move. As we walked to the new house (Plautus had sent our few possessions over during the night, as carts, with only a few exceptions, were not allowed on the streets during the day), I spotted seven more walls on which lines of my poetry had been scratched. If I weren't so full of guilt over my appalling performance yesterday, I would have pointed them out to my father. As it was, I let them pass unnoticed.

Our new home had been cut from the domus of a wealthy family. It faced one of the busiest streets in Pompeii and was little more than a block from the elegant Stabian

Baths. We had two entrances in the front, the doors nearly on top of one another. The first led into our modest atrium, the other into a tiny room that might have been suitable for a doorman. Instead, my father planned to use it as the business entrance to the house. He had become a bookseller, although he did still take responsibility for our former master's library, a duty that would provide a small income. He also offered his services as a tutor, and that task kept him busiest of all, as wealthy Romans always insisted upon a Greek education for their children.

I assisted him, working as a copyist, a job I found tedious because most of his clients were interested in books of rhetoric, law, and bad poetry. I had hoped we could be discerning when it came to our customers, but if we wanted to eat, that was not to be. Even so, the quality of our meals had declined substantially since our elevation from slavery. We purchased most of them from the thermopolium across the street, and even if we hadn't, our senses still would have been constantly assaulted by the odor it produced. No more delicate perfumes wafting through the air like at Plautus's villa, only grease and old beans.

I did, however, have my own room — and

a bed — for the first time in my life. Father encouraged me to have the space decorated any way I liked. He had hired a well-respected artist, a Greek called Melas, who had a business supplying skilled painters of interiors throughout the city. I disliked him the instant he started criticizing the plans I had for my walls, which I wanted covered with scenes from the *Aeneid.*

"A Greek girl like you should prefer the *Iliad,*" he said, his arms crossed over his chest, his eyes disapproving.

"I was born in Pompeii and raised in a Roman household. I'm more Roman than Greek," I snapped, "so don't be impertinent."

"Even if I didn't know your ancestry, your golden hair would have alerted me to your Macedonian roots. You shouldn't be ashamed of them."

I bristled as he said this, hating his words. "I have no interest in discussing anything with you other than the frescoes in my room." He and his crew had already completed much of the rest of the house, and I had to begrudgingly admit that his work was good. Naturally, my father had chosen scenes from Greek mythology and epics; he was proud of his heritage. But it was Melas's miniature landscapes that most captured

144

my imagination. Those, and the delicate floral garlands in our triclinium.

Melas said nothing more about Greece or Rome, about Virgil or Homer, but pulled out a tablet and silently started to make sketches as I described what I wanted. By the time I had convinced him to include a panel showing the scene from the *Aeneid* in which Venus appears to her son dressed as Diana, it was nearly time for dinner, and my father interrupted us.

"Kassandra, my dear, fetch us a meal from across the street. Melas, will you join us?"

"I'm sure he's better things to do, Father," I said.

"I would be delighted to, Aristeides," the painter said. "Perhaps your daughter can explain to me all the ways she finds Virgil superior to Homer."

My father laughed. "Don't encourage her. She will come around to the truth on her own, if we give her enough time and space."

I glowered at them, pulled on a veil, shouted for our slave Telekles — no Roman sees irony in the fact that former slaves own slaves of their own — and went to Galen's wretched thermopolium. Graffiti, painted red, covered the upper sections of the walls on either side of his doorway, begging votes for Cnaeum Helvium Sabinum, who was running for aedile. According to the message, Galen's waitress Maria was doing the asking. I'd never heard her express the slightest interest in politics. Galen greeted me warmly, calling me by name, and, as always, insisted on speaking Greek. I told him we needed food for three and that I didn't care what it was. While he filled containers for me, I ducked into the bakery three doors down and got one of their last loaves of bread. Ordinarily, I went to one further away, where the owner ground his own wheat and baked all day, but I didn't care if what we had tonight was slightly stale. I had no desire to impress Melas.

Telekles chafed whenever he was called on to serve me. He had aspirations of becoming a copyist and much preferred waiting on my father. He carried the tray Galen had prepared only after telling me it was beneath him. Telekles was twelve years old, but behaved more like a man of forty. I quite liked the contradictions in him.

Back at the house, my father and Melas were in the triclinium, reclining on adjacent couches. I cringed. Here we were, entertaining a tradesman, about to dine on street food, and they were sprawled out as if ready for an elegant banquet. I bit back my criticism. As mistress of the house, if I wanted things to improve, I would have to see to it myself.

To be fair, Galen had done a respectable job. His chicken in prune sauce was better than I could have hoped, and he'd put some lavender in the salad. My father always insisted on drinking decent wine, and tonight was no exception. A flagon of his finest Falernian sat on the table in front of his couch. Telekles wasn't pretty enough to serve it; that was the domain of Lysander, another of our slaves, who filled a beaker for me, cutting it with the right amount of water.

"Your father has ordered me to refrain from all comments pertaining to your taste in poetry," Melas said. "He also tells me that you write verse yourself."

"I do, although my talents are modest."

"You exhibit the humility of a true Roman girl." I did not miss the sarcasm in his voice.

"Why do you stay here if you hate all things Roman so much?" I asked.

"I shan't forever," he said. "At the moment, there's no better place for me to earn a living, but once I've saved up enough, I will return to Greece, buy an olive grove, and content myself with pressing oil and indulging in pastoral fantasies. Perhaps, in a

147

nod to Virgil, I'll keep bees as well."

"Won't you miss painting?"

"I won't abandon it altogether, but will no longer rely on it for money. I'll have more artistic freedom."

"My father tells me we're lucky to have you. Apparently, all of Pompeii is desperate for you to redecorate their homes, yet you took this job, which is on a much smaller scale than you are used to. Why?"

"I'm a great admirer of your father," Melas said.

"Because he is Greek?" I asked.

Melas shrugged, leaning on his left elbow. "Because he tutored me in my youth. That, and Titus Livius Silvanus asked me to do it as a favor to him."

"You're acquainted with Silvanus?" I asked. This piqued my interest.

"I decorated his family's villa in Baiae," he said. "Silvanus is a bit of a poet himself, you know. Perhaps you would enjoy his work; I understand it owes more to Virgil than Homer by way of inspiration."

I hated the way he was smiling at me.

15
1902

After dinner, Colin and I took the curse tablet and headed for our rooms, but Kat stopped us outside the door. "Could I keep it overnight?" she asked, addressing her father, not me. "I'd like to photograph it."

"There can't be enough light to do that now," I said. "I'd be happy to give it to you in the morning, but at the moment —"

"I can use reflectors and lanterns. Benjamin showed me how."

"Mr. Carter, not Benjamin," Colin said.

"Mr. Carter," she repeated. "Please, Father, let me take it and try."

I resented her acting as if I were irrelevant to the discussion. "I'd prefer if we —"

"You look tired, Lady Emily," she said, interrupting. "Best that you get some rest now and examine it further in the morning."

"There's no harm in that," Colin said and handed it to her while I stood, stunned by

149

her impertinence. She kissed him good-night, waved vaguely in my direction, and sauntered off. As if nothing unusual had occurred, my husband slipped his arm around me and pulled me close.

"Now we'll have nothing to distract us for the rest of the evening. However shall we pass our time?" He closed and locked the door behind us and kissed me with an urgency that ordinarily would have left me in a pool of desire, but for the first time in our marriage, I was not seduced by his charms. "Is something wrong?"

"No. Yes. I don't know." I sighed. "Forgive me."

He took a step back and rested his hand gently on my cheek. "I know how challenging things are right now. This case is trickier than most. We don't have —"

"It's not the case."

"No? What, then?"

I turned away from him, debating how candid I should be. I crossed to the bed and sat on its edge. I had watched him with Kat, seen how proud he was of her sharp intelligence and buoyant personality, but I also sensed how guilty he felt at having missed so much of her life. She had grabbed a piece of his heart, and I could hardly begrudge her for that. I could, however, begrudge the shabby manner in which she treated me, as if I were some conniving seductress who had lured him away from her mother. Much though I tried to understand her position — the jealousy she inevitably felt for me — I was finding it catastrophically difficult to deal with her, particularly as my husband was blind to her habit of slighting me. How could such an insightful gentleman be so unaware? Was it because she looked so much like his former lover? Was he incapable of seeing the truth about her?

And by *her,* did I mean Kat or her mother? This was my problem. My emotions were in such a tangle. Was I the one infusing tension into my relationship with the girl because I was unable — or unwilling — to forget how her mother had made me feel?

Colin sat next to me and, with deft fingers, started to unhook the back of my bodice while he kissed my neck. When I did not respond the way he expected, he stopped. "Something's distracting you. You're not worried about Bainbridge, are you?"

"You can't possibly believe there's any chance that thoughts of Jeremy could enter my mind when you're doing that."

"I never like to assume."

I should have been enjoying this, but I pulled away.

151

"It's Kat." I could not bring myself to look at him. Maybe it was a mistake to address the subject. Eventually, she'd accept my role in her father's life and stop tormenting me. I ought to be patient. At least, that's what I told myself. In truth, I was too much of a coward to confront Colin about his daughter, and instead, I turned to the other von Lange plaguing me. "Not her, exactly, but her mother."

"Kristiana?" He sat up straight. "Why?"

"Kat is the very image of her and, hence, a daily reminder of . . . oh, I don't know. It's all ridiculous."

He took my face in his hands. "It's not ridiculous if it's troubling you."

"I always felt so inadequate in her presence and now all those old insecurities are creeping back."

"My dear girl, rest assured that you couldn't be inadequate if you tried. No woman — Kristiana included — could hold a candle to you. I've always been honest with you about her. We shared a deep passion and I loved her, but the foundation of our relationship wasn't our hearts. It sprang unbidden, born of the intensity required by our work. You, Emily, you are the only woman who has ever reached inside and grabbed a piece of my soul. I adore you in a way I could never adore anyone else."

"Are there other contenders?" I asked, swatting his arm and forcing something that resembled a smile onto my lips. Talking about Kristiana never improved my mood; I wished I had said nothing.

He put a finger on my lips. "You're letting your imagination run wild."

"Am I? You didn't answer the question. Are there other contenders?"

"I don't deserve that, Emily. When had I ever given you cause — even for a moment — to worry on that count?"

"You haven't."

"So why do you level the charge at me?"

I flung myself back so that I was lying on the bed and draped my arm over my face. "I can't explain," I said. "I can't understand it myself. I don't know why I feel so vulnerable."

"I don't either and could do without your censure. This is a challenging time for me. Kat is —"

I didn't like his tone, but could understand his feelings. "Forgive me. I ought not have said anything. It doesn't matter."

"It matters a very great deal. She's my daughter and —"

I sat up. "I didn't mean *she* doesn't matter. What doesn't matter is my reaction to the way the situation plays on my emotions. I will try harder to master my response so that you don't have another source of difficulty."

He closed his eyes and sighed. "None of this can be easy for you. I wish I had never loved anyone but you, wish I had kept my heart for you alone. All I can do is beg your forgiveness and hope that my transgressions — for that is what they were — don't hurt you more than they already have."

"You're too hard on yourself. No one could say your behavior was outside what's expected of a gentleman."

"I ought to have held myself to a higher standard. I am so very, very sorry." He kissed my hand. "I shall take whatever measures are necessary to earn absolution. In the meantime, let me offer what comfort I can. *Give me a thousand kisses, then a hundred, then another thousand, then a second hundred, then yet another thousand, then a hundred.*" Catullus's lines softened me, and so thorough — and vigorous — were his attentions, that I could hardly remember the countess's name when he finished.

But I did not lose the sinking feeling inside me. If anything, I felt worse. How could I hold anything against him when he was so penitent? I had no right to be hurt by the past, but emotion, as it was wont to do, overpowered rationality.

Breakfast the next morning was a tense affair. To start, Kat made a show of returning the curse tablet to Colin, not so much as acknowledging my presence at the table. I had brought Mr. Walker's *National Geographic* with me and was scouring the article about Pompeii, happy to have a distraction. Published two months before the murder, the article was well-written and insightful, giving an overview of both the history of the site and its present status. Numerous photographs accompanied the piece, including portraits of Giuseppe Fiorelli and Augustus Mau, along with a series of lovely pictures of the ruins. A few of the latter included images of archaeologists at work. I paid the most attention to those, recognizing Mr. Richter, Mr. Taylor, and some of the Italian team, but found nothing that might have catalyzed Mr. Walker to return to Pompeii.

I glanced at my watch, snapped it shut, and closed the magazine. "We'd best set off soon, Ivy."

"Are you going to the excavations?" Kat asked. "If so, I'll join you."

"What a capital idea," Colin said. "I need to go to Naples to check in with the police. Your . . . er . . . Emily would be delighted to spend the day with you."

"I've an appointment to question Mario Sorrentino, but you're welcome to come," I said. We had, at last, managed to track down Mr. Walker's elusive guide.

"I do wish you'd train me in the art of interrogation," Kat said, the comment directed to her father, not me. "I understand you're something of a master. Why don't you send Lady Emily to Naples and inter-view Mr. Sorrentino yourself?"

He raised an eyebrow, but smiled as he drained the last of his coffee. "My wife is at least as talented as I."

"I suppose it would be a nice opportunity for the two of us to spend time together." Her smile was sickly sweet.

Not delighted at the idea of passing the day dodging her barbs and criticism, I wished I could think of a reason to prevent her from coming, but it didn't matter, because the moment we entered the ruins, she begged off to take pictures. Pretending to want to spend time with me was nothing more than a ploy to go off on her own. It wasn't appropriate for a young lady to wander around unaccompanied, but I was not her mother. I knew I couldn't stop her, but I had to try. She met my effort with derision, so I gave up.

Ivy raised an eyebrow. "She shouldn't go by herself."

"If you can prevent her, have at it," I said. "She won't listen to me."

"I'm afraid you're right, but I don't like it. It can't be safe for her to traipse around alone in a foreign country when a murderer is at loose."

"Do you think she'd care if we raised the point? It's not as if we can physically restrain her." I had no wish to discuss the topic further.

We made our way up the Vicolo di Mercurio in the northern part of the city, toward the House of the Vettii, where Mario Sorrentino was to meet us. The vestibule still displayed a considerable amount of its original paint, including a shocking depiction of the god Priapus. If the reader is uncertain as to why this deity of fertility might startle a lady of good breeding, I recommend consulting any book of Greco-Roman mythology; Bulfinch is my favorite. The ancient Romans did not share the prudish values of our current time, as one was constantly reminded in Pompeii, not only by this Priapus, but by the frequent use of the phallus throughout the city. There is an entire room in the National Archaeology Museum in Naples that displays erotic art. Today, it is kept locked — its contents horrified King Francis I of Naples on a visit to the museum with his wife and daughter in the early nineteenth century — and only gentlemen of *mature age and respected morals* are allowed to enter it. Apparently, we ladies are too delicate for such a thing. I managed to lay eyes on Priapus only because the metal shutters covering him had been unlocked for two English gentlemen who paid to have it opened. When they noticed me, they quickly motioned for the guard to close it.

Ivy blushed and went inside, but I remained longer than I would have if the visibly uncomfortable gentlemen hadn't been present. How absurd to hide such a painting from women! Let them bristle a bit. Their nervous tittering made it clear that, gentlemen or not, they were incapable of dealing with the content of the work, and I had great doubts as to them possessing respected morals.

Once I'd tormented them enough, I stepped into the atrium, the central court found in every Roman house, and joined Ivy, who was standing at the edge of a large marble impluvium — a basin that, in antiquity, would have been filled with rainwater — situated directly below an opening in the roof called the compluvium. From there, we had a spectacular view through to the colonnaded peristyle. Cherubs were painted on the pillars that led to it, and on the walls, the decoration consisted of black panels surrounded by cinnabar red borders and blocks of yellow, with painted columns. In the center of each of the black panels was a floating figure: Poseidon, Apollo and Daphne, Perseus and Andromeda, among others. The garden itself held a riot of bronze and marble sculptures, bits of numerous fountains, four marble tables, including one supported by three legs in the shape of lions, and a considerable amount of shrubbery, planted in the spots the archaeologists identified during their initial excavation of the house.

A young man was leaning lazily against one of the peristyle's white columns, and I was about to reprimand him when I noticed a badge around his neck, identifying him as an official guide.

"You ought to know better," I said.

He shrugged. "It survived the eruption. It can survive me." Regardless of this impertinent opinion, he stepped away from the column, looking at me through hooded eyes. The expression in them told me he was too–well aware of his dashing good looks.

"I suppose you're Mario Sorrentino?" I asked.

"Yes, and you are the two loveliest ladies in Pompeii, Lady Emily Hargreaves and Mrs. Ivy Brandon. Please, you must call me Mario. I already feel as if we are old friends."

"I am only interested in speaking about Clarence Walker."

Mario grinned. "Yes, yes, your husband said as much in the many notes he left for me. What do you wish to know?"

But before I could ask a single question, I heard someone calling my name and turned to see Kat rushing toward us, blood streaming down her cheek.

"I'm hurt. Help me, please!"

A quick examination revealed the scratch on Kat's cheek superficial. More concerning was the way she was holding her wrist. "What happened?" I asked.

"I was taking photographs when someone pushed me and I lost my balance. I broke the fall with my hand and injured my wrist. Fortunately, my camera escaped harm."

"Someone pushed you?" Horrified, I felt my heart pounding. Colin would never forgive me for having left her alone. I should have tried harder to stop her. "I wish I knew more about first aid. How does one tell if a bone is broken?"

"Do you want me to fetch a doctor?" Mario asked.

"Let me see what I can do," Ivy said, her face gray, her eyes wide and serious. "Can you move it, Kat?"

Kat twisted her hand and nodded. "Yes, but it hurts."

Ivy gently touched the girl's wrist. "I don't feel a break. Make a fist." Kat did as instructed. "Now wiggle your fingers. Good. There's quite a bit of swelling, but it doesn't appear to be broken. Probably a sprain. Let's get you home and we'll wrap it. The doctor can come to you there."

"How do you know so much, Mrs. Brandon?" Kat asked, all but fluttering her eyelashes at Ivy.

"Six children prepare one for most minor injuries," Ivy said.

"I'm so fortunate you're here. Not everyone is so skilled." She looked at me with a pointed expression.

The two gentlemen who'd been so taken with Priapus must have heard the commotion, and came running toward us. "What can we do to assist? We're at your service."

Kat smiled at them and fixed her gaze on Mario's handsome face. She blushed and then fainted. Or at least did a credible job of pretending. Given her injury, I ought not have judged her, but it was impossible not to notice that she didn't let herself fall until he was close enough to catch her. The performance was nothing short of graceful, a demonstration of perfect timing. And for someone in a dead faint, she had quite a satisfied smile on her face.

16
AD 79

More than a month passed in our new house before I received a message from Lepida, inviting me to spend the afternoon with her. I dressed carefully, in my best tunic, pale blue linen, the color of the sea after sunrise. We didn't have the money to spare for a litter — my father spent everything on books and wine — so I had to walk. As a result, I could not wear my prettiest sandals, but instead had to content myself with sturdier shoes that would stand up to the cobbles and filth on the streets. I hopped across the stepping-stones at the crossroad by the Stabian Baths and continued on until I reached the Forum, which was as crowded as ever. I saw three lines of another of my poems scrawled onto a wall. Encouraged by this, I darted between clusters of merchants and a group of students gathered around their teacher and marched on, past the earthquake-damaged

Temple of Jupiter until I came to the enormous façade of my friend's domus, one of the largest houses in the city. Glorious images of the twins Castor and Pollux with their horses greeted me as I approached, and the doorman called for a slave to take me to his mistress, who received me in a large peristyle garden, lush with greenery and filled by the scent of jasmine.

"It's too fine a day to be inside, don't you agree?" Lepida asked, greeting me with an affectionate embrace and sitting me next to her on a marble couch covered with soft cushions. A slave with a tray stepped forward and handed us each a silver beaker full of cool wine. We sipped in silence for a few minutes, neither of us sure what to say. I didn't consider it my place to speak first, and was relieved when she, at last, did.

"It is too strange, is it not, that we should feel awkward with each other? You have been my closest friend since birth, my partner in every scheme of my childhood, and here we are, with nothing to say to each other? Tell me true, has your elevation from slavery led you to renounce my friendship?"

We both laughed at the inanity of the question. "It's odd to feel no obligation to fulfill your every whim," I said, adopting her teasing tone as my own.

"I prefer it," Lepida said. "I've never considered you anything but my equal."

"Probably because I was no more skilled at doing your hair than you are. I see you're in better hands now." She was the perfect image of a fashionable lady, her raven tresses elaborately styled, enormous pearls dangling from her ears, and a remarkable emerald necklace strung around her neck.

"Silvanus does like to see me well turned out," she said, a sly smile creeping onto her face.

"Married life suits you."

"I am fortunate my father chose for me such a fine husband."

"As fine as you had hoped?"

"Finer," Lepida said. "Extremely skilled in every way he ought to be. Not that I have anyone to compare him to."

"If you have no complaints, he must be worthy of the compliment." My cheeks and neck went hot, but Lepida did not seem to notice my blush. I was embarrassed at having ever longed for the touch of the man to whom she was now married. I had given him very little thought since their wedding — there was no time for it, between moving and adapting to my new life as a freed-woman. But now, in his house, I couldn't help but recall the time I had spent with him. I missed sharing my poetry.

"We must find you a husband, Kassandra," Lepida said. "Have you met any men whose attention you long for?"

"No," I said. "My life is much duller than it used to be."

"Surely not! You have your freedom."

"Yes, but am in a position to do very little with it. Your father's house spoiled me and you know I had the kindest mistress in all of the empire."

"You still write poetry, I hope?" Lepida asked.

"Not so frequently as I used to. The bulk of my time is spent bullying the painter decorating my room into following my orders and copying boring books of rhetoric for my father's customers."

"Then you must start coming to me more often. We're having a dinner party tonight. Stay for it. You will find the company most diverting." She clapped for a slave and asked the boy to send a message to my father, telling him I wouldn't be home until late, and then she turned her attention to my appearance. "You always were prettier than I, with that golden Macedonian hair. I quite envy it. We'll find something of mine for you to wear. When I'm through, you'll be more gorgeous than any princess of Troy."

17
1902

Mario and the English tourists insisted on carrying Kat out of the excavations and helped us put her into a cab. She made sure to regain consciousness before they departed and showered them with a profusion of thanks. The pain of her injury did not interfere with her ability to flirt.

Given how elusive Mario had proved, I made a point of arranging to meet with him the next day so that we might discuss Mr. Walker. He offered to accompany us back to the villa, but I assured him it was not necessary. When we arrived, Kat begged us not to send for a doctor and shut herself up in her room after Ivy neatly bandaged her wrist and secured her arm with a sling. We did not see her again until Colin returned from Naples.

I started for the foyer the moment I heard the carriage, but did not look forward to telling him what had occurred. No sooner had I opened the door than Kat appeared behind me, her pretty face pale, her sling on prominent display. When he saw she was hurt, Colin brushed past me, picked up his daughter, and carried her to a settee in the sitting room, barking for a maid to bring a blanket and ordering a footman to send for the doctor.

"What happened?" he asked.

"I could tell Lady Emily wouldn't be comfortable having me watch while she was interviewing that guide, so I offered to get out of her way," Kat said, her voice barely audible. "I went to the House of the Tragic Poet, where I was taking photographs of a fresco when someone came up from behind and pushed me hard, down onto the ground. I broke the fall with my hand, injuring my wrist."

"I never suggested —" I started, but Colin interrupted.

"The details don't matter," he said. "Not now. Did you see who did this to you, Kat?"

"No. But after I fell I thought I caught a glimpse of heavy black boots, running away."

"Did the attacker say anything to you?" he asked.

"No. It all happened so fast I hardly had time to get my bearings. Could I please have some water?"

Colin, motioning for the maid to bring her some, turned to me. "Why hasn't a doctor examined her?"

"She wouldn't allow it," Ivy said, stepping forward. "And neither Emily nor I did anything to suggest Kat should go off on her own."

"How could you let her do such a thing?" Colin's voice was calm and low, a sure sign of anger.

"We didn't *let* her," Ivy said.

"I'm too weak to talk anymore," Kat said. "Could we send the others away, Father? There's too much commotion with everyone here."

Ivy took me by the arm and dragged me out of the room.

"She is a cunning little thing," she said, after we'd retreated to the terrace. "She's hurt, but not as badly as she's making out. I wouldn't expect Colin to be so easily taken in."

I wished I shared her surprise. The doctor came and went, but we heard nothing about his visit. Nearly two hours passed before Colin came in search of me.

"Will you excuse us, Ivy?" he asked, not turning to me until she disappeared into the house. "How could you stand back and watch her go off like that?" He fairly spat the words at me. I'd never seen his eyes so full of anger.

"I tried to stop her. She doesn't listen to me and does what she pleases."

"She is a young lady who needs to be looked after."

"Quite," I said, biting back the words I wanted to say. "I'm sorry I wasn't able to control her."

"She insists she has no idea who pushed her. Apparently she was alone in the House of the Tragic Poet when it happened. Did you speak to anyone in the area?"

"I thought it more pressing to get her home. By the time she'd reached us, whoever pushed her could have been miles away."

He scowled, but I could see that he knew I was correct.

Ivy and I dined alone that evening; my husband and Kat had trays sent to her room. I spent the rest of the evening on my own, reading in bed, and fell asleep without seeing Colin again. He was already downstairs when I woke the next morning. Breakfast was excruciating as usual, Kat doing everything in her not inconsiderable power to make me as uncomfortable as possible. She was more grating than ever that day, going so far as saying how much she wished I had possessed the strength to keep her from going off alone the day before.

"Instead, here I am, plagued by this injury." She sighed, looking down at her sling. "We all bear our crosses. I only wish mine weren't the design of someone else."

"Lady Emily did not force you to abandon us," Ivy said. "That was your choice alone."

"Oh, I know, Mrs. Brandon. Yet if only she had intervened —" She stopped and looked at her father. "My wrist is more painful than you can imagine. I am so full of regret. I wish that everyone —"

Ivy interrupted. "Emily, isn't it time for you to leave for your appointment with Mr. Sorrentino? I'd like to accompany you. I'm finished with breakfast and could use an excursion."

"I'm off myself," Kat said. "I promised Benjamin I would help him develop plates today."

Colin lowered the newspaper he'd been reading and raised one eyebrow. "Mr. Carter, not Benjamin. You ought not be so familiar with him." I hadn't thought he'd been paying attention. "You're not to go anywhere today. I want you here and resting."

"How could you suggest such a thing?"

171

Kat cried. "I'll collapse under the weight of so much boredom," she said.

"Then I'll stay and keep you company."

"Thank you, Father." Her smile turned salt sweet.

Ivy and I left before the situation grew even less tolerable. My friend had always possessed an uncanny ability to see through me. "Colin's fatherly warmth is something to behold, but he's unconscionably oblivious to the way she slights you. And it's wrong of him to place any of the blame for her injury on you. I could have tried to stop her, too, but I knew it would be futile."

"I find the whole incident perplexing. The House of the Tragic Poet is one of the most popular sites in Pompeii. How could she have found herself alone in one of its rooms?"

"What are you suggesting?"

"I shan't admit it to anyone, even you." Could she have invented the attack to gain her father's attention? He was, after all, spending the entire day with her, his only purpose to entertain and soothe.

Ivy's brow crinkled. "I can make a fair guess. She feels threatened by you, unreasonable though that is. You've had her father all these years and now she wants him to herself."

"No doubt she blames me for her mother's death."

"She's too smart to do that, but it's understandable — even if erroneous — that she views you as the person who kept her from having a normal family. We both know the countess would never have settled for an ordinary life."

"I can't tell her that," I said. "She worships the memory of her mother and I won't be the one to cast the harsh light of reality on the situation."

"She'll grow tired of sniping at you soon enough. She's a bright, cheerful sort of girl, intelligent and witty. If we'd met her in other circumstances, I'm sure we'd adore her."

"I'm trying very hard to adore her in these circumstances. Colin, at least, deserves that. I wish she didn't make it so difficult."

Mario was waiting for us at a small café near the excavations. He ordered coffee for us — ignoring me when I said I didn't care for the beverage — and told us about his background. He had never set out to work as a guide, but there were few other options in Pompeii. As a boy, he had done menial jobs for the archaeologists, carrying baskets of rubbish and fetching supplies. He'd never shown a particular aptitude for more academic work nor had interest in training as an archaeologist. A consummate storyteller, excelling in creating vivid — if often fictional — accounts of the ancient city, he was soon one of the most popular guides in the area.

"What do you remember about Mr. Walker?" I asked.

Mario shrugged. "He was like any tourist, aside from taking many notes as we walked through the site. I recall that he had not before traveled abroad. Signore Walker, he does not like boats. They make him ill. He hated every minute of his crossing of the Atlantic. He came only for his job. I told him he should visit Rome and Florence, but he wanted to go home. He liked the ruins well enough, but had no appreciation for the soul of the place."

"So it would be correct to say you weren't fond of him?" Ivy asked.

"Oh, no, signora. I would not have you so misled. He was a good man — kind, paid me well, and was grateful for my assistance. We cannot all be moved by the same things, and Signore Walker, his passion was New York, his home. He loved the city and wanted to write only about that. The people and their secrets, he said, were richer than those anywhere else in the world."

"Are you surprised that he returned to

Pompeii?" I asked.

"*Si*. As I said, he showed no affinity for the site, but something must have inspired him to come back. This was long ago, Lady Emily, and a guide meets new people every day. It all feels like a different lifetime to me now. I am afraid I can only remember that Signore Walker was a decent, honorable man, who deserved a better end than that he received."

I couldn't fault him for being able to provide no further information. What reason did he have to remember one client out of hundreds?

That done, my mind returned to Kat. In an attempt to ease my guilt about her — no matter how stubborn she was, I ought to have prevented her from going off on her own — Ivy and I spent the bulk of the day seeking out anyone who might have witnessed the attack on her. I questioned guides, tourists, archaeologists, and guards. The only person who had pertinent information was the man stationed at the entrance of the House of the Tragic Poet.

"There was no moment, signora, when the house was empty. You see how busy it is. We are full with tourists all through the day. I don't remember seeing the young lady with the camera, and I swear there was no com-

175

motion, no attack, not here."

"Have you heard any talk about an attack occurring elsewhere?" I asked.

"No, signora," he said. "That sort of thing, it does not happen in Pompeii."

"There's been a murder here," I said. "That sort of thing does, in fact, happen in Pompeii. Please be alert, and should you learn anything that might be pertinent, let me know."

"This is most unexpected," Ivy said, as we started the long walk back to the villa. I was in no rush to reach it. "Will you tell Colin?"

"What good would it do?"

"None that I can see. But dishonesty is a dangerous path, Emily. He should know the truth."

"Do *we* know the truth?" I asked. "She was injured and upset. She might have been confused about where the incident took place. Or her attacker might have done his work quietly. There's no point bothering Colin with it. He'll only be angrier if I come to him and suggest she's lying. I don't need more strife."

We walked the following two miles in silence. At the villa, I found Colin coated in a layer of fine dust, the tub filling in the private bath connected to our bedroom. "Kat got tired of staying home and begged

176

me to take her to Taylor's dig," he said sheepishly, tossing aside his now-grimy tweed jacket and unbuttoning his shirt.

"How is her wrist?"

"The injury is nominal," he said. "Though it ought never have happened."

"No, it shouldn't have, but I will not stand here and take the blame for it. You've said your piece on the subject and there's no sense discussing it further."

"It's not that I —"

"You've already made your feelings clear," I said. "All I will say is this. You wanted her to rest today, yet she convinced you to take her on an excursion. It is not so easy to bend her to your will, is it?"

He did not reply. I hated the tension hanging in the air between us.

"There was a telegram downstairs from Mr. Walker's editor at *The New York Times*." I held the paper up to him. "Apparently, their correspondent in Rome was one of his closest friends. I thought I'd arrange to meet him."

"An excellent plan," he said. "That could prove most enlightening." Finished undressing, he lowered himself into the tub and looked up at me. "I'm sorry, Emily. I shouldn't hold you responsible for what happened. It was wrong of me."

I nodded and pressed my lips together. "Did anything of note occur when you were at the dig?"

He looked grateful for the change of subject. "I heard more about Callie's romantic history than I'd ever care to," he said.

"She talked to you about that? I'm shocked."

"She didn't, her brother did."

"Not very sporting of him to gossip about his sister."

"I wouldn't call it gossip," Colin said. He took a breath, ducked under the water, came up, and lathered soap in his hair. "Concern, more like. She has a certain amount of money at her disposal, not so much that she would be a target for fortune hunters, but enough that she's self-sufficient. He fears this will discourage her from ever settling down."

"Is that such a bad thing?" I asked. "She's an intelligent lady of independent means. I don't imagine there are many husbands who would tolerate her working as an archaeologist."

"A fair point." He disappeared under the water to rinse the soap from his hair, pushing his curls back from his forehead as he reemerged. "There was something off about all of it. I'd swear Carter was as uneasy about Bainbridge getting hurt as Callie. Pass me a towel, will you?" He rose from the tub, temporarily shattering my ability to think rationally or speak. What a pity Praxiteles had not lived to sculpt him; it would have been the master's finest work.

"Another thing. Stirling wouldn't let Kat photograph him. I'm not sure she noticed, but I did. She'd removed her arm from her sling and was taking candid shots. Every time he might have been in a frame, he'd turn away," he said. "I invited them all to a picnic dinner tonight, Taylor's crew, but at the dig, not here. The tables are being set up even as we speak. I'm hoping that a combination of wine, good company, and a complete lack of formality will encourage them to give something — anything — away that might help us better understand what we have on our hands."

When we informed the others of the plan, Jeremy balked at the idea of informality and insisted on full evening kit, but Ivy and I, after consulting each other, decided to wear walking suits and sturdy boots. Kat took our approach a step further, donning a slim pair of trousers, a fitted jacket that reached to her mid-thighs, and knee-high boots. Her father's eyes widened with horror when he saw her, but he said nothing.

By the time we reached the site, servants from our villa had set up a long table laden with a sumptuous array of cold food: thin-sliced prosciutto and salami, hunks of savory cheeses, olives, figs, crusty bread dipped in buttery olive oil, dried apricots, and a velvety red wine. Most of Mr. Taylor's workers had filled their plates and eschewed the table, gathering instead on rocks near where they'd spent the day digging. Social-izing at a distance from their employer was, no doubt, more enjoyable than staying close and being on their best behavior. Their laughter — fueled by the wine — brought an air of merriment to the evening. The rest of us congregated closer to the buffet. Jeremy sat next to Callie, who started to lecture him on excavation reports. I as-sumed he was feigning interest, but some-thing in his eyes suggested otherwise.

"She likes a captive audience," Benjamin said.

"She's fortunate to have a brother willing to put aside his own interests to forward her own," I said.

"She would tolerate nothing less." He sat next to me, putting a plate heaped with meat and cheese in front of him. "The experience here isn't a total loss for me. I do enjoy photography and have done two paintings I'm rather proud of, both of the Bay of Naples. On my own time, of course."

"What do your parents think of your work?" I asked.

He blanched, ever so slightly. "I'm afraid I lost my parents long ago."

"I'm so sorry."

"Don't be. My father never approved of me."

Callie interrupted. "That's absurd and you know it. He would be oozing pride if he could see your landscapes."

"I'd prefer not to discuss it."

"There's no need to be tedious," she said. "Your work —"

"Could we please move on to something else?" He glared at her.

Callie's tone dripped sweetness. "It's only that —"

His voice rose to a shout. "Must you insist on returning to a topic about which you know nothing?" He threw his napkin onto the table.

"Now, now, let's all calm down," Mr. Taylor said. "I, like you, Benjamin, have very little patience. It's not in my nature and I long ago gave up on trying to cultivate it, the same way I abandoned learning to draw once it became clear I lacked any talent for it. We must accept ourselves for who we are and no one, not even your sister, should force you to try to be something you aren't."

"My wife has made great strides in curbing her impulsive nature," Colin said, "but I'm skeptical that anyone can change his fundamental nature."

"Spoken like an aristocrat," Benjamin said. Jeremy bristled and Kat laughed.

"Perhaps you should excuse yourself," Callie said. "You're making everyone uncomfortable."

Her brother leapt to his feet, knocking against the table, and sending two wineglasses flying. "Perhaps you should stop trying to force me to bend to your will. I've already done more than enough, haven't I? I have half a mind to —"

"Carter, my good man, get a hold of yourself," Mr. Stirling said, his tone sterner than I'd heard from him before. "You'll come to regret your words. *An angry man is again angry with himself when he returns to reason.* Publilius Syrus."

"Naturally I'm the problem, not her." Benjamin scowled. "I've had quite enough." He stormed off.

"There's not enough moonlight for him to get far without a lantern," Mr. Taylor said. "I'll go after him and soothe his ruffled

182

feathers."

"Forgive me," Mr. Stirling said. "I ought not have interfered."

"It's not your fault." Callie reached across the table and took his hand. "When his temper flares, there's no stopping it."

"I should have known better," Mr. Stirling mumbled. "Confrontation never leads to anything but trouble. Do excuse me. I'm afraid I'm no longer in a mood conducive to social discourse." He shambled off.

"Poor man," Ivy said. "He did nothing wrong."

"No one ever benefits from crossing my brother," Callie said. "I apologize for his behavior and his vile temper."

I considered the events of the evening. Benjamin needed to better control his emotions, but that came as no surprise. Mr. Stirling's incongruous interference was another matter entirely. The dynamic between the two men made me wonder at their relationship. Could one be our murderer and the other his accomplice? It took little imagination to picture Mr. Stirling adopting oblique methods — like the ostraca and the curse tablet — to warn us off our investigation. He knew Benjamin's propensity for outburst. Did he also know it could lead to violence?

A thundering crash and a hideous scream interrupted my thoughts. With his usual fluid grace, Colin dashed toward the sound. I gathered my skirts and followed, our friends close on our heels. My husband stopped short as he approached a spot where, moments earlier, a towering pile of debris had stood. The heap had collapsed, burying someone, leaving only his booted foot visible.

The workers who had dined closer to the excavations reached the scene of the accident before us and had set up a semicircle of lanterns to illuminate the area. We all worked furiously to uncover the man, but no effort could save him. Amidst the rubble sat a large boulder with a pattern of bloodstains that mirrored the gash on the back of the dead man's skull.

"It's Jackson," Alan Powell, one of the American archaeologists, said, his voice shaking.

"Was anyone else with him?" Colin asked. "Do we need to keep digging?"

"Yes, keep digging. He was talking to someone — I heard voices." Tears left damp trails through the film of dust on Mr. Powell's face.

"Is everyone accounted for?" I asked. While they continued to dig, we listed the names of everyone who had come to dinner. Everyone save Benjamin, Mr. Stirling, and Mr. Taylor was present.

"I don't think there's another body," Colin said. "Ivy, would you please take my daughter back to the villa?" Kat made a noise of protest, but the look on her father's face warned her off argument. "Bainbridge, find Carter, Stirling, and Taylor — they may have gone to their digs — and bring them back. Someone else summon the police."

"We're too late to need a doctor," Mr. Powell said.

"I'm sorry." Colin rested his hand on the man's shoulder. "He could not have survived the blow to his head, no matter how quickly we'd found him."

"But why the police?" Mr. Powell asked. "This is obviously an accident. There's been so much rain lately. We should have expected a landslide."

"In the midst of a murder investigation, we cannot assume anything is an accident," I said. "Why was Mr. Jackson here, away from the rest of you?"

"We'd all had a certain amount of wine," Mr. Powell said, "but Jackson more than the rest of us. He decided to head home."

"Had he been arguing with anyone?" Colin asked.

"No," Mr. Powell said. "We'd had a jolly evening, absent of all strife."

"You heard him talking to someone after he left?" I asked.

"Well . . . I heard voices coming from this general direction. I can't be certain his was one of them."

None of the others could confirm who was speaking. Two of the men thought the conversation had come from our table and started arguing with the rest about the vagary of traveling sound. When Jeremy returned nearly an hour later, he brought only Mr. Taylor with him. He had not managed to locate Mr. Stirling or Benjamin.

"I am . . ." Mr. Taylor's voice trailed. "I don't know what to say. We're careful about how we stack debris. The pile shouldn't have been unstable, but why was anyone near it in the dark? Did he have a lantern?"

"We didn't find one," Colin said.

"Then there must have been someone else with him," Mr. Taylor said. "You're quite certain there's not another body?"

"Yes," my husband said.

Mr. Taylor looked at the bloody boulder and winced. "Please tell me there's no chance this was deliberate?"

"We'll know more after the coroner has examined the body," Colin said, wiping sweat and dust from his face with a handkerchief. "In the meantime, could you please tell me where you've been since you left our table?"

"I followed Carter, as you know. Caught up with him quickly enough, but he refused to talk. Went off in a huff, headed toward town. I decided there was no point in pushing him, so let him go."

"Why didn't you return to us?" I asked.

"Truth be told, I was more than a little irritated with the boy," he said. "Didn't feel much like a party anymore, so I went back to my house."

"Did you walk?" Colin asked.

"Yes, it's only half a mile from here."

"Did you see anyone en route?" I asked.

"No."

Colin nodded. "We'll need to speak with Stirling and Carter as soon as possible."

"Of course," Mr. Taylor said. "What a dreadful thing. We won't work tomorrow. It wouldn't be respectful. I'll contact Jackson's family and arrange for his body to be sent to them. Another fresh death in the shadow of Vesuvius. It doesn't sit right." He glanced in the direction of the volcano, but the night was too dark to reveal its hulking shape. "Makes a person start to wonder . . ."

"Wonder what?" I asked.

He shrugged. "Maybe nothing good comes from disturbing the ancient dead."

18
AD 79

I succumbed to the attentions of Lepida's slaves with pleasure. My friend chose for me a gap-sleeved tunic of the finest silk, pale rose in color, and put strands of pearls around my neck and silvered sandals on my feet. She removed the earrings she had worn that afternoon and handed them to me. When I looked into her polished silver mirror, I hardly recognized myself. My lips bloomed with color, and the shadow painstakingly applied to my eyelids with a tiny spatula made them look bluer than ever.

If I was like a pale rose, with alabaster skin and golden hair, Lepida was the richest jewel in the empire. Her amethyst tunic set off her dark eyes, and her gem-encrusted gold bracelets, necklace, and earrings glistened in the light of the oil lamps that filled the triclinium where we now reclined. My inclusion in the feast had thrown off the numbers, but rather than have another couch brought in, Lepida insisted that I sit next to her, crowding the one she shared with two of their other guests.

Silvanus greeted me warmly when he saw me, exclaiming that he was happy to count me among his friends. His words were kind, but formulaic. From where I was sitting, I couldn't easily speak to him, but as those around me, Lepida excepted, showed little interest in my presence, I took the opportunity to watch him. He was even handsomer than I remembered, his face an ideal example of Roman nobility, with an aquiline nose, square jaw, and pleasingly full lips. Most attractive of all was his voice, deep and rich, full of authority. I looked at the synthesis he was wearing — a tunic bordered with wide braid — and the heavy gold cuffs on each of his wrists and could not help recalling the first time Lepida and I had seen him, when we wondered if he had been a soldier and pictured him in leather pteruges and a gleaming cuirass. I remembered hiding near the door of her father's tablinum, flushed with excitement at the sight of this new visitor. And now, I could not help but laugh, thinking of it.

"What is it you find so amusing, Kassandra?" Silvanus asked. He stared directly into my eyes, his face ever so slightly flushed, but not with wine.

"Nothing of consequence, I assure you, sir," I said, my cheeks turning at least six shades darker than the rose of my tunic. I couldn't bring myself to return his stare. There was a brief pause in conversation. I was certain he'd expected me to say something witty, but I could think of nothing. The poet had lost all her words. Soon enough the moment passed, and everyone went back to discussing whatever it was they had been discussing before. And then, they started talking about a poet whose work had captivated the city.

"No one knows who he is," the man said, "but everyone is obsessed with the lines of his that keep showing up in graffiti. He has an unparalleled talent. Plays with words in a way that I wouldn't have thought possible. The rumor is he's written an epic worthy of Virgil."

"I've heard the same," Silvanus said, "and am quite certain there's no more talented poet in all of Pompeii." He stared directly at me.

"How do you know he lives here?" Lepida asked. My heart was pounding. Could they be talking about my own verse?

"It's much discussed by reliable sources," her husband replied. He glanced at me, and our eyes met, for the barest instant. I knew then, without doubt, that it was my words being complimented. I hardly knew what to think. I was delighted and terrified and utterly unable to form a coherent thought while they continued to laud my work, going so far as to quote their favorite bits. Bits that Silvanus had paid to have written on walls throughout the city.

When the conversation veered in a different direction, Lepida leaned closer to me. "Are you enjoying yourself? You're awfully quiet."

"I'm wholly out of my element."

"Not any longer, you aren't," she said. "You're free now and this is your world. You don't belong in a poky little house with no entertainments. You must spend more time with me, so that you get used to moving in fashionable company."

"I don't think your fashionable company knows what to do with me."

"They'll learn. You're too pretty not to attract their attention. Give them time, my dear, and before you know it, we'll find you a husband who suits you."

"Lepida, you're too kind to me," I said. "We both know the men of your acquaintance have no need for a recently freed slave who has no hope of ever acquiring a fortune."

"Your father could easily acquire a fortune," Lepida said. "He's the most sought-after tutor in Campania and now a bookseller as well. All he needs to do is save up enough to buy a few vineyards, and he'll be well on his way."

Much though I adored my friend, she did not grasp my economic circumstances. It was true, many freedmen earned vast fortunes, but not as tutors or booksellers, and my father had no interest in other, more lucrative business endeavors. But there was more to the issue than simply money. Romans cared about their history and their ancestors. Yes, a citizen of good family desperate for an infusion of cash might be persuaded to take a rich bride of decidedly lower social standing, but that was far from the ideal.

After dinner, when the guests began to depart, Silvanus, faultlessly polite, put me in one of his litters and instructed the bearers to take me home. As I sat on the cushioned bench, he leaned in through the curtains, his face close to mine.

"You see how everyone adores your verses. It's time, Kassandra, that I hear more of your poetry."

This time, I had no trouble meeting his stare.

19
1902

The next morning, Colin woke me with a cup of tea and a small bouquet of wildflowers. "I need to interview Carter and Stirling this morning, as well as speak with the coroner, and I want Kat nowhere near any of this." His dark eyes met mine. "I know you planned to leave for Rome today, to meet with Mr. Walker's friend, *The Times* correspondent. Would you take her with you? I have no right to ask given the way I treated you after she was attacked, but I hope you know that despite my dreadful mismanagement of that situation, there's no one I trust more than you."

I tamped down a smile, irritated at the pleasure his words brought me. "Of course. She can keep me company."

"I'll inform her of the plan. Thank you, my dear. Thank you." He squeezed my hand and kissed me on the cheek.

The trip was somewhat less pleasant than

195

trekking through the Sahara on an ill-tempered camel and with inadequate supplies of water. Kat spoke not a single word on the way to Naples, nor while we waited for our connection on the overnight train deluxe that would take us to the capital city. We sat silent at our table in the dining car. I didn't try to engage her in conversation, instead focusing on the book I'd brought with me. She made no effort to hide her relief. The next morning, soon before our arrival in the city of Caesar (Julius, that is; I have never been able to tolerate that wretched Octavian, or, as he and his enormous ego would have it, Augustus), she slipped into our washroom to dress. When she emerged, I hardly recognized her. I couldn't quite ascertain how she'd done it, but she had utterly transformed her appearance. Gone was the forward-thinking, direct young lady who had worn trousers to a dinner party; in her place was a beguiling rural Italian girl with a sly smile who gestured wildly when she spoke. She'd removed her sling, but that did not surprise me.

If she meant to provoke me, she would not get the reaction for which she hoped. "What a lovely dress. The color suits you," I said and bustled her into a cab that would take us to our appointment at a café near the Trevi Fountain.

"You don't object?"

"Why should I?" I asked. "If you choose to visit Rome as a fetching peasant, who am I to argue? You've made a nice job of it."

"I only remember meeting my mother a handful of times." She wasn't looking at me, but her voice had lost the hard edge it usually had when she spoke to me. "Each time she took on a different persona and introduced herself to the nuns as a close relative. I now realize she didn't want anyone to know her true identity. But she always told me — whispering in German although they insisted we speak French at school — that she was my mother. I was in awe of her ability to slip effortlessly from language to language, and applied myself to studying as many as possible, in an attempt to emulate her. And then, when I could, I turned my attentions to the art of disguise. The nuns weren't helpful in that regard, but I've done a credible job, don't you think?"

"Indeed you have," I said. "How many languages do you speak?"

"German, obviously. I may have grown up elsewhere, but I'm Viennese at heart. French, English, and Italian are second nature to me. I'm competent in Russian and can translate Latin with ease. I've never bothered with ancient Greek." This last she stated as if it were a challenge, knowing my passion for translating the works of Homer. I didn't rise to the bait.

"A most accomplished young lady."

"Are you being ironic?" she asked.

"A bit, perhaps, but only in a manner that might offend Lady Catherine de Bourgh."

"You reference *Pride and Prejudice.*" She laughed and then her eyes narrowed. "I adore Austen. You're well read, but also no slouch when it comes to academic achievement. Where were you educated?"

"At home, with a governess who was more interested teaching social skills that would endear me to eligible gentlemen than in serious studies. Fortunately, my father was not averse to expanding my horizons. His library provided me with everything I could want."

"So you taught yourself?" She met my eyes for the first time since we left Pompeii. "I did the same, with languages, but they come so easy to me it's not much of an accomplishment, truth be told. There were loads of foreign students at my school. I talked to them; it's the simplest way to learn."

"Not many people would have figured that out," I said. "Don't ever denigrate your talents."

She looked away from me again. The cab was approaching our destination, so I said nothing further. Mr. Richards, waiting at a small table, leapt to his feet and greeted us warmly. Kat introduced herself as Floria Tosca — she was fortunate the journalist was not an avid fan of opera — and answered all of his questions in Italian, giving the impression that she could understand but not speak his native tongue. I let them banter for a few minutes before inserting myself into the conversation and asking Mr. Richards about his friend.

"I only heard about Walker's death last week — I'd been hiking in the Dolomites and missed the news when it was first reported. He was a good man, Lady Emily. A good man."

"I understand you knew him well," I said.

"We both started at the newspaper in the same month and shared an atrocious room near the Brooklyn Bridge for six months, until we could afford something better. There's nothing that bonds two men together like trying to keep rats out of their beds. He was a big personality. Friendly, outgoing, and strong as an ox, the sort of gent who would get caught up in a so-called brilliant idea and throw himself into it, heart and soul. He was the man you wanted at your side in a fight, as much for his strength as for his pigheadedness. Once he decided he was on the side of right, he wouldn't back down, even when everyone else around him was ready to go home and lick their wounds. A dog with a bone would have given it up to get rid of him. He could be relentless, but relentless in a good way."

"Have you met his family?" I asked, as Kat motioned for the waiter to bring her a second cup of coffee.

"No. He had a brother, Fergus, somewhere in Montana, and a sister who lives in Virginia, but he wasn't close to her. Walker spent considerable time in Montana as well. Rather, I should say he wasted time there, looking for gold near a place called Last Chance Gulch. It won't shock you to hear he didn't find his fortune. His brother had even worse luck. Got into a bar fight and wound up beaten to death. Some sort of argument over gold. Rough places, those mining towns."

Kat batted her eyes at him. *"Non mi piace pensare a te in un posto così pericoloso."*

She did not like thinking of him in such a place? What was she playing at?

"Nor do I, Signorina Tosca." He cocked his head and looked pensive. "I feel as if

I've heard your name before. Is that possible?"

I recognized the source of her words. Quoting Puccini's libretto seemed to me taking things a step too far, particularly as she was making no useful contribution to the conversation.

"It's a common enough Italian name," I said. "What happened after Mr. Walker's brother died?"

"Walker gave up on mining, came back east, and turned his attention to journalism. He'd written a fair number of pieces for the paper in Helena and was a good enough operator that he managed to persuade *The Times* to give him a couple of assignments after he arrived in New York. The editor liked them, and pretty soon he was on staff."

"I understand he didn't travel much."

"No, not after his adventures out west," Mr. Richards said. "Those were hard years, to hear him tell it, and he didn't want any more like them. Said all a man needed was a clean room, a good pub, and decent friends. And a job to pay the bar bill, naturally. He loved New York City; you can't understand Walker without understanding that. Loved it like it was his own blood. That's why he did cultural pieces — they let him expound on the merits of the city."

201

Kat had remained quiet through all this, but she was listening with such attention I suspected she was memorizing every bit of the conversation. Clever of her to refuse to speak English, as it now gave her the opportunity to focus on listening.

"How did he wind up in Pompeii?" I asked.

"You don't refuse a piece you're assigned," Mr. Richards said. "Not if you want to keep working. His editor thought it would be a good fit for him, as he did a bang-up job on cultural articles in the city. So Walker went, and he wrote something competent, but unimpressive. Wanted to be sure he wouldn't get sent abroad again. He hated the ocean. Hated boats."

"Why did he come back?" I asked.

"I wish I knew. I was still working out of New York when he was here the first time, but I can't understand why he didn't get in touch when he decided to return. His editor said it wasn't for work. I can't imagine what would have induced him to make the trip again. I'd love to be more useful, but I don't know anything else. Do the old boy good, will you? He didn't deserve to die like that."

I could have sworn I saw a hint of moisture in Mr. Richards's eyes as he spoke. I thanked him for his candor and watched him stroll away across the piazza after he made a meal out of kissing Kat's hand by way of farewell.

We sat at the café for another hour. Kat drank a shocking amount of coffee while she scribbled furiously in a notebook. How fortunate that her injury had not affected the hand she needed to write. I collected my thoughts and penned a series of messages, finishing in time to drop them at the telegraph office at the railway station. We boarded our train and I opened the novel I'd brought with me, Mary Elizabeth Braddon's *Wyllard's Weird,* while Kat changed back into her ordinary clothes, erasing all evidence of Floria Tosca. She emerged from the tiny room housing the washstand in our compartment looking uncharacteristically sheepish.

"I'm aware that sometimes I'm too brash and too impulsive for my own good." She'd gone back to her habit of not meeting my eyes.

"The latter is a fault leveled at me more times than I care to count," I said, closing my book.

"I've a shockingly good memory for conversation, cultivated by years of using it as a party trick. I wrote a complete transcript of your meeting with Mr. Richards." She handed me her notebook. "I hope it goes some way toward making up for my bad behavior. I wanted to try my disguise and got carried away. It's fortunate my father wasn't here to see it. He'd probably send me away forever."

"I can promise you he will never do that."

"I do so want to get to know him and, through him, come to learn something of my mother. I realize that's uncomfortable for you. I don't know much about my parents' relationship, but it takes no leap to deduce that you're bound to find it painful."

"It all happened long before I met your father," I said, "and he and I are well versed in awkward pasts. I was married to his best friend."

"No! How scandalous. Are you divorced?" There was, perhaps, a bit too much excitement in her voice.

"Heavens, no. Philip died not long after our wedding trip. It was only after I was out of deep mourning that Colin and I became close."

"How frightfully romantic," she said. "I had no idea. Was he very tortured over it, my father? He strikes me as the sort of man who could brood beautifully."

"Tortured enough, but he would never allow himself to get carried away."

"No Heathcliff, then?"

"Never."

"I arrived in Pompeii determined to despise you," she said. "If he'd never met you . . ."

If Colin had never met me, very little in Kat's life would've changed. Her mother had chosen to marry someone else. But the way Kat swallowed when she choked back those last words made me see the little girl she'd once been, a girl who dreamed that her mother would collect her from school, take her home — to a real home — and give her a reassuringly ordinary life. The countess would never have abandoned her work, not even for her child, regardless of the circumstances. Kristiana's choices reflected a devotion to Colin, but little consideration for Kat. Not that I would ever say that to her.

"Your mother did what she believed best for you. As for her relationship with your father, it never fell within the bounds of society's norms. There's no reason to think it would have, even if he'd never met me. They made their choices and we're left to live with them."

"I've read my mother's diaries, but she

never once mentioned him or me. She never mentioned anything of interest. Every page was staggeringly dull, as if written to deliberately put off anyone reading them."

"Given her work, she may have done just that. It wouldn't have been sensible for her to keep a detailed, intimate diary, and she wanted to protect your father — you know as much from the letter her solicitor gave you."

"Yet you do not share her fears."

"No, I don't," I said. "I'll never understand his work so well as she, who was engaged in the same occupation. She was privy to much more than I can ever be."

"Yet you aren't — weren't — jealous of her?"

Just when I thought we were starting to get along, that hard edge had crept back into her tone. She wanted me to be jealous. Wanted me to feel threatened. "I was consumed with jealousy when I first met her. She was everything I was not — sophisticated, experienced, and essential to Colin's work. And stunning — absolutely gorgeous, but not in a sweet, pretty way. She possessed a beauty that went beyond her perfect features. Her intelligence and independence shone brighter than her eyes. Next to her, I always felt insignificant and awkward."

She turned away, looking out the window. "And now I'm a reminder of something you'd prefer to forget."

She did have a way of seeing the truth about people. "Not everyone can marry his first love, your father included. I wouldn't change anything in his past, for to do so would inevitably alter the man he is today."

"I'm sorry I set out to despise you."

I hesitated for a moment, but then reached across and took her hand. "Don't be too hard on yourself."

The train was pulling into Naples, so we both fell silent. Colin was waiting on the platform when we emerged. He took our bags from the porter, gave me a kiss, and quickly — if a bit awkwardly — embraced Kat.

"If we don't dawdle, we can catch the next train to Pompeii," he said.

"I'm afraid we'll have to go to the telegraph office first," I said. "I'm expecting a reply." Fortunately, it was waiting, and, after I ascertained it did not require immediate response, we rushed to catch the train. Once settled into our seats and *speeding* away (I employ the term with irony; it would be difficult for a train to move at a more sluggish pace than the local from Naples to Pompeii), I recounted for him my conversation with Mr. Richards, not mentioning Kat's disguise. She didn't utter a word and gave every impression of being wholly uninterested.

"This is from the sheriff in Last Chance Gulch, Montana. Helena, Montana, actually, as that's what they call the place now." I held up the telegram. "I sent a message asking for information about Mr. Walker's brother, Fergus, who died in the aftermath of a nasty bar fight there. In effect, he was murdered, and Felix Morgan, the man who struck the fatal blow, fled the scene. These American territories are violent and backward; it's a wonder anyone survives them. I've already requested that the American Embassy in Rome check if they have any record of Mr. Morgan having come to Italy, but I don't hold up much hope. Surely he would have changed his name."

"And adopted a new identity as an archaeologist?" Colin asked.

"Possibly. But most likely not. What if he invented a new life for himself, settled down, got married, had children, and one of those children caught the attention of Mr. Walker?"

"Benjamin?" Kat sat up straight, her eyebrows raised. "Never."

"Mr. Carter," Colin said. "He was in the

States the first time Walker came to Pompeii."

"Precisely," I said. "And nothing happened to Mr. Walker on that trip. Then, a few years later, the journalist returns, because, on the ship, he spotted Benjamin's striking resemblance to his father, Felix Morgan."

"Why would he have got on the ship in the first place?" Colin asked.

"Mr. Walker wrote cultural pieces about New York. Surely that would have included openings of exhibitions at the Metropolitan Museum, where we know Benjamin spent a considerable amount of time drawing. It's where Mr. Taylor first met him."

Colin nodded. "It's possible. But why wouldn't Walker have confronted him there? Why come all the way to Pompeii?"

"For all we know, he did. Benjamin turned down Mr. Taylor's initial offer of employment. It was only later — perhaps after Mr. Walker approached him about the true identity of his father — that he agreed to join the staff. He wanted to protect himself and his sister from a man bent on revenge."

"Benjamin would never hurt someone," Kat said.

"Mr. Carter." Colin frowned. "If Walker was bent on exposing Carter's father and tempers flared — which we know Carter's is prone to do —"

"Benjamin might have killed Mr. Walker in a blind rage," I said.

"He wouldn't do that," Kat said. "Furthermore, his father died years ago. What would it matter if he were exposed?"

"Do we know where Carter was when you were attacked?" Colin asked her.

"At Mr. Taylor's dig," she said, crossing her arms and pulling them tight against her chest.

"His work doesn't always take him there," I said. "If he was painting, he could have been anywhere in the excavations, including the House of the Tragic Poet."

"You've gone completely off the rails with this one," Kat said. "Benjamin — Mr. Carter — would never hurt me. I believe I'm on safe ground claiming to know him better than either of you."

"Be that as it may, I'd prefer to see you spend less time with him," Colin said.

"Now you'll tell me better safe than sorry, I suppose." Kat was fuming, but for once, her ire was directed at her father instead of me.

20
AD 79

Oh, that I had ignored those words uttered by Silvanus as I sat in his litter, ready to go home after the banquet! But I did not. Nor did I refuse to see him the next morning, when he appeared at my father's house. I'm ashamed to admit that every noble virtue I possessed flew out the window when I saw him standing in our modest atrium.

"Your presence last night took me by surprise," he said. He greeted my father like an old friend and, after ordering copies of three books, pulled me aside, into our tiny garden that struggled to let even an insufficient amount of natural light into the house. "You look content, which pleases me. I know you've always meant a great deal to my wife and I'm glad to see you so happily settled in a lovely home."

"More like a suitable home," I said, scowling. "Don't pretend it's more. It's small, but serves its purpose."

"The wall paintings are of the finest quality. Your father was right to ask me to secure Melas for him."

"I don't imagine you've come here to discuss a Greek artist," I said, suddenly feeling ill at ease.

"No, I did not. I find myself missing your poetry, Kassandra."

"Did you hire someone to do the graffiti?" I asked. "I've seen it throughout the city."

"Yes, I wanted to share your words with the world. They're already wildly popular — your work resonates with everyone in the city — and now I'm hoping to persuade you to write more for me."

I shrugged. "There's no reason I wouldn't. You only need ask."

"It's not so simple. I should like to keep our connection private at present." He was standing close to me — a habit, apparently — and held his hand up to my cheek, but did not touch it. I could feel his heat, and my skin prickled.

"Why?" I asked. "It's not as if reading poetry is scandalous. Especially not mine." He wasn't looking at me, but instead gave a decent impression of having a serious interest in the unremarkable fountain that took up most of one end of the garden.

"There are some things, Kassandra, that

must be kept between two people." Now he stared into my eyes.

My heart pounded. Was he trying to seduce me? It wouldn't have been so unexpected when I'd been a slave — and would've, in fact, been expected, had I been a slave in his house. Not even Lepida would have given it a second thought. Such is the oddness of the Romans. But now? Circumstances had changed too much. Did this explain his desire for secrecy?

"No, Silvanus," I said, my voice trembling. "Lepida is my friend. I can't do that to her."

"She has no love of poetry."

"She has a great love for you and she trusts me. I will not betray her."

"I'd never ask you to do that. I'm speaking of poetry, Kassandra, and nothing more. Perhaps I wasn't clear enough." His words did not mirror his tone, which, to my inexperienced mind, sounded heavy with desire.

"She wouldn't care if you read my verse. Why would you think it necessary to hide such a thing?"

"My bride is young and I will not give her any cause — even an unsubstantiated one — to worry. All I ask is that you agree to meet with me and share with me what you've written. I'll come to you, in the tavern of your choice, a place where no one knows us. What harm could come from that?"

I couldn't think of any, which serves only to reveal the limitations of my imagination. I could offer no defense beyond my youth. I agreed. Melas, who was working in the atrium, glowered as he watched Silvanus depart. I tossed my head and ignored his impertinence. It only strengthened my resolve to do what Silvanus asked.

And so it started and so it grew, for there is little more infectious than clandestine acts. A hard lesson for any of us to learn. The evil truths of such deceptions, small though they may seem, are never revealed until it's too late to stop what they have set in motion.

21
1902

Colin and I sequestered ourselves in our room after returning to the villa. Kat had gone off in a huff, muttering that she knew Benjamin better than we did. "The coroner was unable to determine whether Mr. Jackson's death was deliberate or accidental," Colin said. "The landslide could have been catalyzed by rain, but also by someone pushing the boulder over the unstable pile of debris. Stirling claims he went directly back to his digs after he left dinner, but that he found himself too agitated to sleep, and went for a walk. No one saw him."

"He's staying in the same place as the Carters. Wouldn't he have had to collect his key from the desk?"

"He's moved from there into a rooming house. Hence no desk and no one to notice his comings and goings."

"And Benjamin?" I asked.

"He admits to having been in a rage —

we all saw as much, so there'd be no point denying it — and went to a tavern not far from the train station. The owner confirms he was there, but wasn't sure about the time. I also spoke to Taylor's servants. He did go home, but could have left again without anyone noticing. His dressing room has direct access to the garden at the back of the house."

"What do we know about Mr. Jackson?"

"He'd worked at Pompeii for the past five seasons. Studied at Harvard, has published several well-received articles, and is a respected scholar. Got along well with all of his colleagues. No one had a word to say against him. He was a shy sort, spending more time on his own than socializing, but was never awkward about it. He was to be married this winter in Connecticut."

"His poor fiancée," I said.

"Quite." Colin blew out a long breath. "His father is coming to collect the body. Doesn't want his son taking this final journey alone."

"It's heartbreaking."

"The only discrepant thing I could un-cover about him concerns Stirling. He told me Jackson loaned him a not insignificant amount of money, enough to cover the rent on his rooms for three months."

"Might he have murdered Mr. Jackson to escape the debt?"

"Money is a powerful motivator," Colin said.

"But we don't know if we're dealing with a murder."

"No, we don't. If someone killed Jackson, the murderer pushed the boulder down the debris pile. When Kat was attacked, she was pushed."

"You suspect the same person was responsible for both incidents?" I asked.

"I do, and I'd very much like to lock her up to keep her safe."

"She won't tolerate it. You'd do better keeping her at your side. She'll adore the attention."

He shot me a quizzical look, but said nothing.

The next morning, I set off for Mr. Taylor's dig, leaving father and daughter safely ensconced at the villa. Benjamin waved at me as I approached, then bowed his head and offered an apology for his behavior the night of Mr. Jackson's death.

"My temper occasionally gets the better of me," he said. "I know I must learn to master it."

"I would encourage you to do just that," I

217

said. "In the meantime, could you please account for your time the day before the incident? Were you here, at the dig?"

"I believe so . . ." His voice trailed. "As I recall, I took a few photographs here and then spent the rest of the day painting in the main excavations."

"Where, exactly?"

"The House of the Vettii. I was copying one of the frescoes of cupids."

"What time did you get there?"

His cheeks colored. "I don't remember exactly. Fairly early, well before noon."

"You're certain?"

"Of course."

"Ivy and I were at the House of the Vettii that morning. You weren't there. Why are you lying to me?"

"I'm not! I can show you the painting. I must be confused about the day . . . let's see . . . the day before Jackson died. That's right, I'd already finished in the House of the Vettii. After that I moved on to the Forum Baths, in a room with a vaulted ceiling. I can't remember what it's called."

The Forum Baths stood almost directly across from the House of the Tragic Poet, the site of Kat's attack.

"Did you see Kat?" I asked. "She was near there all morning."

"No, I didn't, but I was quite focused on my work. Which I ought to get back to now."

"Before you go, what do you know about Felix Morgan?"

"Morgan?" He shook his head and turned on his heel. "Never heard of the man." He stalked away.

I turned my attention next to Mr. Stirling, whom I found cataloging a collection of small objects discovered at the site. Rather than repeat the questions Colin had posed the previous day, I instead tried to draw out more information about his background. Why did the director of an important excavation need a loan to pay his rent?

"How do you find working for Mr. Taylor?" I asked. "Does he take good care of his staff?"

A sad smile crept onto his face. "There's no need to be subtle, Lady Emily. You want to know why I couldn't afford my rent. As I told your husband, I'm a disaster with money. Always spend more than I make. No matter how hard I try to reform, I get myself into predicament after predicament. There's no one to blame but myself."

"How bad is your situation at present?"

"I'll be able to pay off my debt to Jackson by the end of the season. I moved into cheaper digs a few days ago."

"Mr. Jackson worked under you, so presumably his salary was smaller than yours."

"It was, but Jackson had family money."

"Where did you work before you came to Pompeii?"

"I was in the States, digging up native burial mounds in Illinois and Missouri. Incalculably different from Pompeii. We know so little about the culture of the tribes that built them. I was always a classicist, fascinated by Latin literature, so quite the fish out of water, but I managed to enjoy it well enough. I was able to further hone my archaeological skills. Sometimes, we must take the job that is offered rather than the one of which we've dreamed."

"How did you come to work for Mr. Taylor?"

"Pompeii was always my dream. There's no site comparable to it," he said. "I did my best to keep current on all the work being done here — I memorized Mau's excavation reports and attended every academic lecture I could on the subject. It was at one of those that I met Taylor. He shares my love for this place, and we hit it off immediately. He asked me to join his team the following season."

"How do you feel about working for a nonprofessional? I'm aware that they often prefer methods that aren't the best, scientifically speaking."

"Taylor's a decent man. He's no treasure hunter and wants things done properly. He's hired a top-notch staff, doesn't try to impose his own agenda on us, and thinks conversation is more important than racing through an excavation. Exposure to the elements takes its toll on ancient paintings from the moment they're uncovered. As Ovid tells us, *the workmanship excelled the materials.*"

"Is he aware of your financial difficulties?"

"No. I prefer to keep those close to my chest."

"I was not the one who interviewed Mr. Jackson about Mr. Walker," I said. "Do you know if the two were acquainted?"

"He didn't recognize the sketch, if that's what you mean, but he was working here when Walker was researching his article."

"Are you acquainted with a man called Felix Morgan?"

"Morgan?" He frowned and looked toward the horizon. "The name is vaguely familiar. Is he an archaeologist?"

"I'm not sure."

"If so, Taylor's more likely to know him. He's been here longer than I." He shouted for his employer, who was nearby — spade

221

in hand, but not working on the trench he was standing by — to join us. "Felix Morgan. Do you know him?"

Mr. Taylor cocked his head as he approached. "Sturdy fellow, red hair? He was here for part of a season some years back. Can't recall who he was working for — the Italians, most likely. Definitely not the Germans. Didn't take to it, but seemed a decent sort."

"Can you recall exactly when he was here?" I asked.

"Golly, Lady Emily, I don't know. There are an awful lot of people who come through Pompeii."

"Could it have been about the same time Mr. Walker was researching his article?"

He removed his hat, wiped his brow with the back of his hand, and shook his head. "I wish I could tell you for sure, but the best I can guess, it was before that."

"Why did he leave before the end of the season?" I asked.

"That's a question for him," Mr. Taylor said. "I didn't know him well. Wanted to try his hand at archaeology but discovered it was more dust than treasure and lost interest."

"How did he get hired if he had no background?"

"We occasionally get young men in the midst of a Grand Tour who are convinced archaeology is for them. Sometimes they're persuasive enough to worm their way into a dig. It's harmless enough, and they're generally bored within a week."

"So Mr. Morgan had been on his Grand Tour?"

Mr. Taylor shrugged. "I couldn't swear to it. You might ask the Italians if they remember him. You've never met him, Stirling?"

"Not that I can recall. I've heard the name, but couldn't say more than that."

"I could swear you were both from St. Louis, but maybe I'm wrong."

"I have no memory of him," Mr. Stirling said. Something in his voice tugged at me and the way his eyes darted made me question his sincerity. I wanted to talk to him more, but away from the dig and his colleagues.

"You told me you don't work on Sundays," I asked.

"That's right," Mr. Taylor said.

"Then you won't mind if I steal your director for the day." I smiled broadly. "Ivy and I have been hoping he'd give us a tour of the ruins."

"A capital idea, Lady Emily," Mr. Taylor

said. "You couldn't find yourself in better hands."

"Only if you've no other plans, of course, Mr. Stirling," I said.

"I'd be delighted."

After we'd arranged the details, I went back through the city walls to speak to the Italian excavation team. None of them remembered Felix Morgan, so I asked their director if I could see the records of employees over the past ten years. The name was not listed.

"Perhaps, Lady Emily, he worked for the Germans," the director said. "More likely he was a dilettante tourist who spent a week or so amusing himself by playing archaeologist. It happens sometimes. We humor them, let them dig a trench, and hardly notice when they go. Whatever his story, I can assure you he is not an archaeologist who specializes in the ancient Romans. I'd recognize his name from the literature, if nothing else."

To be thorough, I checked with the Germans, but they had no memories or records of him either. Felix Morgan seemed more ghost than man.

Sunday morning, the carriage dropped Ivy and me at the ticket office by the Porta Marina, and we walked toward Pompeii's basilica, on the southwest edge of the Forum, where we were to meet Mr. Stirling. Once there, we saw a crowd of tourists congregated near one of the walls. A lady of a certain age staggered from its midst and collapsed in an inglorious heap on the dusty ground. No one appeared to take even the slightest notice of this, so Ivy and I rushed to her assistance, my friend pulling smelling salts from her reticule. One whiff and the lady blinked her eyes and shambled back to consciousness.

"Too horrible — too horrible!" She threw one arm over her face. "Don't make me look at it again!"

Mario stepped out of the crowd, grinning. "Tourists, eh?"

"What's going on?" I asked.

He whistled and shouted "Luigi! Your client!" Another guide emerged, looking irritated to be pulled from the excitement. He nodded at Mario, gave himself a little shake, and knelt beside the woman.

"Come, come, it's not so bad. We will sit in the shade for a little before we continue. My friend will collect your husband." He got her to her feet and led her away. Mario shrugged and went back to the crowd, evidently in search of the woman's woefully unconcerned spouse. I followed him, pushing my way to the front, where I saw eight dead ravens, arranged in a circle around a beautifully rendered chalk drawing of a man and a woman, dressed in contemporary clothes, the spitting image of Colin and me.

Ivy, close on my heels, started and turned away. I was as disturbed as she by the sight, but forced myself to take a closer look, only to feel Mr. Stirling take me firmly by the arm and pull me away.

"What a dreadful thing. I should've intercepted you so you might have been spared horror instead of standing here gaping." His face colored and beads of perspiration dotted his forehead.

"I would've looked, no matter what you did to intervene," I said. "Ivy, I know it's unpleasant, but could you please make a copy of the drawing so we have a record of it?" I shouted for those gathered to be quiet and asked if anyone had noticed the grisly scene being arranged, but got no sensible answer. Two guards were standing away from the crowd, amusement on their faces. They, too, denied having seen anything. I rounded up the guides in the vicinity, who pled ignorance as well. Useless, the lot of them. I suggested to the guards that they ought to clear up the mess. They didn't hide their distaste at being ordered around by a lady, but set about the task and shooed the tourists away while I tried to decipher the graffito scrawled in the wall above the ravens.

"Mr. Stirling, my Latin is not good enough to read this. Could you translate?" I asked.

"It's not your Latin that is lacking, Lady Emily. It's difficult to even make out the letters. Let me see . . . *Minimum malum fit contemnendo maximum.* The smallest evil, if neglected, will reach the greatest proportions."

"Ominous," Ivy said. "And quite fitting, don't you think?"

I nodded, tapping the tip of my parasol on the ground. "The tableau is reminiscent of the first omen that predicted the death of Alexander the Great: Ravens fell dead at his feet as he approached Babylon."

"I don't like where you're headed with this, Emily," Ivy said. She'd finished copying the drawing. "Is this meant as a portent of your demise? Perhaps we should skip our tour and see what Colin thinks."

"That's a sensible suggestion, Mrs. Brandon," Mr. Stirling said. "I wouldn't want to do anything that might compromise your safety."

"If I had even the slightest inkling that

this message suggested there's some vicious criminal hiding in the ruins, ready to dispatch me, I would seek shelter," I said. There was something about the graffito that made me think, once again, that we were dealing with two villains. The murderer might have ordered the tableau, but could his accomplice have chosen the location? And, by doing so, was he suggesting the path to Mr. Walker's death — and Mr. Jackson's — started with some small evil, the sort of thing likely to go unnoticed? Mr. Stirling knew we would be here this morning. Was he behind it?

"Perhaps it would be best if we postponed our excursion," he said, wiping sweat from his forehead with a handkerchief.

"This is likely just another warning meant to discourage us from continuing our investigation. I shan't be daunted. Lead on, Mr. Stirling."

He looked nervous. "Only if you're quite sure."

"I am," I said.

He looked at Ivy who nodded. "We'll skip the rest of the basilica for the moment and go back to the Porta Marina, the gate through which those arriving from the ancient port would have entered the city. Imagine, if you will, the sounds that would have greeted you. Donkeys carrying loads. Merchants hawking their wares. Look down at the street — do you see the small white stones between the larger dark ones? They were set that way deliberately. The bright color reflected the moonlight, making it easier to pass this way even at night. Pompeii was nowhere near the size of Rome, but it benefited from every ingenious advance made in the empire."

The picture he painted of the ancient world was striking in its detail, and all the more moving because he focused on the people who had lived here rather than on the buildings or the politics of the place. He took us through the Stabian Baths, with their ornate ceilings, and left me half expecting to see a slave with a strigil, ready to scrape from his master's glistening skin the olive oil massaged into it. When we stood in the atrium at the House of the Silver Wedding (named, not for some ancient event, but for the twenty-fifth anniversary of the marriage of Umberto I, King of Italy, and his wife, Margherita of Savoy, celebrated the year the house was discovered), he asked us to picture the life of the family who had inhabited it.

"This is the largest atrium in the city, more than fifty feet long," he said. "It had

Corinthian columns. The wax masks of the family's ancestors would have been displayed here, and large chests, filled with their wealth, would have lined the walls. The patriarch would have met with his clients in this room here, the tablinum." He pointed to a room at the far end of the atrium. "Some of the family's slaves might have shared tiny rooms, or cubicula, but many of them would have slept on the floor, spreading out bedrolls after their masters had gone to sleep."

Much as I was enjoying our tour, I was focused more on observing Mr. Stirling than on the stories he was sharing. As always, he quoted poetry and appeared good-natured and even tempered, but I could not deny he seemed nervous, starting when I asked questions and frequently looking back over his shoulder, as if he expected someone to be following us.

In this, he wasn't alone. Twice I caught glimpses of shadowy figures in buildings, but found nothing when I tried to catch them. As Ivy and the archaeologist explored the atrium, I felt a prickling on the back of my neck, like someone was watching me. I turned around, but no one was there. At least not that I could see, so I went into the room that was behind me, its window looking onto the atrium. It was empty, except for an artist's pencil, stamped A.W. Faber, its barrel painted dark green. Had someone been there, keeping an eye on me? Benjamin, perhaps? He always carried drawing supplies with him.

I dismissed the idea. No one could've left the room without me seeing — there was only one door, and it led directly into the atrium. Countless visitors to Pompeii sketched the ruins. Anyone could have dropped a pencil. I returned to my friends, making no mention of the discomfort I felt.

We continued on. Mr. Stirling talked about the theater and the games — Ivy peppered him with questions about gladiators — and translated for us bits of the graffiti so prevalent through the city. He pointed out the holes cut into the curbs outside shops, through which a rope could be slipped to secure a donkey while its owner shopped. By the time we had completed our circuit and were back in the basilica — all evidence of the morning's grisly scene now gone — I felt a deeper connection with the ancient Pompeiians than I ever would have thought possible. Mr. Stirling had a profound understanding of the people who had lived in this town.

Could a man with such sensibilities and

so innate a sense of humanity commit a brutal murder? Something about him made me unable to trust him, but I couldn't quite identify the source of my unease. Perhaps there are things capable of driving any of us to that darkest of deeds. I was still contemplating this when Ivy and I returned to the villa. I sought out my husband, who was playing chess with Kat, and pulled him aside. She glared at me and stormed out of the room. Colin gave no indication of having noticed this, but as he studied Ivy's copy of the chalk drawing, a mask of grave concern fell over his handsome face.

"Is it a coincidence that the birds appeared the very day after I started asking questions about Felix Morgan?"

"It certainly supports the theory that Morgan is a critical component to our investigation," Colin said. "And I agree it's likely the graffito is a significant clue. Who might be hiding some small evil from his past?"

"Mr. Stirling could have any number of old debts," I said. "He might have done something underhanded to avoid paying one of them."

"And Carter's temper could easily have got him in trouble."

"If only we could find some connection between either of them and Felix Morgan."

"The American Embassy has no record of anyone of that name coming through Rome," he said.

"We could ask *The New York Times* to search their files."

"I already did. He's never been mentioned in the paper."

"Perhaps he adopted a nom de guerre after the incident in Montana." I shook my head. "No, both Mr. Stirling and Mr. Taylor recognized the name. We'd best go back to focusing on Mr. Walker. Mario is the person here who spent the most time with him. Now that we know more about Montana and Morgan and all the rest, let's question him again. Mr. Walker may have mentioned something about it that seemed insignificant to Mario — and to us — until now. Let's find him without delay."

22
AD 79

With what innocence a tangle of lies begins!

I met Silvanus the next day, in the middle of the afternoon, when I knew the bars would be relatively empty. I chose one as far from his house as possible, by the large theater, near my own domicile. It was a dingy place that gave no indication of ever aspiring to serve a high class of clientele. We sat across from each other at a table in the back garden, although to call it a garden is to give it more of a compliment than it deserved. There were no flowers or shrubs within, only a grimy open space with a pounded dirt floor and an ill-maintained wall surrounding it, covered with obscene graffiti.

A surly waiter with a bad attitude plonked a dish of half-shriveled olives down in front of us and Silvanus ordered two beakers of wine, the best they had. The waiter sneered. If my companion thought we'd get better service by spending more, he was wrong. Eventually, the man brought the drinks. After taking a sip, I couldn't say he deserved any thanks.

Silvanus drained his glass as if he didn't notice how sour the wine was. "Recite for me, Kassandra. Recite."

I hadn't had much time to write since leaving Plautus's house, but knowing I would be seeing Silvanus today, had stayed up half the night working on my epic. My hero was still very much an idealized version of Silvanus, but he didn't seem to notice. In a hushed voice, I leaned across the table and gave him fifty or so lines before passing him a scroll onto which I had copied them — and more — for him.

"You tell a tale of war so unlike any I would expect from a woman," he said. "How do you know the sounds of battle, the way it rings in a soldier's head for days, haunting his sleep?"

"So you were a soldier," I said, ignoring his question. A man of his rank would likely have spent some time as a military tribune.

He ignored my question as well, unrolling the scroll as if he hadn't even heard what I said. "How quickly can you have more?"

"I can't spend as much of the day on poetry as I used to. In Plautus's house, I had more free time. Satisfying my father's needs for a copyist is more consuming than keeping Lepida content."

He grunted. "You have too much talent to waste it on the works of others. I shall speak to your father and arrange something."

"You could hire me to write the poem. That would be the simplest solution."

"Perhaps," he said, not looking up from the scroll. He sounded unconvinced. "Meet me back here three days hence and bring whatever else you've managed to compose."

"I don't know what to make of you, Silvanus. Why all this secrecy over a little poem?"

He looked at me and now it was his turn to lean over the sticky table. His eyes burned into mine. "You are so wonderfully unaware of your charms. I can't decide if this is due to some mystical innocence or if it's a well-calculated act."

"Why would I need a well-calculated act?" I asked.

"I know you expected something else from me that first night I asked to see you in private. It put me in a most awkward position in the house of my betrothed."

"If that's true, it resulted from no deliberate action on my part." I could hear my heart thudding. I couldn't deny I had wanted him then, nor that I still did, now.

"There's something rather dangerous about you, Kassandra." He reached toward my face and touched my lips with his fingertips. "A wiser man than I would flee and never speak to you again. But I am not so wise, even if you will prove my undoing."

23
1902

Given our past experience, we suspected Mario might not be easy to track down, so Colin left messages for him both at the excavation ticket booths and at his rooms, inviting him to meet us for dinner. This garnered a quick response. He told us to meet him at a restaurant owned by his brother, Pietro. When we arrived, he greeted us like long-lost friends, introduced us to his mother and grandmother, and ushered us to a table near the window. After asking about Kat and accepting that her injury was not serious, he refused to discuss anything further until we agreed to eschew ordering off the menu and instead let him bring us whatever he wanted, starting with a carafe of house wine. Once we had put ourselves in his hands — and he had filled our glasses — he asked how he could help.

I explained to him what I had learned from Mr. Richards, and the moment I mentioned Montana, a broad grin spread across his face.

"Oh, yes, Montana," he said. "Signore Walker told me about this place. There, the skies are bigger than the ocean, and the weather unimaginable. He says there is snow as high as a man's shoulder in the winter and that the wind will burn the skin right off your face."

"Did he mention his brother?" I asked.

"No, only said that he lived there for some years before going to New York. Maybe New York is where his family was."

"What else do you know about his time in Montana?" I asked.

"He was like some Spaniard from many centuries ago who crossed the sea to find a city with streets paved in gold. That Spaniard, he told me, conquered a whole people, but Signore Walker had nothing to show from mining. He did not speak of it much, only when we sat to have lunch in the amphitheater. I decided it was best not to tell too many tales of gladiators while we were eating, so I asked him about his life."

"Did he tell you anything about his colleagues in New York?" Colin asked.

"No, only described the city, which to me, it sounds marvelous. Bigger than Rome."

"Can you remember anyone else — a client, perhaps — who has mentioned Montana?" I asked.

"You are very curious about this place, Lady Emily," Mario said.

"I think it may be the key to figuring out who killed him," I said. "Are you absolutely certain that you did not see him when he returned to Pompeii?"

"I am. But, then, I was not working at the time. I'd gone to Naples to visit an old friend. That is why it took me so long to speak to you in the first place."

"Can you think of anything else that might be significant?" I asked.

Mario closed his eyes, contemplative. "I cannot remember anyone else speaking of Montana, but I can tell you this. You have told me when, approximately, he died. In the weeks before then, there was a strange atmosphere in the ruins, as if nothing would be right ever again. The birds did not sing. The rain did not come. I began to wonder if Vesuvius, she was going to erupt again. I sent Mamma and Nonna to the north, just in case. But nothing happened, nothing at all. At least that is what I believed until Signore Walker's body was found."

"What are you suggesting?" Colin asked.

Mario shrugged. "I do not believe in ghosts, Signore Hargreaves, but something, somewhere was trying to warn of a great tragedy. I cannot prove it is so, but we men do not know everything, do we? There are signs, omens, that we miss, who knows how often. I have heard there was a circle of dead ravens in the basilica today. What evil does that portend?"

When we'd finished eating, we thanked Mario and his brother, gave his mother and grandmother compliments on the excellent food, and stepped outside. We had a carriage waiting, but Colin ordered the driver to meet us some distance away.

"I am in need of a little walk," he said, looping his arm through mine. We crossed the tree-lined street and strolled alongside the wall of the excavations. "I don't believe for an instant that there are mysterious forces at work, warning of imminent danger. Odd things happen before volcanic eruptions, but that's not what these things Mario described point to. There's no sign of seismic activity or of the springs drying up. Yet . . ." His voice trailed and he stopped walking.

"There's something about this place," I said. "Perhaps it is a result of the immense and tragic loss of life that feels so close one can almost touch it. It's otherworldly, but simultaneously all too familiar."

"It's unnerving and at the same time deeply and profoundly moving."

"Precisely. Could this so-called strange feeling Mario described have, in fact, been managed by the murderer? Not the weather, obviously, but it's simple enough to convince people something's afoot. Man has a seemingly insatiable desire for the inexplicable, as if always looking for something supernatural."

"So what are you saying, my dear?" Colin asked. "That we are looking for a person skilled in the art of deception, who deliberately manipulated the way the broader populace here — that is, those working in the immediate vicinity of the ruins — viewed natural phenomena before the murder?"

"Quite possibly so," I said. "But more importantly, could this individual have used those same skills to lure his victim here?"

"You think Walker came to Pompeii because he was summoned?"

"Not in those precise terms," I replied. "But I do think it possible that the murderer reached out to him, somehow."

Colin laughed. "I fear we are in danger of letting tonight's wine go to our heads, Emily. Walker came here to research a story. Perhaps in the course of doing so, he learned that someone involved in his brother's death was connected to the site, but we have no evidence to suggest the murderer exerted some sort of pull over him. He returned, so far as we can tell, of his own accord, and although we don't know his motive for doing so, I refuse to believe he was driven here by some mystical force."

"We know he didn't plan to stay long. His return ticket told us as much. He had some specific purpose, and that purpose must have got him killed almost as soon as he arrived. He never returned to his hotel after dropping off his bag," I said. "When I asked Mr. Richards about it, he didn't even know his friend had returned to Italy. You'd think that an uneasy traveler would have wanted to rendezvous with — or at least speak about the journey to — someone he knew and trusted."

"Unless he wanted to keep the trip a secret. So what, my dear, was Mr. Walker trying to hide?"

Colin and I agreed that one of us should speak to Benjamin again. He had lied to me about his whereabouts the day Kat was attacked and stalked off before I had finished asking him about his father. I sent him a note when we returned from dinner, asking him to let me know where I could find him the next morning. My husband stayed back with Kat, still uneasy letting her out of the villa, while I set off for the House of Marcus Lucretius Fronto — arguably the most elegant and sophisticated in all of Pompeii — where Benjamin had said he would be copying a fresco showing Bacchus and Ariadne in triumph, oxen pulling them in a chariot.

When I arrived, he was packing up his easel. "Hoping to avoid me?" I asked.

"Not at all. I wouldn't have left before you got here, but I do need to get back to Taylor's dig."

"I'll walk with you, if you don't mind. I have a few questions for you."

"Should I be nervous?"

"Only if you've something to hide."

We passed through the garden, with its frescoes depicting wild beasts and hunting scenes, and left the house through a smaller entrance rather than the main one, Benjamin explaining this enabled us to cut through an unexcavated part of the city and reach the dig through the Vesuvius Gate. "It's far less crowded. The longer I spend here, the less tolerance I have for tourists."

"I sympathize. Had you been to Pompeii before this trip?" I asked.

"Never. As I may have already shared with you, my father was a shopkeeper. My family didn't have the sort of money required for a Grand Tour, nor did we move in that echelon of society where such things are de rigueur."

"Tell me more about your father."

"What is there to say? He was a hardworking man, but narrow-minded and judgmental when it came to me."

"Where was he from?"

"New York. Lived there all his life."

"And your mother?" I asked.

"They were childhood sweethearts."

"Did he ever tell you about his days in Montana?"

"Montana? I'm afraid you're mistaken," he said. "He never traveled."

"What about you?" I asked.

"I haven't been west of Connecticut, but there are striking views to be found in New England." He went on to describe in intricate detail — and at a pace so rapid I could hardly keep up with his words — the splendor of the red maples in the autumn, and the way the sun, at a certain time in the afternoon, illuminated to glowing the riot of colorful leaves that covered the mountainsides.

"Where did you study? In New York?"

"I've had no formal training," he said. "There wasn't money for it. My parents didn't discourage my interest in art, but they could not financially support the study of it."

"Callie went to Radcliffe," I said. "I'm shocked they paid for her education and not yours."

"Some things are best not thought about," Benjamin said.

Had his shopkeeper father been so progressive that he preferred to see his daughter educated over his son? Unlikely, unless the expectation was that Benjamin would take over for his father. Archaeology and classics for a daughter, who they likely believed would never need to find employment — she would be married instead — might have proven more palatable to them than an artist son.

As we neared the Vesuvius Gate, Benjamin stopped walking.

"What's that?" he asked. I looked in the direction he was pointing, and saw a flash of red fluttering from high up on an unexcavated section of the city. Colin and I had combed these areas when searching for a location where Mr. Walker's body might have been encased in plaster, and I was certain I hadn't seen anything red on that occasion. I started to climb the hill — it wasn't really a hill, rather an immense amount of earth covering ancient buildings — motioning for Benjamin to follow.

At the top, I found a piece of bright fabric caught in a thorny bush. "How very strange," I said. "It's almost as if it were left here deliberately. It looks like a piece of a scarf of some sort, but I don't see how it would have been accidentally torn by the bush. It's too low to the ground."

"Maybe someone had been carrying it rather than wearing it," Benjamin said. "He might have dropped it and bent to pick it up, causing it to rip. Is it important?"

"Given what else is here, I'd say so." A few feet further back, stood the remains of an abandoned camp. Someone had cleared a small circle in the brush and ringed a firepit with rocks. Narrow holes in the dirt marked the spots where tent poles once stood.

"Who would want to sleep here?" He frowned. "And even if someone did, it can't be allowed."

"I imagine not." I searched for any sign as to who had been here, or when. The remains of the fire were cold. A largish rock had been moved close to it — the perfect impro-vised seat. I shifted it and found, almost underneath, a battered cuff link mono-grammed FM. Rather than show it to Benjamin, I slipped it into my jacket pocket. How convenient, to stumble upon such a thing so soon after I'd started asking questions about Felix Morgan. Someone had deliberately staged this scene. There were a few footprints on the ground, made with ordinary-looking boots, not deep enough to reveal anything specific, but nothing else of note.

"Do you think this is connected to the murder?" Benjamin asked, a little too eager.

"No, I don't. It appeared that way initially, but it's probably just some tourist who didn't have enough money for a hotel."

"Are you sure? Maybe we should look again, see if we can find anything." He went over to the rock, as if he expected to see something there. He kicked it over and looked surprised. "I guess there's nothing."

I started for the pavement below, taking a slightly different route than that we'd come up because I could see that someone had recently broken through the brush. Halfway down, I spotted a pencil on the ground, different from the one I'd found in the House of the Silver Wedding. This one was from Staedtler, and some of its blue paint was scraped, as if it had been in a pencil holder.

I picked it up, careful that Benjamin didn't see. He had denied knowing Felix Morgan. Yet he'd taken me on an out-of-the-way route through the excavations that just happened to bring us to a spot where someone had — purposely — dropped a cuff link with the man's initials on it. Benjamin chatted, as we continued to walk, tearing through an immense span of topics at a manic pace, hardly pausing to let me reply. When we reached the dig, he rushed off to help dig a trench without so much as saying good-bye.

I looked for Callie and found her, covered in dust, her titian hair gray and dingy. Hadn't Mr. Taylor described Felix Morgan as having had red hair?

"Do you have a moment to answer a few questions?" I asked.

"Only if you'll help me apply mortar in an attempt to stabilize this wall," she replied. "What we ought to do is build a roof over our excavations, as has been done elsewhere within the city, but, unlike my colleagues, I favor a technique using new supports rather than having it rest on the actual ruins. That way there is less chance of the ancient structure being adversely affected by the weight. In the meantime, all I've got is this canvas. A drainage system would be helpful

249

as well, so that the rain wouldn't cause so much damage. When it's heavy, it can destroy everything in its path."

"That doesn't sound simple to construct," I said.

"It's less complicated than you might think. A good start would be to unearth and then unblock and repair the original Roman drains. The infrastructure is still there and it's criminal not to take full advantage of it." Her suggestion, simple and elegant, had not, she explained, been appreciated by those in charge. Not surprising, but disappointing. Had one of her gentleman colleagues proposed the idea, it likely would not have been summarily rejected. "Forgive me. I'm wittering on. You had a question?"

"Can you think of any reason why someone would have wanted Mr. Jackson dead?"

"Jackson? Heavens, no. I didn't know him well, but he seemed altogether ordinary, boring even. A top-notch archaeologist, and that's all any of us care about here. I'm sure you'll find his death was an accident. He wouldn't have inspired murderous passion in anyone."

"Are you acquainted with Felix Morgan?"

"No," she said. "I don't recognize the name. Did Jackson know him?"

"It's possible, but Mr. Morgan also might

have been a friend of your father's from Montana."

"If so, I was never aware of it. My father certainly never went to Montana, and never introduced me to anyone who lived there."

"Your parents must have been quite enlightened," I said. "Funding an expensive education and supporting your pursuit of a decidedly unfeminine occupation."

"The money was the easy part," Callie said. "Convincing them that archaeology is a suitable occupation for me would've been impossible. As I lost both of them soon after I completed my studies, I never had to try."

The money was the easy part? This did not reconcile with what Benjamin told me about the family finances.

"There are few things less interesting to discuss than my family. I really must get back to work."

With that, she dismissed me, leaving me to wonder about this shopkeeper father who couldn't afford an education for his son, but was in possession of an extensive library and enlightened enough to pay a small fortune to send his daughter to Radcliffe. One of the Carter siblings was not being altogether forthright.

24
AD 79

I saw Lepida the day after I met her husband in that wretched bar near the theater. She came to my house, six slaves carrying her litter, bringing with her an antique Greek vase that she presented as a gift for my father. "To brighten your new home," she said. She would never before have been in a dwelling so unfashionable as the one in which she now stood. Embarrassment colored my cheeks, but my friend gave no indication of finding it any less splendid than her own. My father thanked her for her kindness and returned to his work. Lepida took me by the hand and demanded to see my room. I did as she asked, knowing that Melas's paintings would dazzle her.

On this count, I was right. The painter had completed three of the four walls, and his scenes from the *Aeneid* were nothing short of breathtaking. They, however, were not what best impressed my friend, who had enthusiasm only for his delicate floral garlands until she noticed the sweet expression on Venus's face.

"Why he's made her face yours!" she said, stepping closer to the image of the goddess, appearing to her son, Aeneas, in the guise of Diana.

"I don't see that at all," I said.

"Either you're a liar or you have no idea what you look like."

I didn't argue with her because she was quite correct; I was a liar. I'd been so shocked when I first saw the fresco that, had Melas still been in the house, I would have violently reprimanded him. But Fortuna favored him; he had finished work for the day. By the next morning, I had reconsidered my actions, not wanting to draw attention to what he had done. Surely he meant it as an insult of some sort, a criticism that implied I viewed myself as worthy of being portrayed as a goddess. So I said nothing and made a point of avoiding him for the following week.

"You must tell me more about this painter," Lepida said. "I know he's Greek — Silvanus mentioned it. How long as he been in love with you? Do you welcome the match? I'm sure your father would."

"He is not in love with me," I replied,

queasy at the thought. "We can hardly hold a civil conversation. He's judgmental and impossible."

"He brings to mind a certain quote from Ovid of which you've long been fond: *Let love be introduced in friendship's dress.*"

"We're not friends, and even if we were, I would prefer a Roman husband, as you well know."

"Then I shall make it my mission to find you one. Have you seen anyone you like? I caught a glimpse of a rather handsome wine merchant a few blocks from here."

My heart clenched in my chest. I didn't want to marry a wine merchant, handsome or not. But I knew I would never have a husband as noble as Silvanus. Men like him did not take former slaves as their wives. Maybe the wine merchant wasn't such a bad idea. If he was wealthy — or on the way to becoming so — I would at least stand a chance of being mistress of a house with a spacious atrium, and my children would be well and truly Roman. What more could I ask than that? But then I remembered the way Silvanus looked at me — the heat in his eyes — and I couldn't control the fluttering of my heart.

"Tell me, friend, do you find married life to your liking?" I asked, desperate to change the subject. "Would you recommend it?"

Lepida giggled. "I certainly would. Silvanus is all kindness. I don't see that much of him, but I've plenty to occupy myself — you wouldn't believe how my skills at the loom have improved. When he does come to me, he's most attentive, an ideal husband. He's pushing me to become a priestess of Venus, something to which I have no objection. It's natural for a woman of my rank, and I've always had an affinity for the goddess of love."

"I've always longed to serve Isis," I said.

"A foreign priestess for a foreign goddess."

"Not so foreign," I said. "My parents may be Greek, but I was born in Pompeii." I had never before questioned my devotion to Isis, but seeing it through Lepida's eyes, I wondered. Without meaning to, I had chosen a foreign god.

"One only need to look at your golden hair to see that you are no Roman, Kassandra. Don't frown, I know all too well your thoughts on this matter. But you should embrace your heritage. It makes you an exotic flower in a tedious world, which means you will be all the more appealing to that handsome wine merchant. Or, maybe to another, who owns vineyards as well as a shop. You'd stand out from the stolid Roman girls who would bore him to death."

Standing out was something I had never desired, but I could see the wisdom in her words. "I'll consider your advice."

"I assure you, it's sound. Now, *carissima,* I have a favor to beg. You are so skilled with words. Would you write me a little poem for my husband? I want to give him a gift, one that's personal and a bit romantic. Something not too sweet but perhaps not so shocking as Ovid." She blushed as she asked.

"Of course," I said and promised to bring it to her the day after tomorrow, only later realizing that was the same day I was to meet Silvanus. After she left, I retreated back to my room, telling my father I was unwell, blaming a badly made pie I'd had for lunch. I closed my door and spent the rest of the day bent over the wax tablet on my table. By the time I was satisfied with the result, it was too late to copy the poem onto papyrus. I snuffed out my oil lamps and crawled onto my couch. There, enveloped in darkness, I contemplated what to do now. For I had not written what I'd promised Lepida. Instead of her love poem, I had scrawled more than two hundred lines of my epic.

Two hundred lines that more than primed
me to compose an ode worthy of Silvanus.

25
1902

When I returned to the villa, I recounted for Colin the events of the day. "I'm most suspicious of Benjamin," I said. "We already knew he lied about where he was the morning Kat was attacked and then he admitted to having been practically across the street from her when it happened. And now we have that ridiculous camp. Yesterday, I asked him about Felix Morgan, and today he takes me on a walk where I find a strategically placed cuff link."

"He had plenty of time after receiving your message last night to stage the scene," Colin said. "But he's not the only one you asked about Morgan. Stirling or Taylor had opportunity as well."

"Yes, but neither of them brought me to the site. And I could see that Benjamin was expecting to find the cuff link when he moved the rock under which I had found it. It was as if he already knew it was there."

"In the morning, I'll take the pencil you found at the camp and the one from the House of the Silver Wedding and compare them both with those in Benjamin's art supplies."

We stayed up half the night discussing the case. He was already gone when I awoke the next morning, and had left a note for me:

Sleep, rest of nature; O sleep, most gentle of the divinities, peace of the soul, thou at whose presence care disappears, who soothest hearts wearied with daily employments, and makest them strong again for labor!

Heed Ovid's wise words, my dear. I could not bear to wake you.

I dressed and went to the terrace, where I found Jeremy alone, still breakfasting. "Ivy went off to the ruins to draw and your industrious husband is long gone. Kat shut herself up in her darkroom after he refused to let her accompany him and then forbade her to leave the house unaccompanied. What are your plans for the day, Em?"

"Colin let me have an unexpected lie-in, so I'm at loose ends. What about you?"

He brushed a stray crumb off his otherwise immaculate tweed jacket. "I'm going to the summit of Vesuvius. You should join me. Thomas Cook operates a funicular railway that reaches the top from a road partway up the mountain. I'd hoped to persuade Callie to skive off work, but she was insulted I suggested she would even consider such a thing. I need to stop giving her reasons to despise my aristocratic upbringing."

"She knows your background. There's no hiding it from her."

"I agree, but I can't figure out how to convince her I'm not all bad."

"Perhaps because you *are* all bad?" I suggested.

"I do adore you. No one else knows me so well. Come explore Vesuvius with me. We can make an offering to Vulcan. You can ask for help solving the murder — or is it murders now that we have poor, dead Jackson? — and I can beg for assistance in winning Callie's heart."

"I have grave doubts about the efficacy of petitioning pagan gods," I said, "but the excursion is appealing. It would give me a break from the investigation, which might allow my thoughts some much-needed percolation time. Shall we collect Ivy from the ruins and bring her, too?"

"If you don't mind, I'd prefer we go alone. I'm not in the mood to be on good behavior today and I'd hate to horrify Ivy. She's a lovely, sweet thing and shouldn't be subjected to me at my worst."

The carriage he had ordered arrived at the villa as I finished breakfast, and we set forth across the sweeping, fertile ground that led to the slopes of the mountain. Oh, the irony of that land! Vesuvius was at once a blessing and a curse. The very things that made this area appealing to its ancient residents — the tremendous crops that could be grown in the volcanic soil — had led them to their doom. And now, more than eighteen hundred years later, the slopes were as verdant as they had been before the catastrophic eruption.

While the ancient Pompeiians had no idea Vesuvius was a volcano — it had not erupted for seven hundred years — their contemporary counterparts could not claim that same ignorance. They knew all too well what the mountain could do, yet this neither dissuaded them from living in its shadow nor from farming the same fields destroyed so long ago. Today, a small stream of smoke was rising from the peak, and I asked Jeremy if it was unwise to ascend the slopes.

"That happens with great regularity, I'm told," he said. "Even your Baedeker's mentions it. It's nothing to cause alarm. We aren't ancient Romans, Em. We're armed with science now, and there are no signs of imminent eruption. If you want something more exciting, you only need turn to Mount Stromboli, south of here. It's constantly erupting. I'm quite taken with the idea of visiting — apparently one can climb it when the smoke isn't too dense."

"I never expected you to have so much knowledge of volcanoes."

"I can't take credit. Callie told me most of it. She puts my ignorance to shame."

"I thought you've always cherished your ignorance," I said. "It's a much-lauded pillar of your charm."

He frowned. "Quite. But perhaps it's time to expand those pillars. Or rebuild them. Or . . . I don't know. Insert whatever architectural metaphor you think appropriate."

The sky had begun to clear and Vesuvius loomed directly in front of us. I tried to imagine what it must have looked like before the eruption, when it rose far above its current height, in the shape of a perfect cone. As much as it dominated the landscape now, it would've been even more impressive prior to that infamous day in August, AD 79.

Our carriage snaked up the steep road, winding through vineyards and the lush farmers' fields that fill the Campanian countryside, navigating terrifying hairpin turns until we reached a wire rope railway. Jeremy had already procured tickets, and soon we were zooming up the steep slopes of the mountain. A short while later, we alighted from the funicular and were greeted by a Cook's guide, required at this part of the site. He led us over the path, strewn with ash and pumice, to the crater. We passed several ladies who refused this short walk — it would take even the least energetic individual no more than a quarter of an hour — and were, instead, carried in porte-chaises that looked monstrously uncomfortable as they bounced along. These conveyances may have been direct descendants of the litters used by the ancient Romans, but they were a poor imitation. No ornate boxes with curtained windows here, only stiff wooden chairs with poles attached to the sides, each carried by two unhappy looking men. It could not be a pleasant way to earn a living.

At the top, we peered over the edge into the smoking crater. The guide assured me, as had Jeremy, that this was not indicative of imminent eruption, and after we had made a thorough exploration of the area, took us to a spot where we could see soft lava. We trod carefully, not wanting to burn the soles of our boots, and Jeremy pressed a coin into the not-quite-liquid stone. That done, we picked a pleasant spot to stand and take in the view. The city of Naples sprawled below us to the west, a labyrinth of buildings and streets impossibly close together. Looking straight ahead through the sparkling waters of the Bay of Naples (most of the morning's clouds had blown away, leaving the sunlight to dance on the waves) we could make out the Tyrrhenian Sea, dotted with rocky islands.

We remained there for some time, mesmerized by the scenery, our guide keeping a tactful distance. At last, sated with beauty, we headed back toward the footpath, but before we reached it, Jeremy came to a dead stop and grabbed my arm.

"What is Callie doing here with him?" he asked, pointing at two figures standing next to the crater.

"That's Mario Sorrentino, the guide who took Mr. Walker around Pompeii. She must have hired him to bring her here," I said.

"Only Cook's guides are allowed on this

side of the mountain," Jeremy said, "so he's not acting in any sort of official capacity. And Callie refused to come with me today because she had work that could not be neglected. Something about a wall she thought might collapse. Yet here she is. Apparently the wall was not so important as Mario." The tone in his voice made it all too clear what he suspected Callie wanted from Mario. They were standing awfully close together, engaged in a conversation that could be described either as heated or passionate, but without seeing their faces more clearly — or hearing their words — I couldn't tell which. Jeremy made a sound akin to that of a bear growling. "She knew I would be here and is deliberately slighting me."

"You have no evidence for such an outrageous claim. There's no sense standing around writing fictions when we can so easily learn the truth." I took him firmly by the arm and we trudged back to the crater, our guide keeping an even greater distance than he had before. I hailed Callie as we approached, careful to ensure that my tone was all enthusiasm. "I see you, too, decided it was an excellent day to explore the summit of Vesuvius."

"Not quite," Callie said, turning to avoid

looking at Jeremy. "Mario told me he had found some artifacts up here yesterday and thought I would be interested in them. I was skeptical, as the area is so well traveled it's unlikely anything new would turn up. My concerns were merited. Our expedition has proved a complete waste of time. If you'll excuse me, I've a great deal of work to do." She turned on her heel and started for the footpath. Jeremy pressed his lips together, his brow furrowed.

"Bloody hell," he said. "I'm going after her."

This left me with Mario. I glowered at him. "Let's have a little chat, shall we? Artifacts on the summit of a volcano?"

"I did not tell her that," the Italian said. "I cannot explain why she would lie so shamelessly."

"How do you know her?"

"I see her and Signore Carter around the ruins," he said. "We all work there, so it is no surprise, is it? She stops to speak with me on occasion, and sometimes goes to my brother's restaurant."

I could well believe Callie would talk to him. He was far too handsome for her to ignore. "So why were the two of you here, if not for archaeological purposes?"

"It is irrelevant."

266

"I should prefer to draw my own conclusions after hearing all the facts," I said. "If it was for a romantic assignation —"

"Why would you think that?"

"The duke invited Miss Carter to come here with him today. She refused. And now she comes with you. Why?"

Mario shrugged. "Perhaps she does not like *his grace*." He all but spat the words.

"If you and Miss Carter are . . . attached in some way, I will not sit in judgment of you. You're both adults, free to do as you choose."

"Forgive me, Lady Emily, I should not have let my temper get the better of me. I bear the duke no ill will. No doubt he is an excellent man and I would be lucky to count him as a friend. But as for Signorina Carter, there is nothing between us. You have reached the wrong conclusion. *She* asked *me* to meet her, so that we might speak about a topic that has lately been of much interest to me, and I suggested this location as it is a place where one's conversations will not easily be overheard."

"What is this topic?" I asked.

"Nothing that concerns you. I will say nothing further, as I gave my word to keep what we discussed private, but I swear to you that there is no romantic attachment. I would never involve myself with such a lady. Nor, if he is wise, should your friend."

"Why do you say that?"

"Signorina Carter is not what she seems. There is nothing more he needs to know. Trust my advice and tell him to protect his heart."

The Cook's guide, hovering some feet behind us, was looking at his watch, pretending to find it utterly fascinating. "You cannot leave me with so little, Mario," I said. "My friend is quite fond of Miss Carter. If his feelings put him at risk, I need to know why."

"I can tell you nothing more. Is not my warning enough?"

"Not without an explanation. Please, Mario. This feels like something more than the suggestion that she will toy with his affections. You know a murder occurred in the excavations. Does your warning have something to do with that?"

A shadow crossed his face — not a change in the hue of his complexion, but an actual shadow, the sun disappearing behind a stray cloud, as if the ghosts of Pompeii were making a point. "If Signore Walker had found himself involved with her, he would not have been murdered, Lady Emily. He would have fallen on his own sword, like a good Roman."

26
AD 79

"I can't keep doing this," I said the next day, sitting across from Silvanus in the sad little dirt garden of our wretched bar. The same surly waiter from our previous visit had scowled at me when I crossed the filthy threshold, and I promised myself I would not come back again. "Your wife is coming to see me later today. How am I to pretend I didn't meet with you earlier?"

"Why would the subject arise?" he asked, motioning for more wine.

"Why would it not? She's going to ask me what I did today and I don't like to lie. There's no need for this secrecy. You should tell her you're interested in my poetry. Such generous treatment of an unknown poetess would make you rise in her esteem."

"I have no need to rise any further in her esteem," he said. "And my wife has little interest in poetry."

Perhaps he did not know his wife so well

270

as he thought. "I have no need to deceive my dearest friend and will not be persuaded to do so. I'm no longer a slave who must obey whatever you command."

"You were never compelled to do what I asked." He leaned in close to me. "I wasn't your master."

"Then what are you?"

"I'm trying to be your friend and your patron." Once again, the intensity of his tone and the fire in his eyes belied his words.

"A patron does not hide in the shadows."

"Is that so? You are an expert on how patrons behave? Have you given any consideration to what I'm trying to do for you? You're a woman, a Greek, only recently freed from slavery. You have no money and no status. Do you think the intellectuals of Rome would embrace you as a poet? Speak of your work as they do that of Virgil or Horace? You're nothing to them. They wouldn't deign to read you, nor would they hire anyone to recite your work at their dinner parties."

Angry tears smarted in my eyes, infuriating me even more than his words. I didn't want Silvanus to think I was some feeble-minded woman with wounded feelings. "I had no such expectations and did nothing to seek out your support. I know my place

271

all too well."

"I want to change that place," he said, his voice soft now. "I want to elevate you, and I have proved that by making sure the entire city has seen your work. Everyone here reads graffiti. By keeping my patronage a secret — even from my dear wife, for despite her best efforts, I fear she would be unable to resist telling others of your gift for verse and how I'm trying to nurture it — we ensure that no one knows your identity. Not yet. Let them come to love your poetry. Let them clamor for more. And only when they know your talent is as great as Virgil's will we reveal who you are."

"You're mad," I said. "My talent is nowhere near that of Virgil."

"Spare me the modesty. You're too intelligent to be unaware of your worth. Finish your epic. Keep bringing it to me here. I'm a busy man, Kassandra. Memorizing poetry is a time-consuming act, but one I'm willing to do for you."

"You're memorizing my poetry?"

"So that I can recite it for a group of specially chosen guests when the time is right." There had long been a craze for poetry recitation at banquets, and some patrician men had proven expert at the art; others hired poets or actors to do it. I should have expected that Silvanus was one of the former. "Why do you make this difficult for me? I can easily walk away and never speak of this again. I can find another poet, but it is you, Kassandra, whom I want."

"No, don't find another." The words escaped my lips before I could even think. "I'll write for you, and we will keep it secret until you're ready."

He reached across the table and squeezed my hand. Every nerve in my body trembled with pleasure. "Great things will come from this. I promise you that."

One ought to trust the promise of a well-respected nobleman, but I was anxious when Lepida arrived at my house. I had penned her poem in the heady moments after returning from my meeting with her husband, flush with ambition and hope and no small measure of lust. The emotion readily transferred to my tablet. There was not enough time to copy it before she arrived, so I let her read it and decide for herself if it was good enough. She liked it, so I suggested that she copy it in her own hand. She balked at the idea.

"I'm not trying to claim I wrote it myself," she said. "And your handwriting is far superior to mine."

"Will you tell him *I* wrote it?" I asked.

"I had thought I would, why? Do you think I shouldn't? You needn't worry — he would never think you were writing it from your own emotions. A poet can use her words however she chooses, summoning the feelings required for each piece. Silvanus understands that, but if you'd prefer, I won't identify you as the author. We can let him think it's Sappho, if you like."

"He would recognize my verse as unlike hers. I haven't that much talent. Perhaps you would be happier having me copy something of hers. *Once again Love, the loosener of limbs, shakes me, that sweet-bitter irresistible creature.*"

"No," Lepida said. "I want him to have something uniquely his, commissioned by his loving wife. I'll be vague as to who wrote it. I can tell him I hired someone my father knows. There are countless poets in this city."

I considered her last statement as I carefully copied my poem onto papyrus, knowing that my identity would be no secret. Silvanus would recognize my handwriting. There was no shortage of poets in Pompeii. So why had Silvanus singled me out? He might claim to appreciate my talent, but he had no real knowledge of it when he first approached me. What, then, had spurred him to pull me aside that night at Plautus's house? He said he had heard I was a poet. Perhaps Plautus had told him, as he'd initially led me to believe. Or perhaps my friend's noble husband was hiding his true motives alongside the identity of his hired hand. Did he want more from me than poetry?

27
1902

When I returned from Vesuvius, alone, Jeremy having stayed behind to speak with Callie, I found the villa empty except for Kat, who was still holed up in her darkroom. I retreated to the terrace and gazed across the bay, thinking about Mario. He had not budged, refusing to utter a single word more about Callie and why he was meeting with her at the top of a volcano. The entire situation was so bizarre I hardly knew what to make of it.

Even if the archaeologist and the guide were romantically involved, that would not explain such an odd rendezvous. Callie wouldn't have ignored her duties at the dig for a tryst. She'd revealed nothing to me during the weeks of our acquaintance that led me to believe she harbored tender feelings for Mario, but, given her not-so-secret views on marriage and attraction, it wasn't inconceivable that she had embroiled herself in some sort of dalliance. He was the perfect picture of a dashing Italian lover — dark, curly hair, liquid eyes, and a lean, muscular physique.

Kat emerged from inside, carrying the latest batch of photographs she had developed. She had an uncanny ability to capture the essence of individuals, never letting her subjects pose formally, preferring to catch them unaware. She revealed the wicked gleam not often visible in Ivy's eyes and the loneliness that occasionally crossed Jeremy's face. My favorite was one that revealed an undeniable passion emanating from Colin as he looked at me. While I would have preferred her to have had the sense to show it to no one but me — I reminded myself that she was very young and either too romantic or bent on embarrassing me — I treasured the image.

"I don't suppose you have any of the guides who work in the excavations?" I asked.

"Not many, particularly as my father's unreasonable refusal to let me leave the house had paralyzed my ability to work."

"Could you show them to me?"

"Is it for the case?"

"It is."

She smiled slyly, rushed off, and returned

quickly with a stack of pictures. Only one showed Mario. He was in constant motion and used expansive hand gestures, so I was not surprised to find it half-blurred. She'd captured him looking sideways at someone out of the frame. There was something shifty in his expression that I had never before noticed. More significant, though, was that I recognized the location, as well as the two tourists in the background. She had taken the picture from the entrance of the House of the Vettii the day I met Mario there, when she was supposedly being attacked.

"When did you take this?" I asked.

"I don't recall exactly." She pulled the photograph away from me. "I have others that will interest you more." She bustled off to her room again and returned with a series of shots she'd taken of the archaeologists at work. Mr. Jackson was in several of them, always staring at Callie.

"Was she looking at him when you took this one, do you remember?" I asked, holding up an image of Callie scowling.

"Yes, she was. I don't think she much liked him," Kat said. "He watched her in an unseemly way."

"I wonder if she ever confronted him about it?"

"Not that I ever saw."

"No one else has mentioned it," I said.

"I don't think most of the others would have noticed. Except Benjamin. He's always keeping a close eye on her. You can keep these if you think they may prove useful. I've more work to do." She slunk back to her darkroom.

I had no doubt now that she had lied about being attacked. She'd been spying on Ivy and me while we talked to Mario. Yet I hesitated to question her story. What good would it do? She wanted her father's attention and had sunk low to get it. If she knew I was onto her, it would not improve things between us.

Colin did not return until much later, but did not share with me the results of his day until after we were alone in our dressing room, getting ready for dinner. "Benjamin uses Faber pencils," he said. "There was no other sort in his supplies, which isn't surprising, as artists get attached to their favorite kind. That doesn't prove the one you found at the House of the Silver Wedding is his, but it could be. The Staedtler likely belongs to someone else, unless he bought and left it deliberately. How was your day? Did you enjoy your lie-in?"

"I did, thank you, and managed to be unexpectedly productive despite it." I detailed for him everything that had happened at Vesuvius.

"It's unlikely any of this has a connection to the murder and, beyond that, Bainbridge does not need you to interfere," he said, fastening the studs on his shirt. "He has a not inconsiderable amount of experience with the ladies. However things turn out between him and Miss Carter, he will come through it unscathed. At least in the long run."

"But what of Mario's warning about her?"

"Darling, he's hot-blooded and passionate. Who knows what he meant? It may be nothing more than a jealous desire to prevent another man — a duke, in particular — from receiving the favors he could not persuade her to give him."

"He doesn't seem like that type of person," I said.

"We're only slightly acquainted with Mario." Colin turned to the mirror and tied a cravat. "Let me talk to him. He may be more comfortably speaking candidly to another man than he was with you."

Colin was correct about Mario being more comfortable with him. The guide insisted that there had never been a liaison between him and Callie; if anything, he had appeared alarmed by the suggestion. He said nothing that could lead us to believe his comments to me at Vesuvius pertained to the murder of Mr. Walker. Most important, perhaps, he gave my husband — who possessed an unparalleled skill for reading the silent signs that someone has something to hide — no indication of being anything less than open and honest. Colin and I agreed it was a personal matter and, hence, none of our business. Jeremy could make his own decisions. We might have quite forgot the whole incident at Vesuvius had Mario not turned up at the villa two days later, long after midnight, his face battered and bruised.

I had never seen such dreadful evidence of a violent beating. We brought the injured man to one of the house's empty bedrooms. Ivy, with her preternaturally gentle touch, tended to his wounds, cleaning them up and bandaging them as necessary, while Kat took photographs, insisting they be recorded as evidence of the attack. All the color had drained from my Ivy's face. I knew she was struggling at the sight of so much blood, but she did not let her emotions prevent her from the task at hand. Only when she was done did we let Mario speak.

He had gone to bed early, he explained, and had been awakened from his slumber by the sound of insistent knocking. Assuming it to be his brother, coming to inform him of some calamity afflicting either their mother or grandmother, he leapt from his couch and flung open the door. Instead, he saw a man dressed all in black, wearing a strange mask, with wide openings for the eyes and mouth, over his face. He said it might have been made from clay. It reminded him of those worn by actors in ancient Rome, similar to the ones depicted on the walls of many of the ruins of the houses in Pompeii.

"I was terrified, as anyone would be," he said, accepting the glass of water Ivy handed him. "Before I could speak or even think he grabbed me and flung me down the stairs. I smashed into the landing and could hear his boots on the steps, coming for me again. I tried to stand up, so that I might fight him, but I was too unsteady to rise. He beat me badly and kicked me many times. Then he goes. He says not one word the entire time. I waited for a while, to be sure he would not come back, and then, I somehow find the energy to drag myself here."

"You walked the entire way?" I asked. The villa was at least four miles from where he lived.

"I had no choice. I did not want to trouble

my brother with this. To do so, in the middle of the night, would only upset Mamma and Nonna. So I come here, knowing you will help."

"Many families live in your building, do they not?" Colin asked. "Did anyone open a door when they heard what was happening?"

"No, Signore Hargreaves," Mario said. "They know better than to interfere when they hear such a thing."

"Are you suggesting the Camorra is behind this?" Colin asked, his face deadly serious.

"No, no, it's not them. They do not wear masks. They want you to know who they are."

"Who, then, do you suspect?" Kat asked.

Mario has sunk back into the soft pillow on the bed. "I have no idea, Signorina von Lange. I am very careful not to anger anyone."

Except Callie, I thought. The doctor we had summoned arrived, shooing us ladies from the room.

"Do you think, Emily, that we should return to England?" Ivy asked, her face still pale and drawn.

"And abandon Mario after someone has savagely beaten him? No, I don't think that would be the right course of action," I said. "It's time I have a long, candid conversation with Callie. She's lying about something, but I don't know what."

28
AD 79

It was growing more and more difficult to hide from my father what I was doing, first because it was a time-consuming endeavor, and second, because it took me away from my work as his copyist. He was too generous — and too indulgent — to reprimand me for the latter. He knew I was spending all of my free time writing, often staying up half the night (our slaves would have reported this to him, Telekles in particular), and he admired my diligence. Poetry, he told me, when I confessed that was the object of my work, was a far better occupation than making copies of exemplars. He would hire someone else before telling me to abandon my verse. This heaped more guilt upon that already consuming me over my feelings for Silvanus. Nausea plagued me whenever I saw Lepida. Was it my fate to deceive everyone I loved?

Melas and his assistants had finished the

decoration of our house. I had hoped this would mean I'd no longer have to see him, but, unfortunately, he and my father had struck up a friendship, and he dined with us at least twice a week. A boon for the painter, as it saved him from paying for his own food.

"Your father tells me you're writing," he said, helping himself to a heaping portion of one of Galen's less-successful dishes, pork in a caraway sauce too thin to be satisfying. "A noble endeavor. What is your subject?"

"I prefer not to discuss my work."

My father nodded. *"A new idea is delicate. It can be killed by a sneer or a yawn; it can be stabbed to death by a quip and worried to death by a frown on the right man's brow."*

"Ovid," I said. "An extremely wise man. I do not, however, consider Melas the right man to criticize my ideas."

"I don't know whether to be wounded or pleased," the artist said. "Am I the wrong man because you care not for my opinion or because you can trust that I would never seek to undermine you?"

"I'm afraid it's the former," I said. "Ought I have some great interest in your opinion? You've given me no cause to. Instead, you have criticized my preference for Virgil over

286

Homer and balked at my taste in art."

"I didn't take you for the sort of boring girl who wants only to hear her own opinions mirrored back. Perhaps I was mistaken."

"You don't know me well enough to mirror my opinions."

"Then I shall have to work harder to learn them," Melas said.

"I shouldn't bother," I said. "I've no time for idle distraction and, even if I did, why should I argue the relative merits of verse with a painter?"

"You believe that a painter can only appreciate his own medium? Then, I am afraid, you know me no better than I know you. A blow to us both, as anyone engaged in a creative endeavor ought to possess sufficient powers of observation to read the characters of those around him — or her."

"It is precisely because I'm able to read your character that I lost interest in you, Melas."

"You can't lose what you never had." The painter smiled. If I had hoped he was insulted, my words were not having their desired effect.

My father laughed. "You must stop, Kassandra, lest our guest refuses to dine with us again." That outcome would please me greatly, but I was not so unkind that I wanted to see my father abandoned by his friend.

"I wouldn't be that petty," Melas said. "I appreciate your daughter's spirit, Aristeides, even if it is more Roman than Greek."

"Kassandra cannot change her spirit any more than you can, Melas," my father replied. "She is Greek. No matter how much she longs to be Roman, she never will be."

"Perhaps you could keep me locked up at home as they used to do in Athens. We could build a gynaikonitis so that I might be shielded from shocking and inappropriate conversations. Didn't Aristotle believe women to be nothing more than failed men?"

"I have never claimed Aristotle is without fault," my father said. "Now, if we want to discuss philosophy . . ."

I drained the wine from my beaker and raised it for Lysander to refill. This would be a long night.

29
1902

The doctor had assured us that Mario would make a full recovery. The next morning, at the guide's request, Colin and I took him to his mother's house. Signora Sorrentino, after first giving Pietro a hard smack on his arm for not having (magically, so far as I can tell) realized his brother might be attacked and taking action to stop it, set her younger son up in a bright bedroom and ordered his grandmother to sit with him. This freed her up to retire to the kitchen, where she started forming meatballs for a soup that, she explained, would help Mario heal more quickly.

She initially refused my offer of assistance, sizing me up and finding my potential in the kitchen lacking, but eventually was persuaded by Pietro's wife, Gianetta, to let me chop vegetables. Apparently I did not do it well, as before I'd made my way through the stack of celery stalks in front of me, Gianetta pushed me aside and took over. Neither of the women spoke English, but my Italian was good enough to communicate with them, and I soon learned that Mario's mother was more than a little disappointed — in her words, her heart was indelibly wounded — that her younger son had not yet married despite being the most handsome boy in all of Pompeii. When I asked her who she thought might have attacked him, she shook her head and suggested it was some jealous farmer's son. Further inquiries told me she had no specific individual in mind, only, if I may summarize, a firm belief that every other single man in Campania envied Mario. Gianetta, through frequent eye rolls, communicated that she did not agree with her mother-in-law, but she admitted it was long past the time that Mario should have wed. When she started to list the girls in town she considered the best potential matches for him, I excused myself and went to find Colin and Pietro.

Pietro was stunned by the attack on his brother. "It was not the Camorra," he said, echoing Mario's opinion. "There's no one with whom we are feuding, so it is not a family situation. Only a coward would cover his face with a mask, knowing that I would come after him for retribution, and I do not know any men who are cowards."

"Are you acquainted with the Carters?" I asked.

"Signorina Callie and her brother? They come to my restaurant on occasion, but I cannot say I know them well."

"Do you know any of the other American archaeologists?" I asked. "I imagine some of them are patrons of your restaurant."

"Signore Taylor comes with some frequency, and I consider him a friend. He is usually on his own, so I make a point of talking to him."

"Why does he come alone?" Colin asked.

Pietro shrugged. "Perhaps he is tired of his colleagues by the end of the day and desires a little peace. Sometimes, I think it is more that he is not so skilled at excavation as they are. He loves it, and has an appreciation for Pompeii that goes beyond the scientific, but he does not know so much about the methods as his workers. He is no useless dilettante, which makes him somewhat discontent with his situation."

"Discontent how?" I asked. "His staff seem to like him well enough."

"Forgive me, Lady Emily, I use the wrong word. Not *discontent,* but, maybe *embarrassed.* He is a strong man, intelligent, the

291

leader of his expedition. All this is because of his money, not his knowledge. You understand?"

"I believe so. Do you see any of the other members of his staff regularly?"

"Signore Stirling, he comes, too, but not alone. I don't much like his acquaintance — he is with the Camorra. I know better than to interfere when they are around, so I never speak much to them."

"Do you know the man's name?" Colin asked.

Pietro shook his head. "Even if I did, I would not share it with you. I pay the money to them necessary for protection, but otherwise, stay away from the Camorra. He may tell you the man's name, but only if he is irredeemably foolish."

We went straight from Pietro's to Mr. Taylor's dig, where Mr. Stirling proved himself — if Pietro was to be believed — irredeemably foolish. He claimed to have no idea that his friend, Michele Fabbrocino, was connected to the Camorra and offered to introduce us to him. Colin assured him that was unnecessary. He would seek out the man on his own and question him.

That settled, we asked Callie for a private word, walking with her along the Strada dei

Sepolcri, the Street of the Tombs. The Romans did not inter their mortal remains within their cities, and, hence, graves lined the streets beyond their city walls; every informed visitor to Rome is familiar with those found on the Appian Way. Pompeii was no different. The tombs here were not yet completely excavated, and their ruined state contributed to an eerie feeling that chased me as we wound our way through them.

Just beyond these monuments stood the Villa of Diomedes, where the bodies of nearly twenty women and children had been found, huddled together in a cellar, surrounded by supplies. They had hoped to wait out the eruption there. Equally chilling was the discovery of a man, still holding the key to the house, his body close to that of a slave, who clung to his few valuable possessions. Was the man locking the door, hoping to keep his family safe? Or, had he and his slave tried to flee to safety? There was a hideous irony in passing by so many formal tombs only to come upon a house that now stood as the makeshift marker of so many graves.

"Let's stop here," Colin said.

"Should I be scared?" Callie asked. "The two of you, pulling me off for a quiet chat?

Am I about to be accused of murder?"

"What do you think?" Colin asked.

"The fact that Mr. Walker and I crossed the Atlantic on the same ship might have aroused your suspicions," she said, "but I can assure you that if I had killed him, I should never have been careless enough to draw your attention to having seen him before he arrived in Pompeii. And if I wanted him dead, wouldn't it have been easier to fling him overboard than to dispatch him here and have to deal with the disposal of his body?"

"You appear to have given the matter a certain amount of thought," Colin said.

"I have," Callie said, sitting on the villa's stone steps. "I've never before found myself in the midst of a murder investigation, as we ladies are rarely allowed anywhere near such tawdry things. Mr. Walker's death troubles me. I can't claim an acquaintance with the man, but I do remember him, and knowing he was violently struck down is unsettling."

"Violent death is always distressing," I said, "and all the more so when one has any personal knowledge of the victim. But we haven't come here to discuss that."

"What, then?" she asked.

"I'm sure you can guess," Colin said.

"I've already been scolded by Bainbridge for not going up Vesuvius with him. Surely he's not so weak-minded as to have sent you to reprimand me as well?"

Colin leaned against a tree and crossed his arms. "I would never agree to such an absurd errand and, although it pains me to give him a compliment of any sort, not even Bainbridge would stoop to such under-handed methods."

"He didn't seem the type, but one never knows" she said. "So why are you here?"

"Am I to understand that you can think of no other reason we would seek you out today?" I asked.

"Yes, because I certainly cannot."

"What about Mario?" I asked.

"Mario?" She sneered. "So that's what it is, is it? Not even Bainbridge had the audacity to accuse me of that."

I was about to rebuke her, but Colin spoke before I could. "Bainbridge's mind doesn't work that way. So you didn't do it?" He was being deliberately vague to draw out a response from her.

"Mario is a friendly enough man," she said, "but, a certain sailor excepted, I prefer more educated bedfellows."

I know I blushed a shocking shade of crimson, but Colin continued to speak as if she had said nothing extraordinary. "I've no interest in your romantic entanglements, Miss Carter. I'm more concerned with Mario being flung down the stairs."

"What? Flung down the stairs? What stairs?" She looked genuinely flummoxed.

I sat on the steps next to her. "He was attacked in his home last night by a masked individual who beat him badly and left him in a pool of blood." True, the pool of blood was an embellishment, but I wanted to take advantage of her shock and lower her guard.

"Why would anyone do that?" she asked.

"We were hoping, Miss Carter, that you might be able to enlighten us on that point," Colin said. "My wife was a witness to the conversation you had with him at Vesuvius, and it did not appear to be particularly friendly. What is the trouble between you?"

"There is no trouble," Callie said. "Not any trouble that matters on a larger scale, at any rate. He and I had a disagreement — a private disagreement — that concerns no one but me. It wasn't the sort of thing that would lead me to want him physically harmed."

"I'm afraid I need to know more about the nature of this disagreement," Colin said.

"And I'm afraid I'm unwilling to divulge any further details," she said, rising to her feet and stepping to stand in front of him, her hands on her hips, her chin jutting out defiantly. "If you believe me to be guilty of some crime, send the police. Otherwise, I have nothing to say."

"Why are you so defensive about this?" I asked.

"That is no one's business but my own," she replied. "I appreciate that the two of you have taken on the investigation of Mr. Walker's murder, and I'm more than willing to be interrogated on that topic, as I have already proven. The same goes for Mr. Jackson. My private life, however, is not up for public review. I'm quite accustomed to people like you taking advantage of any excuse to nose in and offer advice, but it never endears them to me."

"You misunderstand us entirely," I said. "We have no desire to give you advice. A friend of ours has been savagely beaten — a friend who argued with you not long before the attack. Your private life can be as private as you like, but we have every right to question what happened between you two that might have catalyzed this terrible event."

"If you have evidence that I set out to harm Mario, give it to the police. I assume the incident has been reported to them and I further assume that you will tell them — if

297

you haven't already — every nasty thing you can think of to make sure they are as suspicious of me as possible. In the meantime, as I've already communicated, I have nothing to say on the subject."

"I'm at quite a loss, Miss Carter," Colin said, his voice low and deliberate. "You, of course, have an absolute right to your private life. My wife and I have no desire to create fictional stories in an effort to make the police think ill of you — for fiction is what they would be. I have seen nothing in your behavior that I consider out of line. Perhaps you are so used to being judged for choosing a life more colorful than that usually offered to ladies you can no longer recognize friends when they stand before you, and I find that terribly sad. We won't press you to reveal whatever secrets you want to keep. If you give us your word that you had nothing to do with the attack on Mario, that will be the end of it, so far as I'm concerned."

"Thank you," she said, lowering her eyes and looking cowed. "I apologize for responding with such venom. As you surmised, I am used to being judged: for wanting to pursue a career, for refusing to marry, and for any number of behaviors society considers unladylike."

"I know the feeling all too well," I said. "We have more in common than you realize, Callie. I never would want you to think we're judging you in such an odious manner when, in fact, I find much in you to admire."

"That surprises me," she said.

Her words wounded me. I hated to think that anyone could believe I would sit in judgment in such a reprehensible manner. I had never in my life approved of the rules that shackle us ladies and have suffered from much censure as a result. Had I become the sort of person one could mistake for a society lady, bent on matchmaking and horrified by the suffragette movement? I, who had marched with the Women's Liberal Federation in support of the right to vote? If so, I would have to correct the situation without delay.

30
AD 79

I had fallen into a strange new routine, completing the little work I still did for my father by the time the sun reached the top of the sky, and then retreating to my room, where, under Melas's frescoes of the *Aeneid,* I wrote scroll after scroll of poetry. Every fifth day, I met Silvanus in the bar. And twice a week, I went to his house to visit Lepida, who had not the slightest clue I was seeing her husband so frequently. Although there was nothing but poetry between the patrician and me, I could not help feeling I was betraying my friend, especially now, when I'd started to believe Silvanus wanted more from me. Even if he didn't, aren't all secrets a sort of betrayal? There might be kind ones, ones to which no one would object, the sort when one lies to hide a gift until the occasion on which it will be given, but this was not what Silvanus and I were doing.

I was never at ease when I called on Lepida and was beginning to recognize luxury as less important to me than I had previously believed, for it was only in my father's modest house that I could rest easy anymore. I had grown accustomed to the noisy streets of our new neighborhood. Galen knew my favorite dishes now and made a point of having them on hand at his thermopolium at least twice a week. When I went to buy bread each morning, Telekles in tow, I chatted with the daughter of the man who owned my preferred bakery, and soon we had taken to going to the sumptuous and comfortable Stabian Baths together.

I also found — most unexpectedly — that I had started to miss the banter I shared with Melas when he was working in our house. He still dined with my father on occasion, but they had taken to going out more often than staying in. Initially, this caused me to rejoice, but one day, when I was returning from the baths, I ran into the painter. More like we ran into each other, as we both landed on the same stepping-stone at the same time. I would have fallen into the street if he had not had the sense to grab me around the waist, saving me from toppling into the filthy water flowing through the gutter.

"I should have needed another bath if you hadn't acted so quickly," I said. "Thank you."

"I would do the same for anyone. I'm not such a savage as you think."

"I've never said you are a savage."

"Will the two of you move if you want to have a conversation?" A man with a heavily loaded donkey shouted. "We're trying to get through here."

Melas took me by the arm and we leapt from the stepping-stones onto the pavement. "You may never have employed the term directly, but you have made no secret of your dislike of me."

He was standing close to me, and I took the opportunity to study him. No one would describe his features as handsome, but his eyes were pleasing enough, and his skin clear. "It's not so much that I dislike you . . ." My voice trailed because the fact was, I did dislike him, but until now, I had never really considered why.

"You're not persuading me, Kassandra," he said. "Allow me to buy you a beaker of wine and perhaps we can find a path to friendship. If nothing else, it would make your father happy."

"Why would he care, one way or another?"

"He knows it irritates you when I dine

302

with him. Why do you think we sit at Galen's tables so often? Your father would be more comfortable in his own house, but he does not like to see you unhappy."

"You're both making more of this than you ought. I don't give you all that much thought, Melas." I sighed. "And now you will say my protest disproves my claim. Go ahead, pick a bar and buy me some wine. I will try to be your friend, but do not expect things to change between us too quickly."

He grinned. *"Dripping water hollows out stone, not through force but through persistence."*

The Greek painter could quote Ovid.

31
1902

Colin left Callie and me outside the Villa of Diomedes so that he could interview Mario's neighbors. Callie insisted that she needed to return to work, so I accompanied her. As we walked, the friction between us started to fade. I told her about my childhood and how my mother cared for nothing but seeing me make a good marriage, and then about my first husband, whose proposal I had accepted only because it presented an easy way to escape her house.

"And then he died so soon," Callie said, sighing after I explained how Philip's friend had murdered him not long after our wedding trip. "You, left to mourn a man you hardly knew."

"It was not all bleak," I said. "Had it never happened, I wouldn't have discovered my passion for the ancient world. Society forces widows into lengthy mourning, and in doing so, inadvertently gave me the time to

304

develop intellectually, without anyone judging me for wanting to read Homer or spending too much time in the British Museum."

"We do have more in common than I assumed," she said. "I know how close you and Bainbridge are — he raves about you — but now that I know you better, I find it a most unlikely friendship."

"There are ways in which it appears to be so," I said. "Yet, if you understand his character, you'll find that he and I are more similar than a cursory glance would reveal. I know how much you despise the aristocracy, but imagine the pressure on him to marry and provide the dukedom with an heir. His refusal to do so is anything but easy."

"He doesn't object to the inherent unfairness of the system, only to the rules he's supposed to follow as part of it. He's perfectly happy to embrace the trappings — and wealth — of his title."

"Yes, he is, but don't assume he is altogether content in a role he did not choose. I'm not defending the system, Callie, only asking you to consider this: Is it not as inane to reject a man's affection because he possesses a title as it would be to seek it because of his rank?"

"I don't think it's the same thing at all,"

she said. "He may not have chosen to be a duke, but he is one, nonetheless, and shows no signs of renouncing his title. I cannot, in good faith, ally myself with a man whose life is dependent on a system I find unfair and revolting."

"Why, then, are you spending so much time with him?" I asked.

"Because he is so bloody charming," she said, coming to a stop and flinging a well-formed arm over her face. "I can't recall ever having so thoroughly enjoyed the company of a gentleman. This whole act of his — pretending to want nothing more than to be the most useless man in England — would be maddening if it weren't so obvious that, beneath it, lies the heart of an individual who would sacrifice anything for a friend."

"You do know him well," I said.

"It's not so difficult to crack that silly surface if one is willing to persist."

"Yet you are determined to push him away, simply because he is a duke?"

"You're a beast, Emily."

"I am when it comes to defending Jeremy."

She blushed, ever so slightly, but said nothing.

"How did you get along with Mr. Jackson?" I asked. "I understand he was rather fascinated with you."

She bristled. "I did not appreciate his admiration for my person, but can assure you that it did not catalyze in me murderous impulses. And now, I must return to work." She stalked off before I could ask her another question.

I let her go and returned to the villa, where I found Ivy on the terrace. She had just come from Mario's bedside.

"His mother is terrifying, Emily, but you know that already. An absolute force of nature. If her son isn't fully recovered by the end of the week . . . well, I shouldn't want to be there to see it. He's already much better. Bruised and battered, but more upset that he didn't manage to stop his attacker than he is troubled by physical pain. He claims he could be back at work tomorrow, but fears that the colorful appearance of his face would prevent him from securing clients."

"A valid concern." He was so covered with bruises, it hurt to look at him. "He's fortunate not to have sustained worse injuries."

"The poor man." Ivy's voice faltered, but then she steeled herself and asked about my day. I told her about my conversation with Callie.

"I'm more than a little surprised you and

307

Colin were so quick to accept her refusal to talk about her relationship with Mario," Ivy said.

"I don't think it's a relationship, per se—"

"Call it what you like. I'm not suggesting there's anything serious between them. She may reject the notion of aristocracy, but I see no sign that she's keen to dabble with the lower classes, that sailor excepted. Regardless, she must be the most likely suspect behind Mario's beating. We know she was upset with him before the attack and the fact that she will not reveal the content of their conversation is . . ." her voice trailed.

"What?" I asked.

"It's . . . well . . . if she were not the sort of lady whom you admire, I don't believe you would go so easy on her. You're willing to give her the benefit of the doubt because she shares your intellectual leanings. I don't mean this as criticism, my dear, but I do wish you would make yourself amenable to the possibility that she may be involved in something rather odious."

I frowned. "You raise an excellent point. I shall strive to keep my mind open on the subject, even though I find that I like her very much."

"As do I," Ivy said. "If only she would be

willing to marry Jeremy! That is, should it turn out she is quite innocent. We don't know that she wasn't involved in Mr. Walker's demise."

"She couldn't have killed him," I said. "She's too small."

"Not if she subdued him first and immobilized him," Ivy said. "What if she whacked him on the head with a rock and then tied him up? She could have strangled him then."

"What a ghastly imagination you have, my dear."

"I saw Kat's photographs of her with Mr. Jackson. She could have pushed that boulder onto him, too."

"No, she couldn't have. She was sitting at the table with us at the time, remember?"

"But Benjamin wasn't," she said. "What if they planned to stage his argument with Mr. Stirling so that he could rush off and deal with Mr. Jackson? I recall what happened with absolute clarity. Mr. Stirling was a bit stern with him, but not so much that any rational person would have taken offense. Benjamin was looking for an excuse to run off."

"That doesn't mean his sister knew what he was doing."

"Perhaps not, but neither does it prove she didn't."

When Colin returned from interviewing the residents of Mario's building, he found me in our room, where I'd retreated with a book, tired of watching Kat do her best to ignore me in favor of Ivy. He explained that at first, none would admit to having seen or heard anything at the time of the attack on their neighbor, but once he had managed to convince them that the Camorra were not involved, he discovered two useful clues. First, that the front door had been propped open as early as ten o'clock that night. A man, returning from an evening out with his friends, found it held open by a brick. Assuming someone had lost a key, he left the obstacle in place.

"Which suggests that our attacker neither had a key of his own nor picked the lock," Colin said. "I didn't find anyone who owned up to having opened the door for a stranger or who noticed someone slipping into the building behind him, but it would be easy enough to lay in wait for a resident to come home and slyly catch the door before it closed."

"Someone could have noticed the brick and removed it. I'd wager our intruder kept close, ready to catch the door again, if necessary. Why did he wait so long between opening the door and going to Mario's room?"

"It's sloppy, the sign of a novice," Colin said. "He could have slipped in and hidden somewhere in the building — in the cellar, for example — until he was ready to make his move. That would have been more sensible than loitering outside for two hours."

"So we are not looking for a professional thug who chose a Roman theatrical mask to hide his appearance."

"No, we are not. Which brings me to the other bit," Colin said. He handed me a canvas bag that contained the shattered remains of the mask. "Given to me by an elderly lady who swept it up this morning. She has very strong feelings about the common areas of the building being kept clean."

I poured the contents onto a table and we arranged them, in the manner of a jigsaw puzzle, as best we could. Many of the pieces were too small to be of use — some little more than powdered remains — but, when we finished, we had a fair idea of what the mask had looked like. It was an unsophisticated rendering in ordinary clay of one of a pair of tragic masks featured in a mosaic originally found in the House of the Faun, now in the Naples museum.

"I questioned the souvenir sellers again. They all sell similar masks, but no one remembers anyone out of the ordinary," Colin said. "It could've been purchased at the same time our ostraca were."

"If so, Mario's attack would be related to Mr. Walker's murder, which makes me suspicious of Callie," I said. "Ivy pointed out that she could have strangled him, if she'd first incapacitated him. Do you think we're making a mistake in trusting her?"

"I don't," my husband said. "We have no evidence that suggests any involvement on her part in the murder. Which is not to say we should accept everything she says as a Home Truth. The attack on Mario wasn't pulled off with the delicacy of the killing; it was noisy and messy. Granted, that could be a feint to make us believe that the two incidents are unconnected, but, for now, at least, I think we should treat them separately."

32
AD 79

Despite myself, I came almost to enjoy Melas's company. Which is not to say I still found him anything but immensely irritating. He had that intolerable Greek sense of superiority and an annoying habit of whistling when he started to grow bored with a conversation. Fortunately, he did not do this often with me, only when I started talking about Lepida.

"You would like her, you know," I said one day when he had once again persuaded me to sit in a bar with him. He had a favorite, much nicer than the one Silvanus and I frequented, but as neither of us could afford much, the actual beverages were no improvement. "She's not some vapid girl without opinions."

"Silvanus would never have married a vapid girl," Melas said. "He's far too ambitious to have a useless wife. I wonder that he even stays in Pompeii. A man of his family and fortune could do well in Rome."

"His family has a house on the Palatine Hill," I said, "but he prefers Pompeii."

"Who wouldn't prefer Pompeii? Rome is crowded and filthy."

"And Pompeii isn't?" I snorted. "The streets are a disgrace."

"You know quite a lot about our friend Silvanus," Melas said. "Lepida must enjoy regaling you with stories about him."

I deduced from his tone that he did not believe Lepida to be my source. I shrugged. "Is that so surprising? She's a new bride and enamored with her husband."

"I see," he said. I did not like the way he was looking at me. "What are you working on now? Your father tells me he has hired two new copyists so that you might have more time for your poetry. Do we have a budding Sappho in our midst?"

"I prefer epics," I said. "Not that I would have the hubris to —"

"Spare me the false modesty. So you're writing an epic. Is it of Rome or of Greece?"

"It tells the tale of a hero making his way back to Rome after the end of the Civil Wars."

"A Roman Odysseus?" Melas asked.

"No, nothing like that. The wars took him away from the city, but his discovery of a set of sacred vessels in the deserts of Egypt sends him on a new journey. The thousand-year-old crone who had protected them for centuries is dying and incapable of returning them to their rightful place."

"Which is?"

"I'm not quite sure yet, nor is he. She dies before she can tell him and leaves him with a riddle. If he can solve it, the answer will lead him to the location of the next clue."

"So it's a quest, really, where, I can only assume, he faces tests of strength and bravery in order to set things right, as it were?"

"Yes, and feats that require intellectual prowess as well," I said.

"I'd love to read it."

I laughed. "Not before the entire work is complete. And, then, only if I deem it worthy."

"It worthy or I?"

"It," I said. "You've a decent appreciation for poetry, so if it's not good enough, I'd prefer to be spared your teasing about my shortcomings."

"You could let me see the beginning now, so that I might offer useful insight into what you've already got."

"Not a chance, my friend," I said. "You'll see not one single line before I've written the last."

"You called me your friend," Melas said. "Which makes it likely I will die of shock long before you're finished with your great work. At least tell me the name of your hero."

"Gaius Antonius Vitalis."

"Very Roman, Kassandra, very Roman. Reminiscent of both Julius Caesar and Marc Antony. Do you long for a return of the Republic?"

"My politics don't come into it, and at any rate, everyone calls him Vitalis. There's no reason to consider the rest of his name."

"No need to get defensive," Melas said. "I've always known Antony deserved better than Augustus's slander. But, then, I'm not really Roman, am I?"

"Sometimes, Melas — more often than not — I despise you."

33
1902

I had come to dread breakfast. All the progress I had made in Rome toward forging a civil relationship with Kat seemed to have eroded into nothing. On this particular morning, she asked why I had the bad manners to pour milk in my cup before tea and then informed Colin she was tired of being kept home and out of our investigation. I admired her pertinacity, but her father was having none of it, wanting to protect her from the darker sides of the world, especially after her attack. Rather than holding this against him, she adjusted her sling and blamed me.

"I've little tolerance for ladies who are happy to follow their own unconventional paths but throw stones at anyone else who tries to follow," she said, picking at the eggs on her plate. "They're worse than men because they're hypocrites."

"What are you three planning for the

317

day?" Ivy asked. "I'm going to work on a watercolor of the Forum Baths for Robert. Perhaps it's time you had a family outing, with no talk of murder. Kat, your step-mother knows a great deal about ancient plays. More Greek than Roman, admittedly, but perhaps she could —"

"I despise the theater," Kat said. "And we can't avoid talk of murder. What's more important than bringing Mr. Walker's killer to justice?"

"I quite agree," I said. I understood — and appreciated — Colin's desire to shield his daughter from our work, but suspected it was a futile endeavor. "About the murder, not the theater. But Ivy's suggestion has merit. Let's go to the ruins and play tourist. Perhaps something there will inspire us to see the case in a new way."

"Personally, I'm considering making an offering at the Temple of Isis," Kat said, "in the hope that the goddess can assist in our quest."

Her father laughed. "At this point, that might not be a bad idea."

Fear not, Dear Reader, that my worthy husband had abandoned his religious morals and embraced the pagan, although I cannot in good conscience make any statement on the subject regarding his daughter's beliefs. We headed off to the Temple of Isis. Its ruins included nothing recognizably Egyptian, just the usual sort of Roman colonnade surrounding the ruins of the usual sort of Roman temple, perched at the top of the usual set of stairs.

"Is it marble, or stucco made to look like it?" I asked, stepping closer to better examine the cladding on the cella, the rectangular room that would have originally housed a large statue of the goddess. Kat had removed her sling (as she did whenever it proved inconvenient), pulled the Brownie out of her bag, and was taking pictures of me. Could this be a sign of improving relations between us?

Colin did not respond except with a grunt. I turned around and saw his hand raised to his temple, which was bleeding. I cried out and rushed to him.

"Some sort of projectile hit me," he said. "The injury is superficial."

So far as I could tell, he was right. After pressing my handkerchief against the wound to stop the flow of blood, I told him to keep pressure on it and fairly flew through the temple grounds — Kat close on my heels — in search for the miscreant who had injured him, but found no one. I poked my head out of the entrance. The street beyond was empty. Whoever had struck him had disappeared. "Don't move," I said when we returned to his side. "You may have a concussion."

"I don't have a concussion." Colin grimaced. "And head wounds always look worse than they are. Here's what hit me." He showed us a piece of marble, approximately six inches square, upon which there was painted a finely rendered image of a lion being savaged by a decidedly tame-looking ass.

I recognized the scene. "Alexander again, the second portent of his demise. The noblest lion in his menagerie was kicked to death by a previously docile ass." I wiped a smear of my husband's blood from the corner of the piece. "Did you notice anyone following us? You're better at detecting such things than I."

"Not from the villa, I'm certain of that. Once we entered the ruins, it became more difficult to tell. Someone who knows the site would be able to remain unseen by ducking in and out of buildings."

"You must teach me your methods," Kat said, frowning. "I want to be able to know when someone is following me."

"My methods, such as they are, failed in this case, unless I'm to believe whoever flung this stone at me was lying in wait, which seems unlikely as this was a spontaneous excursion. As for you, I'd prefer you keep out of situations that might lead someone to tail you."

"Naturally," Kat said, grinning. "Still, I should like you to teach me all the same."

"That we shall discuss later," Colin said. "Much later."

If ever, I thought, recognizing the stubbornness in his tone. I looked back down at the stone and touched the lion painted on it. "It's beautifully done. Whoever painted it has considerable artistic talent."

"Someone like Benjamin . . . er, Mr. Carter?" Kat asked.

"Possibly," I said.

"Whoever it was must have kept it on hand, ready to take advantage of the opportunity to fling it at us whenever he could," she said. I noticed she was no longer defending Benjamin, as she had before.

"Not the best strategy." Colin ran his hand through his curls, picked up his hat — which had fallen to the ground when the marble struck him — and sighed. "Let's go find Carter." He took me firmly by the hand and led us to Mr. Taylor's site. Callie hailed us as we approached the excavations and, after we asked where we could find her brother, pointed us to a trench opposite of where she was working. Colin told Kat to stay with her, and he and I went off to talk to Benjamin. He was kneeling on the ground, photographing some small glass objects. Once he was finished, we begged a quiet word, walked with him to the edge of the dig, and showed him the marble.

"This is exquisite work," he said, taking it from Colin and examining it. "Is it ancient? I'm no archaeologist, but the colors look too bright to be old."

"We don't believe it is ancient, no," my husband said. "Do you recognize the scene it depicts?"

"No, I can't say I do. It's certainly unusual. One doesn't expect an ass to be capable of overpowering a lion. Where did you find it?"

"Have you been on site all morning?" I asked.

"Yes," he said, his tone turning harsh. "Why do you ask?"

"You have not left Taylor's dig at all?" Colin asked. "No painting in the main excavations?"

"No, I planned to go a bit later when the sun is lower in the sky so that I might —" He stopped and anger clouded his face. "What are you getting at, Mr. Hargreaves?"

"If I ask your colleagues whether you have been here all day, will they confirm what you have told me?"

"Yes, of course." He looked nervous and started bouncing on the balls of his feet. "What are you implying?"

"Someone threw this piece of marble at my husband, striking him in the head," I said. "You are a skilled artist, capable of having produced the painting."

"I'm more than skilled enough, but surely you're not suggesting I would try to harm anyone? That's outrageous."

"If you didn't throw it at me, you still could have painted it, whether or not you knew the piece's intended purpose."

"I see, I see," Benjamin said. Rivulets of perspiration ran from his temples down his face. "Of course you weren't accusing me of trying to injure you. You know I would never do that. But this painting, while of outstanding quality, is not my work. I don't use this particular shade of blue." He indicated the sky on the marble. "It's cobalt, and I prefer cerulean. Well, that's not entirely honest. Cobalt is considerably more expensive and I can't afford it. Regardless, this is done with oil — see how the paint is still a bit soft? — and I've only watercolors with me."

"So you wouldn't object to us searching

your supplies here as well as in your rooms to confirm that you have no oil paint?" Colin asked.

"Certainly, we can go now." His tone was defiant but then, in a flash, he looked concerned and spoke more softly. "Tell me, are you seriously injured? This is most concerning."

"As you can see, I am not," Colin said.

"That is excellent news, the most excellent." Benjamin, still bobbing on his feet, looked an absolute mess. "Shall we go to my rooms, then? But, no, first, I should show you the materials I have here."

A quick perusal of his painting kit at the site confirmed he had nothing but watercolors and chalk pastels — pastels that could've been used to make the drawing we'd seen in the basilica — as well as a tin of Faber pencils, with him. We then set off for his rooms, Kat, on her father's orders, remaining behind with Callie.

"You can't keep her wrapped in cotton wool forever," I said. "She won't tolerate it."

"You're right, of course, but I'm going to do my best to try."

The Carters were staying in the Albergo del Sole, which provided modest accommodations popular with scholars and those who could not afford the swankier and more convenient Hôtel Suisse. The nondescript building sat almost directly across from the ancient amphitheater, but its exterior belied the cozy atmosphere inside. The man behind the desk, who handed Benjamin the key to his rooms, could not have been friendlier.

We climbed to the first floor. The Carters had a small sitting room between two impossibly narrow bedrooms. The space was surprisingly bright and comfortable.

"Do whatever you will," Benjamin said, standing back from us, hovering near the door. "I've not the slightest idea how this sort of thing works. All I can ask is that you handle our possessions with respect. Callie is unlikely to be happy if she finds her things disturbed."

We uncovered nothing that could connect Benjamin to the marble slab, but it was impossible not to notice the striking difference in quality between his clothing and possessions and those belonging to his sister. Her dresses, shirtwaists, and suits were beautifully tailored, many from respectable fashion houses in Paris. Benjamin's suits, in contrast, were adequate examples of what I believe is called ready-to-wear. It was most peculiar, as if their parents' judgment as to who was held in higher esteem carried on long after their deaths.

What had his parents done to him that Benjamin was willing to accept a station in life so far beneath that of his sister? Callie could have an education, but he couldn't? She had access to a decent income, while he didn't have the money to buy cobalt blue paint? The Carters, truly, were a strange family.

34
AD 79

After I had confided in Melas about my work — despite having given him very few details — I plunged into an absolute crisis of confidence. First, I found myself oddly distracted by thoughts of him. Much as I disliked him, he was more interesting than I had first assumed. He knew poetry as well as art, and had proved capable of valuable insights. He might look Greek, but I no longer found him quite so unattractive as I once did. I tried to force myself to focus on my poetry, not the painter, but my words sounded clunky and banal to me, and, days later, I could not free myself from the cruel bondage of self-criticism. I was paralyzed, unable to think and unable to write.

When I next met with Silvanus, I had no new lines for him.

"The Muses have abandoned me," I said, burying my head in my arms on the table between us. The mistake of this action was immediately apparent; I was sticking to the filthy wooden surface. "Work is impossible."

"Then you must sacrifice to them, Calliope in particular. I can get you an ox —"

"You don't understand how hopeless it all is." I was well and truly wallowing now. "It's not so simple as a sacrifice, especially if *you* are the one buying the ox. You're more likely to win their inspiration than I."

"There's no need for sacrilege," Silvanus said. "All poets feel like this on occasion. It's inevitable."

"How would you know?" I lifted my head and looked at him. His noble brow was creased, his eyes dull. I had never seen him so worried.

"Are not such things obvious?" he asked. "There's always struggle in creation. I've dabbled enough myself to know as much. And you, so favored by the Muses cannot be ignorant of it."

"I tell you, they've abandoned me."

"Well get them back." His voice startled me with its sharpness, but then immediately turned softer and enticing. "We will start with a sacrifice, tomorrow. I'll arrange the details. And then you must work, uninterrupted until you have your stride back. Perhaps you should go to the country. My family's villa in Baiae —"

"I can't go to your family's villa. What would people say?"

He waved his hand as if shooing away an irritating fly. "Of course. A silly suggestion. You must see, Kassandra, how seriously I take your work and your talent. I will find a suitable popa to carry out the sacrifice and speak to the aedituus in charge of the Temple of Apollo. He will know what we should do."

And that was how I found myself, the next day, in the temple, waiting to hear if the priest, after inspecting the entrails of a pig — Silvanus did not have time to find an ox he considered acceptable — would tell us that the signs were favorable. At last, he did just that. And now, Silvanus insisted, the Muses were back at my side, with Apollo taking an interest as well.

"We'll meet again tomorrow. I will expect at least three hundred new lines."

35
1902

The day of Ivy's Roman banquet was now upon us. I confess to having half forgot about it, consumed by our investigation. Benjamin arrived scandalously early that morning, ready to assist my friend in turning the villa into an ancient paradise. He said very little to me when I found them in a charming little room that opened directly onto the courtyard garden. Within this modern version of a triclinium stood the three wide couches we'd found in Naples, arranged to form a U-shape, with a table in the center. Benjamin, following the advice he'd earlier rejected, had painted them to look inlaid and covered them with plump cushions and bolsters upholstered in varying shades of purple silk.

"Imperial purple," I said. "The Republic is well and truly dead."

"The Republic was long gone by the time Vesuvius erupted," Ivy said, "and I mean us to dine in the manner of the patricians in the last days of Pompeii."

"Perhaps I should have suggested a different color," Benjamin began.

I interrupted him. "Not at all," I said. Clearly, our searching his rooms had left him ill at ease. He was back to bouncing on his heels and his eyes, bloodshot, showed signs of strain.

A maid came to fetch Ivy, telling her that the cook had run into some sort of problem and wished to consult her, leaving me alone with the young American. He sidled over to me.

"Lady Emily, I hope to take this opportunity to speak to you privately," he said. "I know you don't entirely trust me — that much became clear yesterday — and I cannot claim your suspicions are entirely without merit, but I must assure you that they are not —" He stopped.

I waited for him to say more, but nothing came. "Yes, Benjamin? What is it you wish to tell me?"

A ragged sigh escaped from his lips as he looked around nervously. "I ought not speak of it now. Tonight, after the banquet, would be preferable. Will you come to me then? We could meet below the terrace at midnight."

"You can tell me now. No one will disturb us."

As if he had been born with the sole purpose of proving me a liar, Jeremy burst into the courtyard, his voice booming. "Look at this toga! Is it not the most spectacular thing you've ever seen?" Yards of heavy white fabric with wide purple borders were half-wrapped around him, the rest of it dragging in his wake. "All I need now is a laurel crown."

Colin, six paces behind, called out greetings. I ignored them both. "Let's slip away for a moment. I can fend them off."

"No, no, Lady Emily. This is not the right time," Benjamin said. "This evening, under the cover of night. That will be preferable in every regard."

"Tonight, then, at the first possible opportunity."

He swallowed hard and nodded. "I am more grateful than you can know. This burden —"

"You, Carter, you're an artist. Can you make me a crown?" Jeremy was upon us now, tripping on his toga, Colin laughing at his antics. I ordered my friend to stand still, crossed to him, unwound the cloth, brushed it off, and folded it over my arm.

"I'm certain I can come up with something," Benjamin said. His cheeks were bright crimson. "There's a bay tree not far from the house. Why don't we see what state its leaves are in and take it from there."

"Capital, my boy, capital. Let's be off at once," Jeremy said.

"You look perturbed," Colin said after they had left. "What happened?"

"Benjamin was about to confide in me. He admits to . . . well, I don't know precisely what, yet — Jeremy is a master of the art of interruption — but he made it clear that we are correct to be suspicious of him. Benjamin, that is, not Jeremy."

"I have many, many suspicions about Bainbridge, my dear, but don't like to discuss them in polite company." He slipped his arm around my waist and pulled me close. "Would it help if I intervened? I could take our friend to find his ridiculous crown so that you and Carter might speak now?"

"He's awfully skittish," I said. "I told him I'll seek him out this evening. There are too many people bustling around here at the moment. He lost his nerve."

"Let's hope he can regain it."

By the time the sun was slipping below the horizon, its fiery fingers splashing the bay with shades of vermillion and bronze, and the sky had turned inky, Ivy's transformation of the villa was complete. Oil lamps in the ancient style glittered from every corner and candles floated in the courtyard's central pool. The scent of jasmine and roses filled the air and strains of harp music greeted our hostess's guests. (Ivy had lamented being unable to find someone who could play the lyre.)

I'd had my hair styled in appropriate fashion, parted in the center and waved around my face, with ringlets behind my ears, and donned a simple, elegant tunic fashioned from fine silk of the palest shade of blue, with a single, darker band around the bottom hem. Unlike nearly every gown I'd worn from the moment I was out of short skirts, it required neither a corset nor any other stiff, binding, or heavy undergarment.

Ivy was resplendent in fringed silk the color of the setting sun. "For once we ladies get the better end of things and the gentlemen are left to suffer," she said, adjusting the heavy gold bracelets she wore on her wrists. "The toga is an absolute nightmare. Difficult to manage and dreadful for the posture."

"Yet not nearly so bad as the corsets we suffer daily," I said, relishing the novelty of being able to draw a full breath while wearing evening dress. "I don't know how I shall go back to my usual clothes."

Ivy had provided crisp linen tunics and soft leather sandals for the servants, who were making sure none of her guests were without honeyed wine. Mr. Stirling chose to dress as a Greek philosopher and sported a perfectly dreadful false beard, explaining that was the fashion, even in Rome, for scholars. Mr. Taylor was fully kitted out as a general, complete with plumed helmet, leather skirt, and reddish-purple cloak. I could not help but think how much better Colin would have looked in the ensemble, with his well-developed muscles and strong legs, but such digressions have no place in this narrative.

Instead of military garb — which he insisted no one would have worn to dinner — my husband was wearing a synthesis, the Roman equivalent of evening dress for men. To my eyes, it looked no different from an ordinary belted tunic.

I had expected Kat would take the occasion to make full use of her talent for disguise, but she had chosen a simple dark green tunic with only a pair of pearl earrings as an accessory. She looked very young, shockingly so.

Callie and her brother arrived late, Benjamin rather disheveled in a nondescript rumpled tunic, keeping a careful distance from me. His sister, instead of dressing as a Roman, had hired a costume maker to create for her a delicious concoction meant to evoke Cleopatra, but not the Cleopatra ignorant persons imagine today, with a heavy Egyptian wig and eyes rimmed with kohl. Instead, she was draped in white silk, her gown cut in the style of a Greek queen — which, as a descendant of Alexander the Great's general and friend Ptolemy, was exactly what Cleopatra had been. A thin golden diadem circled her head.

"If I am Cleopatra," she said, gliding over to Mr. Taylor, "you must surely be Caesar."

"Better him than Antony," Mr. Taylor replied.

"I wouldn't be so quick to say that." Callie poked his arm. "Personally, I prefer Antony, which I mean as a compliment to him rather than an insult to Caesar. But tonight is not a time for argument."

"Then I won't beg you to call me Caesar," Jeremy said. With the assistance of his valet, he had managed to get his toga properly folded and draped and had a neat wreath fashioned from bay leaves and floral wire on his head. Ivy gave Mr. Stirling her arm and ushered us into her makeshift triclinium.

"Tell me the number of guests, and at what price you wish to dine. / Don't add another word: dinner is ready for you," he said. "The poet Martial."

Servants helped us remove our sandals before guiding all of us save Mr. Stirling onto the elegant couches — he alone had no trouble situating himself. The rest of us found reclining to dine not so easy as it looks, and quite a bit of chaos ensued as we tried to make ourselves comfortable. Jeremy, hopelessly tangled in his toga, jumped up, flung it off, and then dropped back onto his couch.

"I understand, now, why they didn't wear these bloody — blooming — things — forgive me, Ivy — to dinner parties," he said, straightening his laurel wreath. "I should've listened to you when you tried to tell me that, Hargreaves. The tunic beneath is far preferable, even if it doesn't look so noble."

"Your aristocratic nature, Bainbridge, shines through regardless of what you wear," Mr. Taylor said. "Clothing does not make the man."

"Cheers," Jeremy said, raising his beaker of wine in response and then glancing toward Callie. "I do hope you can ignore any references to things aristocratic that are directed at me."

"What would be the point?" Callie asked. "If nature, not clothing, makes the man?"

"You are bent on tormenting me," he said, but she smiled at him, her hazel eyes flashing.

Having a quiet word with Benjamin during dinner would have been impossible. Mr. Stirling lay on our couch between me and the young man, regaling us with pertinent epigrams from Martial and quotes from Ovid. He was a delightful dinner partner. I had never before seen him quite so animated, but I could not decide whether to credit the wine or the fact that he so enjoyed poetry.

The servants brought out tray after tray of scrumptious dishes: herbed cheese, dried apricots in honey, mussels seasoned with wine and cumin, fried anchovies, melon dressed in a vinaigrette, and grilled lobster. The flavors were unusual — particularly the melon — but delicious all the same. Exotic and delightful.

For our final course, Ivy gave us a pudding made from pears poached in white wine, pureed and baked with honey, spices, eggs, and milk. There was also a silver bowl filled with nuts and a matching tray heaped with fruit: dates and figs, pomegranates, and sweet oranges.

All in all, I am confident I could have adapted nicely to ancient life, with its comfortable clothing and surprisingly good food. I had quite taken to honeyed wine, as had Ivy. In the end, we all managed nicely on the couches; the wine helped. Sated, we climbed down from them, slipped our sandals back on, and retreated to the courtyard, where I motioned to Benjamin to follow me to the terrace, walking all the way to the far end, so that our conversation could not be overheard.

He closed his eyes, his breath shallow. "I can delay no longer," he said, "but I hardly know where to start."

I directed him to sit on one of the comfortable chairs placed to take advantage of the view of the bay. It was dark, but the moon was nearly full, bathing us in its silvery light. "I find going back to the beginning often simplifies things."

"Yes, I suppose you're right," he said. "It is so very difficult. There are things that once said, cannot be unheard. Pandora could not put all those evils back in her box, could she?"

"Some stories, no matter how painful, must be told, Benjamin."

"Even when uttering them will destroy lives?" He had a horrible glint in his eyes, and for an instant I wondered if I should be afraid of him.

"There can be more evil in keeping secrets than telling them."

He started. "Oh, not evil, this isn't quite so bad. Shocking, yes. Appalling, even. And sure to cause more harm than good, I'm afraid. Unless . . ."

"Unless what?" I asked.

"Well, things change when there's been a murder, don't they? What once could have gone unsaid —"

I had begun to worry that he would never get it out, whatever it was. "Tell me now, Benjamin. No matter how bad it is, I promise I will do everything in my power to minimize the aftermath." Granted, if he had killed Mr. Walker, there wasn't much I could do for him, but I could lend support to Callie.

He did not reply for some time, and as I have found considerable persuasive power in silence, I did not prod him further. Instead, I thought about Callie, wondering if Mr. Taylor could be persuaded to let her keep her position, even if her brother was a vicious killer. I was weighing the possibilities when at last Benjamin spoke.

"Callie is not my sister."

tleast when at last Benjamin spoke.

"Allie is not my sister.

36
AD 79

Praise be to Apollo and all the Muses, Calliope in particular!

Silvanus's sacrifice worked. No sooner had I returned from the temple than inspiration struck. All the problems that had tormented me vanished, leaving my mind once again clear and agile. I had bought three honey cakes on my way home and left them as offerings at our lararium, raising my hands and giving thanks to the household gods. And then, I remembered having told Lepida of my devotion to Isis. I promised myself I would go to her temple tomorrow. No pig this time, but I had some very fine olive oil I was certain the goddess would appreciate.

I retreated to my room, pausing only to give my father a kiss hello, closed myself in, and started to write. After so many days had passed without a single coherent phrase entering my head, I now could not move my stylus across the tablet fast enough.

Ideas swarmed like the Furies.

I brought three scrolls the next time I saw Silvanus and noticed that the wine at the bar no longer tasted so sour to me, which probably meant I'd been spending too much time there. I didn't linger, wanting to get back home to write more. As I rose to leave, he grabbed me, tight around the wrist.

"I have enough now that I can start to introduce your work to my friends."

37
1902

"Callie is not my sister." Benjamin repeated the words.

Shock had prevented me from replying at once, but now, I shook my head (as if the act might render me capable of sensible speech) and stared at him, my mouth hanging open. "Not your sister?"

"No."

I could hardly gather my thoughts. "Yet you are living together, sharing —"

"Yes, I realize how bad it looks."

This news would come as a dreadful blow to Jeremy. He might not care much for society's opinion of him, but continuing to believe oneself in love with a lady who is living with another man would be hard to do, no matter how modern one's morals may be. "Why haven't you married her?"

He laughed, and the sound, almost maniacal, bounced across the water of the bay in front of us. "Callie? Marry? That would never happen. But you misunderstand the situation. We're not lovers — that is, not anymore. We were close, long ago, when she was studying at Radcliffe and I was living in Boston, but we've been friends, and only that, for more than two years."

"So how is it, then, that you are sharing rooms in Pompeii?" I asked.

"She wanted the job, didn't she? And she knew — or at least had good reason to believe — that Mr. Taylor would not hire an unaccompanied lady. She'd been turned down for seven positions, all because of her gender. When I met Mr. Taylor in New York, and he offered me a job, she begged me to pretend to be her brother and ask him to take her on as well. It was not difficult for her to convince me — nor was it difficult to convince Mr. Taylor. One conversation with Callie and he could see how supremely qualified she is. As for me, I was in love with her; there was nothing I wouldn't do for her."

"If your feelings are of such a tender nature, you might, perhaps, have given better consideration to her reputation."

"I deserve your censure," Benjamin said. "But, truly, neither of us believed we were risking anything. My heart, perhaps, but I had no illusions in that department. Callie never loved me and never would. I accepted that and was grateful to at least have her friendship. I don't have such a high opinion of myself that I believe I could change her feelings on the matter. At any rate, we knew we would not be recognized here, and as soon as Mr. Taylor comes to consider her an essential member of his staff, I will be able to leave to pursue my own work. I only agreed to a single season of this charade."

"This explains the disparity in your educations and your possessions," I said. "I couldn't help but notice when I searched your rooms."

"Yes, I'd begun to worry that you were harboring deep suspicions of our relationship, and then I realized that my own behavior was only making matters worse. I was tense and uneasy, and probably couldn't have looked guiltier if I tried. You are kind, Lady Emily, and have an understanding of life that goes beyond most ladies of your station. I knew I'd be safe making my confession to you. Much as I hate to betray Callie, it would be worse if your investigations had uncovered the situation in a more public way."

"You cannot expect me to keep your secret," I said. "You and your — er, friend — have both lied to your employer, taking advantage of his good nature, not to mention that you have practiced a grievous betrayal on all your friends."

He lowered his head. "I know. Your accusations are all true; I can offer no defense. I have proven myself unworthy of your friendship, but all the same, you cannot — cannot — tell anyone. Callie will lose her position and it will all have been for naught."

"Mr. Taylor isn't wholly unreasonable. There is a possibility — slim, I admit — that he will overlook her scandalous behavior and allow her to remain in her job. However, that decision must be his to make."

Benjamin rose from his chair, fell to his knees in front of me, and clutched my hands in his. "Please, please give me a little time. Let me tell Callie you know our secret and, together, we can come up with a way to make the situation more palatable to Mr. Taylor."

I pried my hands from his. "Stand up," I said. "You are debasing yourself, Mr. Carter. I shall give the circumstances careful consideration and speak to Mr. Taylor myself. It would be best if you and Miss Carter — or whatever her true name is — left me to handle the matter. I see no reason, however, that we have to do this at once. I would like a few days" — I was being deliberately vague — "to consider how to proceed."

"You are kindness itself, Lady Emily," he said. "I will never be able to adequately thank you."

"Does anyone else know of your deception?"

"No one, I swear. We wanted to keep it quiet."

"You'd best return to the party," I said. "I want some time to think and if we're here much longer, your absence will be noted."

I watched him all but dance away, back toward the others in the courtyard, and was glad to be rid of him. What an outrageous story! On balance, I believed much of what he said, despite the fact that he was a proven liar, yet I doubted he had told me everything. There was too much glee in his relief, as if he knew he had got away with something more than hiding Callie's true identity.

He and Callie had encountered Mr. Walker as they crossed the Atlantic. Had the journalist uncovered the truth about them, and, learning of their plans to work in Pompeii, decided to come to the site and expose them to Mr. Taylor? Benjamin had admitted to a passionate and unrequited love for the girl. Had he killed the man who stood in the way of his would-be sweetheart's dreams and aspirations? Did he think that eliminating Mr. Walker would endear him to Callie, making her understand how much he loved her?

Considering the boy's devotion to her and his utter lack of concern for protecting her reputation, he wouldn't have left her unaware of his dark deed. He would be compelled to let her know he was her savior. Would Callie stand by in silence, fully aware of the identity of a vile murderer? Surely no one could value a job — any job — above a man's life?

I heard Ivy's soft footsteps. "Are you quite all right, Emily?" she asked.

I rose and gave her hand a reassuring squeeze. "I've had the strangest conversation and it's placed me in a most delicate situation. I can't explain the details right now, but I'm in dire need of your help."

"Of course," Ivy said. "Anything you require."

"Can you, somehow, manage to arrange things so Callie stays here, at the villa, tonight? She mustn't think there's anything behind it — and Benjamin must believe it was her idea. I cannot express how critical this is." I didn't want the two of them to have the possibility of consulting each other before I had decided what to do.

"I am the wife of a politician, Emily. This is the sort of thing at which I excel." She looked deliciously self-satisfied. "Neither of them will have the slightest idea they've been manipulated."

The rest of the evening passed in a blur. As promised, Ivy handled the situation with flawless ease. Expressing concern that Callie had, perhaps, partaken of too much wine, she took her inside and ordered a tisane for her. By then, it had grown rather late, and the guests had started to take their leave. Ivy crossed to Benjamin, brought him to Callie, and softly explained that she was worried about his sister. He wouldn't mind waiting to depart, would he? So that she could be certain the girl was all right? How early was he due at the dig?

I watched her with admiration. It took only a few sentences after asking about the time Mr. Taylor expected him the next morning for Callie to ask Ivy if it would be too much trouble for her to stay at the villa, so that her brother would have at least the chance of a decent night's sleep. To this day, I do not understand how Ivy convinced the archaeologist that she'd had too much wine.

Once Benjamin had gone, Ivy spirited

Callie away to an empty bedroom. Jeremy, his face full of concern, tried to follow, but Ivy rebuffed him.

"She'll be quite fine in the morning, I promise," Ivy said. "But for now, she needs her privacy."

His laurel wreath had slipped and was precariously perched on his head. "Did she really drink all that much? It didn't appear so."

"You're more perceptive than I would have guessed," I said, noticing from the incredulous expression in Kat's eyes that she was no more easily deceived than Jeremy. "Perhaps Ivy could sense that she preferred to stay over tonight instead of going back to the hotel."

"You ladies are extremely strange. Incomprehensible, really. I'm off to bed."

Colin, who had watched the scene from a chair in the corner of the room, walked over to me, his arms across his chest. "It would appear there is a great deal you need to share with me."

The night had grown chilly, so I picked up Jeremy's discarded toga and pulled it around me like a cloak before following my husband outside, down the stairs at the end of the terrace, and onto the path that skirted the rocky cliff upon which the house was

351

situated. We sat on a convenient boulder and I detailed for him my conversation with Benjamin.

"You were right to let him think you planned to take no immediate action," he said, when I had finished. "If he's guilty of more than lying, he won't feel the need to act in haste. The situation to which he confessed does provide him with a potential motive for Walker's murder — and Jackson's, too, if he had discovered the truth about the Carters — but it's still a stretch. We can't explain why Walker boarded the ship in the first place — he hated traveling, did it infrequently, and wouldn't have gone back to Europe without a most compelling reason."

"If Felix Morgan is Benjamin's father and Mr. Walker saw him in New York and noticed a resemblance, he could have deliberately followed the boy to Pompeii."

"It's not inconceivable, but we have no evidence that he encountered the Carters before the crossing. It could have been a coincidence that they were all on the same ship. Once there, though, he might have somehow learned about their subterfuge. Would that have troubled him enough to induce him to come all the way to Pompeii?"

352

"If Pompeii was his intended destination all along — and we have no reason to believe otherwise — Benjamin might have misunderstood the man's motives and assumed he was here to expose him and Callie."

"If Carter killed Walker, he knows admitting the lie about Callie will be a distraction, and, possibly, give him time to flee. I'll keep a close eye on him. In the meantime, you should tell Taylor the truth about his devious employees. Just because you said you would wait, doesn't mean you must." He blew out a long breath. "For the first time in a very long while, I feel like we might be getting somewhere. However, it's the middle of the night, which means there's nothing more we can do at the moment. With the moonlight shining on your hair and the way those folds of cloth are draping across your shoulders, you are the very image of Aphrodite."

"Not Venus, even in a Roman province?"

"I know you prefer the Greeks, my dear. Would you object to returning to our rooms?"

Naturally, I did not.

38
AD 79

The hours moved at six times their usual pace. The summer had been uncommonly hot, something I noticed more in our snug city house than I would have at Plautus's sprawling villa, cooled by gentle breezes from the sea. I was dressing to go to dinner at Lepida's, trying to decide which tunic would look the least shabby next to her fine silks, when my friend appeared, a veil covering her head. Our doorman let her in and Telekles — always fond of Lepida; too fond, I'd say, but given his youth there was no danger in his infatuation — brought her to my room, although this was wholly unnecessary, as she could have walked the short distance herself, particularly as my door was in plain sight from the atrium.

"Kassandra, I had to come myself, because what I have to say is wholly unexpected and more than a little upsetting."

"My dear friend, your hands are shaking."

I made her sit on my bed. "What's wrong?"

"I'm afraid I must rescind your invitation to dinner tonight. I'm mortified."

"Parties get cancelled," I said. "There's no need to feel bad."

"That's not what happened." She swallowed hard and stared at the geometric black and white mosaic on the floor. "When Silvanus arrived home, not an hour ago, he came to me and said I must send word to inform you that you would need to make other arrangements to dine tonight."

"No doubt he's invited guests who wouldn't be impressed by his wife's friendship with an insignificant freedwoman. Don't trouble yourself; I understand."

"It's more than that, Kassandra. He told me I was never to see you again, that you were no longer welcome in our house, and when I pressed him for an explanation, he refused to give one."

It was as if someone had struck me. "Have I done something to offend him?"

"I can't imagine how you would and am sorrier than I can say. If you're not allowed to come to me, rest assured that I will come to you, no matter what lies I have to tell, and I'll dine more happily here with you and your father and that abominable Greek painter than I ever will again in my own home."

My heart was pounding. Had the scrolls left him dissatisfied? Was I in disgrace, having disappointed him? I could say none of this to Lepida, and I started to grow angry at having let myself be persuaded to lie to her. Still, I had given my word, and telling her now would only catalyze Silvanus to turn all the more against me.

The ground began to shake. Pompeii had frequent earthquakes — the most devastating in recent memory had marked the very day of my birth — but, other than that one, they rarely caused severe damage. Enough to keep Melas busy repainting cracked walls, but not enough to cause anyone to take particular notice. We were used to them. Reacting without thinking, as we all did during earthquakes, we started for the doorway, seeking shelter in the sturdiest space we could find, but even before we could cross the room, the tremor had stopped.

Relief relaxed Lepida's face, and she embraced me. "This earthquake shows the gods do not condone my husband's decision. We will have their full support in subverting him. I feel much better now."

I wanted to reassure her. "You shall be

late to your own party if you don't head home. Don't let any of this trouble you, my friend. I'm sure it will all blow over before long."

She kissed me and took her leave. As I watched her slide into her litter, I caught something in her expression — a mixture of confusion and sadness — that made a sob stick in my throat.

But beyond that, lay something else. Something more terrifying than whatever disappointment Silvanus could cause. The earthquake had not struck when Lepida told me I was banned from her house; it started after her promise to keep our friendship, regardless of the lies she would have to tell in order to see me.

I was born during an earthquake. Some people insisted this was a good omen, that it meant I was a survivor, that I could not be defeated. But others say it was a portent of doom, that my birth was cursed. Now, for the first time in my life, I could give credence only to the latter.

39
1902

Colin set off early the next morning, Kat in tow, en route to Benjamin's rooms at the Albergo del Sole. Somehow she'd persuaded her father to start teaching her how to discreetely follow someone. He must have thought the American's walk to the dig an innocuous enough place to start. Ivy, Callie, and I sat on the terrace, enjoying the sunshine, until Jeremy emerged from his room, dressed in a crisp linen suit.

"Callie, my dear girl, might I have a word?" he asked. I cringed, wishing there was some way to keep him from being alone with her until I could share with him the truth about her relationship with Benjamin.

"Only if you accompany me to the excavation," she replied, rising from her chair. We had sent a servant to fetch her clothes so she would not have to return to the hotel. "I'm late as it is." I wanted to keep her away from Benjamin, but Colin, who would reach the dig before her, could do just that.

As soon as they were gone, I told Ivy everything. She was aghast. "I never, ever would have suspected such a thing," she said. "Whatever can they be thinking? The deceit, the utter disregard for propriety! Only imagine what sort of heartache a girl capable of such chicanery could heap upon Jeremy."

"I agree it's shocking, but, after contemplating the matter, I can't judge her so harshly as I did at first."

"Her behavior is unacceptable —"

"It is grievously wrong, of that there is no question," I said. "Yet, I understand why she did it. Is it fair that she be denied employment for which she is amply qualified simply because of her sex?"

"Does she need the income or does she do the job only to satisfy her own whims?" Ivy asked. "If it's the latter, which I very much suspect, she is keeping some more worthy individual from earning honest — and necessary — pay. And that aside, she was living with Mr. Carter!"

"We must not place the blame solely on her. Benjamin is as guilty as she, yet his reputation will not suffer like hers as a result. Society won't care about him in the long run. Oh, he may feel the lash of harsh tongues for a few months after their ruse is exposed, but in the end, it's only Callie's name that will be remembered."

This did not placate my friend. "Then perhaps she is fortunate that no one cognizant of the situation knows her true name."

"Benjamin swears there is nothing but friendship between them, although he did admit to an attachment in the past. He's obviously in love with her, but I've seen no indication that his feelings are returned."

"Well, of course you haven't, Emily," Ivy said. "She's been pretending to be his sister. Anyone capable of pulling off such an act would be far too clever to reveal any of her true feelings."

"He's in no doubt of her indifference to him."

"You believe him?"

"Despite his propensity for deception, on that count, I do."

"*O, what a tangled web we weave, when first we practice to deceive.*" Ivy frowned. "How does exposing these two liars impact your suspicions regarding Mr. Walker's murder?"

"A question, Ivy, I wish I could readily answer. Now, though, I must tell Mr. Taylor the truth about his employees."

"The poor man! He'll be mortified at having been so cruelly tricked."

"More likely, he'll be furious to lose such a skilled archaeologist," I said. "At least he ought to be."

I sent a message to Mr. Taylor, asking him to meet me in the main excavations of the city. "A crowded public place often offers more privacy than a quiet room where one can be overheard," I explained, when he came to me outside the Stabian Baths. The archeological park was more crowded than usual, owing partly to the weather (sunny and warm) and partly to the fact that we were approaching the high tourist season. Someone called Hazel (I am aware of her name because her husband employed it while shouting at her to be quiet) was abusing her beleaguered spouse for having forced her to visit such an uncivilized place. Apparently she had twisted her ankle, but this could hardly be his fault. She was wearing the most ridiculous shoes, with narrow pointed toes, thin soles, and heels inappropriate for navigating ancient cobbles. She could not have been badly injured as she was still walking unassisted, holding her skirts up so that she might step with ridiculous deliberateness.

"Travel does bring out the worst in many

of our fellow humans, doesn't it?" Mr. Taylor asked.

"Too right," I said. Ignoring a twinge of
nerves, I twirled the handle of the parasol
in my hand. (The sun had grown hot
enough that even I wanted a little relief.) "I
cannot in good conscience delay any longer
revealing to you the reason I asked for a
private chat. I've learned something that I
must share with you, difficult though it may
be to hear."

"Now you've alarmed me, Lady Emily."
His face was too brown from years spent in
the sun to blush, but there was no mistak-
ing the concern in his eyes. "Shall we find
somewhere else? It might be an idea to get
out of the sun." We ducked into the baths,
crossed through the palaestra, and took
advantage of its shaded portico.

"There's no easy way to say this. It has
come to my attention that the Carters are
not, in fact, brother and sister." I explained
to him how and why the subterfuge came
about. He listened without interrupting, his
face revealing no hint of emotion.

When I finished speaking, he shook his
head, slowly, back and forth and took three
steps away from me. "Well, now, this is
unexpected. I'm at a loss for words, and
that's something that doesn't often happen.

I like both of them, and they've done good work for me. Thought they were good eggs, but to know that they so callously lied . . ."

I didn't press him to continue, wanting him to have adequate space and time to take in this information and give it due consideration. He turned away from me, walked to the end of the colonnade and back three times, and then, returning to stand in front of me, looked me square in the eyes.

"Did you suspect anything?" he asked.

"No," I said. "Benjamin confessed to me because he erroneously believed I was onto them."

"Did anyone else know their secret?"

"No. If he hadn't told me, I'm confident they would have got away with the scheme. They gave no one any reason to think they were not siblings."

"I half wish they had got away with it," he said. "I'm no monster, Lady Emily, but I'm as vain as the next man, not wanting to be made a fool of. But if no one else picked up on their trick, I'm no stupider than the rest, am I? Which means it would be tough for me to claim I've been embarrassed or humiliated."

"No one could consider this a humiliation," I said.

"I didn't grow up wealthy, you know. My

363

parents were simple folks, content with their lives, but I always wanted more. I was raised in Ohio, in a perfectly ordinary small town, but no matter what I tried, I couldn't make my fortune in America — I went from one failed venture to another — so I came abroad, where I talked my way into a position working for a bank in Vienna. Now, I'm not ashamed to say that when I first met Augustus Baeder, the man who changed my life, he had no reason to hire me, but he was willing to give me a chance, because he saw something in me that he recognized. Grit, probably. That position led me to where I am now, rich enough to do anything I want. Callie Carter — or whatever her name is — came better prepared than I was at that interview with Herr Baeder. She's educated and impeccably trained, and her work is as good — better, truthfully — than most."

"She's capable, efficient, and determined," I said. "And although I cannot condone such blatant lying, I do understand what motivated her. She had already been rejected seven times for positions on other archaeological teams, the sole reason given in each case was the fact that she is an unmarried woman without a chaperone. Hence, the need for a brother."

"She believed I'd be no different than the others who wouldn't take her on." Mr. Taylor tugged at his hat, removed it from his head, and stared at it while he turned it in his hands. "I'd be lying if I said I would've hired her. I'm a creature of my times. Perhaps that should change. She does outstanding work. They were wrong to lie, but it would also be wrong to ignore their respective talents and let one mistake destroy their lives." He plopped the hat back on his head. "That's the only fair way forward and it's what I'm going to do."

"I must say, Mr. Taylor, it's more than they deserve."

"Sometimes, we all need more than we deserve." His entire mood lightened as he offered me his arm and we strolled back onto Pompeii's main street. "Given this conversation, I might as well confide in you that I have a habit of collecting strays. I can't resist it. Stirling, for example, what a mess he was when I found him! He'd got into some trouble over unpaid debts he'd left behind in Cambridge. Our Cambridge, not yours. He studied at Harvard. Had a devil of a time finding a position. Scandals can destroy a reputation, and the world of archaeology is small. He spent years working on small excavations of burial mounds in the United States, but he always wanted to be at Pompeii. He kept up with the current research here — read all the excavation reports and, before he'd so much as set foot in the city, knew every inch of the site better than most people who've worked here for years. A man obsessed, if you will."

"I can well understand being drawn to this place," I said.

"It's unlike anything else. Magical and cursed all at once." He sighed. "I'm grateful to you for telling me the truth. Now, if you'll forgive me for abandoning you, I'm afraid I must return to my excavations and have a conversation with my disingenuous staff members."

40
AD 79

I met Silvanus two days after the earthquake. I had gone to the bar early, wanting
to be there before he arrived. Sitting down,
I waved over the same surly waiter who
always served us and directed him to bring
two beakers of the cheapest wine they had.

"Your friend, he prefers the best," the man
said.

"His preferences aren't my concern."

The waiter shrugged and came back with
the drinks. I had taken Silvanus's usual seat,
against the back wall of the pathetic garden,
with its beaten dirt floor and complete
absence of plants.

Silvanus raised his eyebrows when he saw
me there, but said nothing, only sat down
and took a swig of his wine, which he immediately spat onto the ground. "This is
worse than ever."

"I didn't see the point in having better," I

said. "I assume this is to be our last meeting?"

"You're angry. I understand that and expected as much. I didn't mean any insult by excluding you from the dinner party, but I was ready to recite from your poem, and I didn't think you should be there for that."

"No, gods forbid I would be present to see the reaction of your guests to my own work."

"We've discussed this before. If we are to make it possible for you to achieve the success you deserve, it's critical that no one have even the slightest clue as to your identity until we decide to reveal it. You might have given the whole game away if you'd been there."

"We have discussed this before, yes, but you are not merely keeping me from one dinner party," I said. "Lepida told me I'm not to enter your house again."

"When did you speak to her?" he asked.

"Irrelevant." My voice dripped with venom, but then I thought the better of what I was doing. My friend could get in a great deal of trouble if she went against her husband's wishes. "And I didn't say I spoke to her, did I? Maybe she sent me a message."

"You're correct that it's irrelevant," he

said. "I appreciate the friendship you share with my wife, but right now, I cannot have you coming to my house. By forbidding her to see you, painful though it may be in the short term, I don't have to ban you from individual parties again and again when I want to present your poems. Do you not think Lepida intelligent enough to notice if I never let her invite you to parties when there was poetry? How would I explain that to her? It could make things most awkward, and I have already told you she is likely to expose our secret — even if only out of love and pride for you. Once the truth is known to everyone, you will, of course, be welcome in my house. Everything will be better then."

I folded my hands in my lap. I understood the theory of what he was saying, but it did not feel right. "I don't care what you do, so long as you're kind to Lepida."

"I am always kind to my wife."

Before I could reply, another tremor struck. Small, like the last one, over almost before it started. What were the gods saying now?

41
1902

"And that was it?" Ivy asked, when I returned to the villa. "He wasn't angry?" She had dropped her embroidery onto the floor when I told her what Mr. Taylor said.

"The betrayal made him uncomfortable, certainly, but he exhibited more empathy for them than anything else."

"So, just like that, it's all over? And they emerge unscathed?"

"Not entirely unscathed. He's no doubt in the midst of a most unpleasant conversation with them both, which is no more than they deserve, but they will remain in his employ."

Ivy sighed. "I'm happy for them in that regard, but I can't rejoice in the knowledge that their deliberate lies brought them to such a pleasant end."

"I understand," I said. "Do remember, however, that it's not all over. There's still a murder to solve."

"And you think Benjamin will meet his

just deserts as a result of that?" Ivy asked. "I know you are still suspicious of him. Yes, he has a temper, and yes, he's moody. He's committed a terrible fraud. But can he really be a vicious killer?"

"That, my friend, is a question I cannot answer at present."

"Perhaps we should take a closer look at Mr. Taylor," she said. "He was too quick to forgive them. What does that tell us about him? And what are we going to do about poor Jeremy? I haven't seen him since he left with Callie this morning. Do you think she will have confessed her sins to him?"

"If she hasn't, I'll tell him. He won't take kindly to being made to look a fool."

"You're suggesting he's not so enlightened and ready to forgive as Mr. Taylor?"

"Not even close," I said. As much as I wanted to talk to Jeremy, I also wanted a word with Callie. I may have helped her, but that did not mean I was anything but angry with her. As much as I admired her drive and her persistence, she ought not have stooped to such underhanded measures in pursuit of her goals. Her deception would have no positive effect on the obstacles faced by the ladies who came after her. Once it became public knowledge — and I had no doubt that, eventually, it would —

her methods would provide ammunition for those who wanted to thwart the progress of women.

Colin and Kat returned more than an hour after the sun had set, exhausted and dusty. They'd been at the dig when Mr. Taylor had gathered all his employees around, told them everything, scolded the world at large for forcing young ladies of spirit into constructing such lies, and sent them back to work. Callie broke down into tears and all but flung herself at his feet in thanks. Benjamin took the news more stoically, asking to speak to his employer privately, but upon doing so, he, too made profuse apologies.

"It's turned out well for them both," Colin said as I was dressing for dinner. Ready before me — as gentlemen always are, their toilettes far less complicated than ladies' — he dropped onto a chair with elegant ease. "I'm intrigued by the story of Stirling's difficulties. It sounds like Taylor glossed over them to you. I don't see how a handful of unpaid debts at university would entirely destroy a man's career prospects. Surely not even the Americans can be that puritanical."

"No doubt there's more to it," I said. "Mr. Taylor admitted to collecting strays, so it might be worth interviewing his staff again. Mr. Stirling may not be the only one of them with a checkered past."

After my husband assisted me with the pale green sash on my dress — a delicious Worth concoction of cream silk and lace covered with chiné flowers that reminded me of a Monet painting — we went down to dinner. Well, not precisely down, as all the rooms in the villa were on a single level. We found Ivy, Kat, and Jeremy on the terrace, drinking champagne and engaging in a lively, lighthearted conversation. My temples started to throb.

"You're in awfully good spirits," I said, as Jeremy pressed a glass into my hand. "Might I speak privately to you, for a moment?" I hated to destroy his mood — and the evening — but I could not stand by and let him believe Callie's lies any longer. She'd had her chance to do the noble thing; I was disappointed she had not shown the moral courage for it.

"Naturally, Em, I'm always delighted to be pulled aside by you. Hargreaves becoming tedious, is he? Can't say I'm surprised. What else can you expect from a Cambridge man? You can always count on me for a bit of excitement."

"I can't think of anything more tedious —

not to mention more wildly inappropriate — than your idea of excitement," I said. He was grinning broadly. I took a deep breath and looked him square in the eyes. "I must tell you something quite serious, something that pains me on more levels than I can count. You know how fond I am of you and that I want nothing more than to see you happily settled, whatever that may mean. I am aware that your own feelings on the subject are somewhat complicated, and I have always done my best to respect that. Now, however —"

"Criminy, Em, what are you getting at? You're babbling and incoherent. What has you so tied up in knots?"

"It's just that —" I stopped. "This is extremely difficult for me, Jeremy. I have never, ever wanted any part in seeing you hurt. That whole dreadful business with Amity still haunts me, and now —" I stopped again, this time not because I was unsure of how to best proceed, but because he was laughing.

"It's all clear to me," he said, once he'd managed — rather inelegantly — to stop his guffaws. "There's no need for you to explain. You found out about Callie, didn't you?"

"*I* found out? Does this mean you know

the truth about her identity?"

"Of course I know," he said, an insufferably smug look on his face. "She told me the first time I tried to kiss her. She doesn't like dishonesty and considers herself a — what do Americans call it? They have some charmingly crass phrase. Oh, yes, I remember — a real straight shooter. Thought that if I was going to have the misfortune of falling in love with her, I should at least know the truth."

"So you have known, this entire time, that she was living with Benjamin even though he isn't her brother?"

"That's one way of putting it," he said, and shrugged. "Can't say that it made the slightest difference to me. No one in their right mind would worry she'd fall for a moody artist. Good bloke — I'm fond of him myself — but he's not the man for her. Even Carter knows as much."

"Does he know that you know?"

"Yes, Callie told him. They're absolutely candid with each other and both agree it is critical they be fully informed about the status of their little game."

"I'd hardly call it a little game," I said, feeling rather irritated and unable to identify the object of my ire. Was it Callie? Benjamin? Jeremy? All of them? Yes, it had to be all of them. But then, as I continued to consider the matter, I remembered that Benjamin had lied to me yet again — he had sworn that no one knew their secret but me. "What do you really think about Benjamin? How well do you know him?"

"He's harmless enough," Jeremy said and pulled a silver cigarette case from his jacket pocket. "You don't mind if I smoke, do you?"

"Do whatever you like. You will regardless of what I say."

"You're not angry at me, are you? Callie told me her secret in confidence, and a gentleman —"

"Callie is the least of my concerns at the moment," I said, not being entirely honest. "It is Benjamin who worries me more. He's been rebuffed by the girl he loves, publicly exposed as a liar, and is one of the few people in Pompeii capable of producing the painting on the marble thrown at Colin. We know what his temper's like. How will he react if he finds himself accused of murder?"

42
AD 79

The weeks became months, and still I wrote almost without stopping, like a woman possessed, inspired not by the Muses, but the Furies. I sent word to Silvanus that I would not be able to meet him until I had completed my work and assured him the end was as close as Odysseus came to being destroyed by Scylla and the terrible Charybdis. He replied that my words had not given him comfort. They were not meant to.

Late on a stormy autumn night, I scratched the final words on my tablet. My hero had escaped the wrath of countless enemies and, once again, gazed upon the seven hills of Rome. As rain cleansed Pompeii around me, I transferred my verse onto papyrus and then gathered my scrolls. I had made two copies of each book of the poem, one for Silvanus, and one for myself. Tomorrow, he would have the last installment, and our clandestine relationship would come to an end.

I no longer cared about him reciting my work to his friends. I no longer craved fame and glory. My words were enough; they had to be, for once a poem is complete, it is out of the grasp of its creator, and will do — and be — what it will.

And so, once again, I made my way through the worst neighborhood in the city, to the wretched little bar and its wretched little garden. I had come early, wanting to arrive before Silvanus. In this, I was successful.

I did not, however, arrive before Lepida, who was sitting at our regular table, on the bench usually occupied by her husband, a look of incandescent rage on her face, rage that would have been worthy of Achilles himself.

43
1902

I was of two minds after conversing with Jeremy. On the one hand, I was pleased that Callie (whose true surname, he told me, was Piper) had not lied to him about her identity once she became aware of his affection for her. She wasn't so devious and depraved as I had feared. But at the same time, could I rejoice at seeing one of my dearest friends so blind with love that he would attach himself to someone with a known capacity for deception? I could not entirely share Mr. Taylor's confidence that, given a second chance, she would never again turn to such tactics if faced with adversity.

Colin and I arranged to reinterview each of the members of Mr. Taylor's staff, hoping that one of his strays might reveal something that would enable us to bring Mr. Walker's and Mr. Jackson's murderer to justice. Most of them, however, proved to have mundane, if murky, pasts. One had been sent down from university and never finished his degree. Another had been caught having an affair with the wife of a friend. A third, who was entirely self-educated — a result of having grown up in abject poverty — had approached Mr. Taylor, begging to be allowed to learn the science of archaeology on his dig. It was still early in the season, but already he had proven himself capable of quick learning and an unrelenting desire to work. His was an entirely admirable character, working hard to, as the Americans say, pull himself up by his bootstraps.

"Taylor may consider them strays," Colin said, "but they're hardly a motley group. Their indiscretions are less nefarious than I've seen elsewhere."

We were waiting for Mr. Stirling, the last member of the staff to whom we would speak. From the moment I had met him, I'd been fond of him — he with his sensitive poet's soul and a gentleness one does not often find in the members of his sex, but, at the same time, there was something about him I didn't trust. Why did he refuse to have his picture taken? He sat across from us, his hands folded and resting on the table in front of him, and explained away the troubles from his Harvard days easily; they were ordinary enough, a student overspending his allowance.

"The piece I don't understand, Stirling, is how this stopped you from getting a job," Colin said. "There's no question that unpaid debts are dishonorable, but they're not uncommon, nor, unless they are enormous, do they categorically ruin a man."

"No, they don't," Mr. Stirling said. "More often than not, someone steps in and pays the bills. One's father or one's uncle or some other responsible — and, no doubt, disappointed — relative. I, unfortunately, had no such person in my life. My father and I were never close. As his only son, I expected to be his heir, but we argued frequently, and he never hid his disdain for me, even when I was a child. I was thin and weedy and he considered my appreciation of poetry effeminate. He expected me to take over the family business when he retired, but I had no interest in managing textile factories, no matter how profitable an endeavor it was. He supported me at Harvard, thinking eventually I would accept my fate and do as he wished."

"Obviously, you did not," I said.

"No, and I made a great show of telling him this immediately after receiving my degree. He was furious. That very night, he changed his will, completely cutting me out and, at the same time, he stopped my allowance. It was the latter that made it impossible for me to cover my debts. Two days later he was dead from a stroke."

"I'm very sorry," I said.

"Thank you, but I am not worthy of your condolences," he said. "Finding myself unable to settle my accounts, I made a terrible decision. I was out with a group of friends and one of them, the eldest son of a family of fabulous wealth — you would recognize the name — had taken rather too much to drink. Seeing the state he was in, I helped him back to his rooms and put him into bed, where he passed out at once. I removed his coat and his boots and then" — he closed his eyes, ashamed — "I noticed his watch had come out of his waistcoat pocket. It was an old thing, a family heirloom: gold, quite heavy, and attached to a thick chain and fob. I took it from him, knowing I could pawn it for an amount that would pay off my outstanding debts. And then, it was as if I was possessed by some awful spirit and no longer in control of my actions. I took the money from his purse and everything else of value that I could carry easily from his rooms."

"And everyone knew you were the thief," Colin said.

"Yes. I was the one who took him home. I never tried to deny it and am mortified I was capable of doing such a thing. Word spread, of course. Who would want to hire a man who would steal from one of his closest friends? No matter how desperate I was — and, believe me, I was in dire financial straits — I ought never have stooped to stealing from a friend."

"Did you confess all this to Mr. Taylor?" I asked.

"Not in as much detail as I would have liked," Mr. Stirling said. "I knew my reputation was ruined, and that the story was known in the archaeological community. As a result, I was aware I couldn't hide my awful past from prospective employers. I broached the subject with Taylor the first time we met to discuss the job. He had heard the gossip, but did not press me to explain myself. It was enough, he said, that I was willing to take responsibility for my actions."

"How did you take responsibility for your actions?" Colin asked. "Were you arrested? Tried for your crime?"

"No, no, that's not the way things are done for we people of the higher classes, is it?" He frowned. "My friend refused to press charges, not wanting the scandal to wind up in the papers. I returned to him everything I had taken and begged his forgiveness. Believe me, there is nothing I would not do to erase the dreadful incident altogether, but one can never escape one's past. My punishment is living with my crime. *The first and greatest punishment of the sinner is the conscience of sin.*"

"Seneca the Younger?" I asked. Mr. Stirling nodded.

When he had first sat down across from us, the archaeologist had placed a notebook on the table, the notebook in which he recorded the daily results of the dig. I asked him if I might look in it; he nodded. Page after page was filled with his neat handwriting. More interesting, in the current circumstances, were the sketches he had also included. They showed him to have considerable talent as an artist.

"These are lovely," I said. "What sort of pencils do you use?"

"Faber and nothing else. They're the best."

He returned to work and Colin leaned toward me and spoke in a low voice. "There's something about him that doesn't ring true. He's admitted to being a thief who succumbed to desperation, and his

384

notebook proves him a capable artist. Could he have painted the scene of Alexander? I want to search his digs. Will you remain here and make sure he doesn't leave?"

I kept Mr. Stirling distracted until Colin returned, all smiles, to collect me. "Stirling, old chap, I've not seen my wife look so radiant in ages. Is she basking in your attention or has she discovered a passion for archaeology?"

Mr. Stirling sputtered a reply. "I'd never do anything that might lead her to —"

Colin slapped him on the back. "I'm only teasing. A passion for classics, which Lady Emily has in abundance, naturally leads to a passion for archaeology."

The archaeologist sighed. "Forgive me, I'm a bit flustered. I'm not used to —"

"Nothing to forgive." Colin grinned at him and took me by the arm.

"What was that about?" I asked as he helped me into the carriage.

"Testing the waters, my dear. I wanted to see how agilely he'd react to an unexpected situation."

"What did you find in his rooms that made you want to test the waters?" I asked.

"Four notebooks in which he's collected research on Alexander the Great. Complete with detailed descriptions of each of the omens foretelling the Macedonian's death. Not what I expected of a man who claims to be obsessed with Pompeii and nothing else."

That evening, after dinner, a maid brought us a small parcel that had been left on the stoop. It contained a scroll of papyrus covered by a scene painted to look like a mosaic. The informed Reader will already have guessed its subject: the third, and final, portent of Alexander's death. A man, bound as a prisoner, was shown seated on a throne, dressed in royal robes, a Macedonian diadem on his head.

"Does this confirm that Mr. Stirling is our man?" I asked, after retiring to our room to dress for dinner. We hadn't told our friends about the scroll.

"It makes him a prime suspect, but we still can't connect him to Walker," Colin said. "And what would have been his motive for killing Jackson?"

"They could've argued about the money Mr. Stirling owed him. Or perhaps Mr. Jackson discovered that Stirling had killed Mr. Walker and threatened to expose him."

"We still can't tie Stirling to Walker."

"But we can connect Benjamin to Mr. Walker, even if only tenuously."

"I recall Taylor offering to give us a tour of Herculaneum on the Sunday of our choice. Let's see if it's possible to do the excursion tomorrow, and include Carter, Stirling, Callie, and all of us here. Our suspects might be at ease if they believe we're playing tourist and we might be able to encourage one of them to admit something significant."

I sent a note to Mr. Taylor, who replied without delay, delighted to organize the expedition. Colin and I rose early the next morning and took breakfast in our room rather than with the others on the terrace, hammering out the details of our strategy. We would approach Mr. Stirling first and then, if necessary, turn to Benjamin.

We made a large — and lively — party as we piled into carriages and set off. Kat insisted that Colin sit next to her, leaving Ivy and me across from them. I've no doubt that if she could have got me into a different vehicle altogether, she would've. As it was, she monopolized her father's conversation during the drive. This irritated me less than usual, as it gave me time to collect my thoughts, review our plans, and compose myself.

The *scavi* at Herculaneum are much smaller in scope than those in neighboring

Pompeii. Most of the ruins remained buried, not only by approximately eighty feet of solid, volcanic rock, but also by a modern city. The original excavations at the site were conducted on behalf of the Kings of Naples, and, as at Pompeii, were done with an eye toward enhancing the royal collections. Instead of systematically removing the layer of rock over the ancient structures, early excavators dug narrow tunnels into the buildings, enabling them to pop in, search for treasure, and pop back out. The rediscovery of the Roman city was made by Ambrogio Nocerino, while he was digging a well in 1709. He did not hit water, but instead found something of far greater value: the remains of Herculaneum's theater. Thrill — and terror — must have filled him as he descended into the shaft, probably with nothing more than a single candle, to find himself standing on an ancient floor, staring into the eyes of long-forgot bronze statues, while he breathed in air that had been sealed away for more than a thousand years.

Years of plunder followed that accidental discovery. The theater, whose marble decorations had been almost completely intact when Nocerino found it, was now completely stripped. In the 1750s, a Swiss mining engineer, Karl Weber, excavating for the king, happened upon an astonishing find: a villa, nearly a thousand feet long, containing, among other treasures, the contents of its owner's library: approximately eighteen hundred papyrus scrolls, the only complete ancient library known to modern man. The gasses that swept over Herculaneum during Vesuvius's eruption resulted in temperatures much hotter than those in Pompeii, instantly carbonizing and preserving the organic material there instead of consuming it by fire.

Imagine the excitement that must have passed through the soul of every scholar of classics upon learning that, at last, the world would have access to volumes of ancient writings previously believed lost. And then, if you can, envision their disappointment, not only because the King of Naples planned to keep most of the scrolls for himself, but also because every attempt to unroll them caused the papyrus to crumble. In 1753, Antonio Piaggio, a Vatican priest, developed a machine that enabled him to gently open the scrolls without damaging them too badly. The process was painfully slow, and the revealed text difficult to read, but it was better than nothing. To this day, scholars continue the struggle to find a more effective method for dealing with them. Most have been left untouched, in the hopes that someday a better way will be found. What else waits to be discovered? The lost plays of Aeschylus? Early copies of Homer's epics? Someday, I hope, we will know — and be able to read — the complete collection of this astonishing library.

As we approached the site through the Vicolo di Mare, Colin gave Kat and Ivy a cursory explanation of our plans. Kat, naturally, wanted to play a part, but her father refused.

"This is not the time for someone of so little experience to lend a hand," he said. She glowered. "Emily and I will pull Stirling aside first. You can help by keeping the others away from us when we're with him."

"I'd rather interrogate him," she said.

"No one is interrogating anyone," Colin said. "We're going to draw him out in casual conversation. It's a delicate procedure."

"Kat and I will distract everyone else," Ivy said, "and ensure it doesn't appear that you're speaking to Mr. Stirling for a specific purpose. If he's not the murderer, whoever is might be put on alert if he — or she — thinks you're conducting interviews."

"Quite right, Ivy," Colin said. "You've a much more devious mind than you let on."

Ivy blushed, pleased with the compliment.

We alighted from the carriages, and Mr. Taylor gave us each a candle, explaining that the excavations were far below the modern city. We followed him down to an ancient street and walked until we reached a two-story house whose spectacular garden still had all of its twenty columns standing. Callie let Jeremy take her arm, while Ivy positioned herself between Mr. Taylor and Benjamin. Kat, sulking a bit, followed behind.

"Stirling, can you explain the makeup of these neighborhoods?" Colin asked. "Obviously, a wealthy family lived in this house, but what about the buildings surrounding it? It appears that there was living space above the shops."

"Quite right," Mr. Stirling said. "As soon as the others are done, I can take us to one of the best-preserved examples, a caupona, which is something like our modern taverns, a place where one could get food, drink, and lodging."

"I don't think we'll be able to pull them away from the frescoes," I said. "Let's go ahead. They can follow when they're ready."

He led us to a remarkable structure. The front wall of the building was missing, leaving it open like a dollhouse, but what was inside more than made up for that. On the ground floor, large amphorae stood, still stacked against the wall, the wooden racks above them empty. In the neighboring room, a balcony, its wooden railing intact, would have served as a storage area. Higher up, the second story, red, black, and cream paint visible on its walls, contained the remains of a bronze bed.

"I adore getting these glimpses into ancient life," I said. "It reminds me how similar the Romans were to us. Tell me, do any other periods of history speak to you the way this does?"

"When I was in Illinois, excavating mounds, I was tantalized and frustrated at the same time," Mr. Stirling said. "We know so little about the daily life of the tribes who built them. I desperately wanted to learn more. But that was nothing more than flirtation, really. The Greco-Roman world is my first love."

"Was it always Pompeii?" Colin asked. "At school, I ran through any number of obsessions — Julius Caesar, Genghis Khan, Alexander the Great."

"All little boys are taken with Alexander," Mr. Stirling said, the words tumbling too quickly from his mouth. "Fascinating man. So much to admire. But for me, nothing compares to Pompeii."

"Stirling!" Mr. Taylor popped his head out of the house next door and called down the street. "We're heading for the theater. Join us?"

"I believe that was an order, not a suggestion," Mr. Stirling said. We returned to the others, hanging back, so that we might continue our conversation.

"Taylor's lucky to have you," Colin said. "You've an admirable intellect and both the patience and the eye for detail so critical to archaeologists."

"You're kind to say so, but I'm fortunate as well. Given my history, I'm relieved to have any position."

"We all make mistakes," I said. We reached a gloomy flight of steps, damp and chilly, and it felt more like we were descending into some icy version of Hades than into a theater. "I can't count the number of mortifying things I've done. Some situations offer no decent way out."

"True words, Lady Emily. None of us like to act dishonorably, but sometimes, there's no other option."

The Stygian darkness at the bottom of the stairs swallowed us, our candles all but useless. Benjamin, Jeremy, and Callie were far on the other side of the theater, standing on

393

the stage, their location revealed by the dim dots of their candles. We couldn't see them well, but could hear their voices, growing louder and louder until Callie shouted.

"Oh, for crying out loud! I can't believe you would mention that, of all things, here and now!"

"Maybe you should've owned up to it long ago," Benjamin said. The anger in his words echoed against the ancient walls. "But he's dead now, so it doesn't matter. As usual, everything's neatly taken care of, at very little cost to yourself."

"What are you suggesting, Carter?" Jeremy asked.

"You'd best keep out of it," Benjamin said. I heard scuffling and footsteps and then the sound of a fist against flesh. Jeremy grunted. Then another punch and the thud of a body hitting the floor. Colin raced forward, barking orders.

"Callie, get upstairs! Emily, make sure she obeys."

I grabbed Callie's arm and propelled her toward the daylight at the top of the steps, the noncombatant members of our party close behind. The sounds of fighting followed us, and in a few minutes, the remaining gentlemen emerged, Benjamin sporting a split lip and Jeremy limping, ever so slightly, his left eye turning dark purple. Colin had a firm grip on the American and motioned for me to come to him.

"I don't think Stirling's our man," he said to me in a voice so low it was difficult to hear. "Callie slipped up and said something that caused Carter to accuse her of having had an interlude with Mr. Walker on the ship. She admitted it, infuriating the boy, who started hurling abuse, accusing her of ill-treating every man of her acquaintance. Bainbridge stepped in to defend her honor, such as it is. I stopped them before they could do too much damage to each other. I'm taking Carter back to the villa, where I can interrogate him in private. It would be best if no one else followed. Give me three hours, at least."

44
AD 79

I almost fell over when I saw Lepida there, in the grotty garden of that awful bar. She was scowling at me, rage evident on her noble face and in her clenched fists. I bit my lip so hard I drew blood and considered turning around and running away. I would never have to see her or her husband again.

It was tempting, but I couldn't do it. I owed her more than that.

"I never believed you capable of so thoroughly betraying me," she said. "Sit, why don't you. I've ordered wine in the hopes that it might dull the pain of your evil deeds."

"I've never betrayed you, Lepida," I said.

"For a poetess, you have an inadequate grasp of the meaning of words. Have you not been meeting my husband here, in this disgusting place? Don't bother to deny it; I know the truth. I had a slave follow him and he saw the two of you. I didn't think he liked the slums so much, but I am told men have strange and varied tastes. He took you first when you were still a slave, I'm sure. I may not like it, but I accept that such things are common and to be expected. Does he like it better now that you're free? Now that your relationship is forbidden and illicit?"

"Lepida, you misunderstand entirely. I've never been intimate with Silvanus. We did meet here, yes, but not for any nefarious purpose."

She raised one perfectly arched eyebrow. "That you have the audacity to try to foist such a feeble lie upon me is a worse betrayal still."

"Silvanus came to me, like you did, wanting a poem," I said. "That is all. We met here, yes, but only so that I might give him more of my poetry."

"Your poetry." Her words, venom-laced, matched the hatred in her dark eyes. "I don't deny you have a certain talent, but you are young and maudlin. What use would he have for your verse?"

I paused, conscious that I had promised Silvanus I wouldn't tell Lepida what I was writing. "He could tell you better than I. All I can do is plead with you to believe the truth: there is nothing but poetry between Silvanus and me. Nothing."

"My husband is a skilled poet himself. Why would he want the verses of some worthless slave? The only explanation is that you're some sort of sorceress, a Circe who seduced him, taking sick delight in the knowledge you were stealing the husband of your closest friend. I have no one to blame but myself. Who is stupid enough to take a slave into her heart, to believe her as close as a sister? We were born on the same day, both daughters of a great earthquake. You know what they say about us, either that we are favorites of the gods or that we are cursed. It's only now that I see it all clearly. Apollo is the sun and Diana the moon, but we're twins of another sort: good and evil. I have the favor of the gods, but you, you vicious, untrustworthy wench, you are cursed. You bring misery to those who love you. You steal what is not yours. And there's no doubt — not even the smallest sliver — that you will come to a terrible, terrible end."

Tears stung in my eyes, but this time, they did stem from sadness and hurt, not anger. "Lepida please." I reached for her hands, but she pulled them away. "You have this all wrong. I swear on all the gods that I've never touched your husband. Ask him — ask him what has transpired between us."

"I've already done that," she said. "Why

do you think I'm here? He told me everything, every sordid detail. Unlike you, he doesn't lie about his actions."

"I'm not lying! You must believe me. It was only poetry."

She rose from the bench, knocking it over behind her, but not seeming to notice. She walked around the table, pulled me to my feet, and spat in my face. "I curse you, Quinta Flavia Kassandra. I curse your life and mind and memory and liver and lungs mixed up together, and your words, your thoughts, and your memory. I bind your tongue, so that it will be twisted and devoid of success. I beg the goddesses to end your life in a torment of fire and rock from which you cannot escape, a death more painful than that known by any human before." She spat in my face again, pushed me onto the ground, and stormed away.

45
1902

Colin dragged Benjamin in the direction of the carriages, leaving the rest of us behind, a subdued and silent group at the edge of the excavations, sitting on benches that faced the Bay of Naples.

"I can't say I expected the day to turn out like this," Mr. Taylor said.

"None of us did." I shot a withering glance at Callie. "Perhaps you could enlighten us as to what happened?"

"You've got the wrong idea, Emily, and, as I've had occasion to tell you before, I will not discuss my private life in public."

"Callie —" Jeremy reached for her, but she stormed away. He followed.

"We should return to Pompeii," Mr. Stirling said. "I'm not entirely clear as to what is going on, but it strikes me as unsporting to leave Hargreaves alone with Carter."

"Unsporting?" I asked.

"Carter's proven himself a bit of a brute, hasn't he? We all saw the state in which he left Bainbridge."

I had almost forgot that none of them — save Ivy and Kat — knew much about the details of Colin's work. Subduing Benjamin would not prove a challenge. "You're kind to worry about him, but I've no doubt he can manage."

"Do you really believe Carter is responsible for Walker's death?" Mr. Taylor asked.

"I do," I said, "but we still need a way to prove it. Colin will get a confession from him."

"What about Mr. Jackson?" Ivy asked.

"Kat's photographs revealed his feelings for Callie. Benjamin may have lashed out at him for the same reason he did Mr. Walker," I said. "Jealousy."

I had every reason to believe that Benjamin was guilty, but we could not yet prove Mr. Walker's motive for having returned to Pompeii. He might have followed Callie, but why had he boarded the ship in the first place? Something wasn't right.

We sat in silence, gloom hanging over us. After nearly a quarter of an hour had passed, Mr. Taylor spoke. "Would it be inappropriate to continue our tour? I don't see what good will come from us sitting about and moping."

"There's nothing we can do to help in the current situation, and I would like to see the Villa dei Papiri and its library," I admitted.

"I'm afraid you're bound to be disappointed on that count," Mr. Taylor said. "There's been no excavation in Herculaneum since 1877, and the tunnels dug at the villa are all but forgot. They lie beneath private property and are inaccessible."

"All but forgot," I said. "Not entirely. Surely you know how to access them?"

"Years ago, I greased a few palms in order to get in myself, because, like you, I was desperate to see the place. It's not what I had hoped. Narrow tunnels, difficult to navigate, and all of the sculpture, as well as most of the wall paintings, are now in the museum. We'd be better off exploring the rest of the excavations."

"It can't be all that disappointing if the work was thorough enough to result in a detailed floor plan of the house, which we both know it did. I brought my copy," I said, pulling it out of the notebook in my reticule and handing it to him. "If I were to, as you say, grease those same palms, would you lead me through?"

"It would be more like visiting a coal mine

than a villa, Lady Emily," he said. "But if you're bent on doing it, I would consider it an honor to accompany you. And I'm more than happy to re-grease the palms myself."

"I, for one, am intrigued at the prospect of seeing my dear friend at last lay eyes on an ancient library," Ivy said. "Small, dark spaces have never bothered me."

"Nor me," Kat said. "I wouldn't miss it for anything."

"I'm afraid you won't be able to manage it," Mr. Taylor said. "The only access is via a long ladder, and climbing it with an injured wrist is absolutely out of the question."

Kat scowled. "I haven't needed the sling for days, but kept it on as I've grown fond of everyone's sympathy. Let me at least try."

"No," Mr. Taylor said. "I can't risk you falling. I'm sorry."

Kat continued to plead her case as we followed him to the house through which one of the Bourbon tunnels was accessible. The owner was more than happy to let us in — in exchange for a generous contribution to his well-being — but when he saw the sling on Kat's arm, joined Mr. Taylor in forbidding her from joining us. Subdued but unhappy, she accepted the chair he offered her in his garden near the opening of the tunnel. The rest of us started down the ladder into a deep shaft. Mr. Taylor had brought with him two safety lamps that he and Mr. Stirling now carried.

"Candles made for a romantic exploration of the rest of the site, but these tunnels are too dark for them," he explained.

When we reached the bottom, the smallness of the space took me aback. The roughly hewn tunnel was only three or four feet wide, and in spots, so low we had to crouch. My breath caught in my throat when we had walked far enough that we could no longer see any hint of the daylight that had illuminated the shaft in which the ladder hung, but I was too excited at the prospect of the villa's library to give into any feeling of unease.

We covered a significant distance before we saw a bit of ancient wall, and it became evident that the Bourbon excavators had mined along the side of it, creating a corridor of sorts parallel to the structure. Eventually, we came to a room, dark and close, bare patches marking the spots from which its frescoes had been hacked. From there, the tunnel diverged in three directions. Ivy was no longer showing signs of enthusiasm.

"How do we prevent ourselves from getting lost down here?" she asked. "I'm all for exploration, but I've no intention of winding up trapped in some endless warren. I'm not sure continuing on is a wise course of action."

"Fear not, Mrs. Brandon," Mr. Taylor said. "I've been through here before and we have Weber's map."

"We should have brought bread crumbs, like Hansel and Gretel." Ivy's breath was coming fast and ragged. "I'm ashamed to say it, but I'm not comfortable going on."

"What about you, Lady Emily?" Mr. Taylor asked. "Should we abandon our scheme? It's not a pleasant place."

I was torn. The labyrinthine passages were dark, damp, cold, and claustrophobic. But somewhere, further along, was the only intact ancient library in existence! The scrolls were now in museums, but I longed to see the room in which they were originally housed.

"Don't go back on my account, Emily," Ivy said. "I could never forgive myself if I kept you from a library. Mr. Stirling is more than capable of escorting me out of this dreadful place." Perspiration dripped down her face, despite the chill in the air. "I'm half expecting the walls to collapse and it's all I can do to ward off panic."

"I'll take you back up," Mr. Stirling said. "We'll wait for the two of you at the top with Miss von Lange, and I expect a full report on what you see." The archaeologist took Ivy by the arm and we watched as he led her back through the tunnel until we could no longer see the light from his lantern. Mr. Taylor and I continued on, into the main part of the house. The peristyle was enormous.

"Do you recall the bronze statues of dancers in the museum in Naples?" he asked. "They were found in the southern portico, over there. A bit further now and we will come to the tablinum, where the first papyri were discovered."

A thrill coursed through me — we were so close to the library! — but when we reached the tablinum and then the room to its south, where more scrolls had been found, it was all but impossible to imagine what the space would have been like before the eruption. The savage methods of those early archaeologists (if we can even call them that) wreaked havoc on the villa. Its paintings had been ignominiously removed, and the complete absence of natural light, combined with the mazelike tunnels made it difficult to get a sense of the structure as a whole. In truth, Weber's map gave a better impression of what the villa had been like than struggling through the place itself.

I will admit that I was beginning to feel closed in by the stale air. Yet I went on, firm in my desire to see the library.

"You've gone very quiet, Lady Emily." Mr. Taylor asked, "Is something troubling you? We can turn back if you'd like."

"No, I want to see the library." I would not succumb to fear and weakness, even as it fought to consume me.

"It's not much further." He removed my copy of the map from his jacket. "We're here, and the library's here." He reached into his pocket again, pulled out a pencil, and marked both locations on the map, but I could only look at his pencil. The barrel was painted blue, and I could just see STAEDTLER stamped in the wood above a silver holder, engraved with Mr. Taylor's monogram. The pencil was a perfect match for the stub I found at the abandoned campsite in Pompeii along with the cuff link engraved FM. My heart started to pound. He had mentioned his lack of artistic talent more than once. Had that been an attempt to remove himself from our list of potential murderers? He'd admitted to having met Felix Morgan, which sent us on a useless search for information about Morgan's time in Pompeii. Furthermore, he had time and time again mentioned Benjamin's temper, always sounding sympathetic to the boy, but ensuring we would consider him a suspect.

My head was throbbing. Perhaps Mr. Taylor collected strays because he was one as well. All his talk about it being impossible to change one's nature was an attempt to hide his own darkness. His magnanimous spirit was carefully cultivated. He forgave others' sins because he wanted to forget his own.

"Perhaps we ought to turn back," I said. "I'm ashamed to say it, but I'm starting to feel closed in, as if the walls are pressing in on us."

"Surely not, Lady Emily. You've too much courage for a narrow tunnel to intimidate you."

There was something in his tone — a cutting edge — that made my limbs go cold. If the tunnels of Herculaneum had seemed claustrophobic before, now they all but slammed in on me.

"I'm not convinced I deserve the compliment," I said, trying to sound as blasé as possible. He stepped closer to me and I backed up against the wall. There was a horrible hardness in his eyes.

"There must be something more troubling

you. If you felt closed in, you would have returned to the surface with Mrs. Brandon. And thinking on it, you weren't troubled in the least to see your husband go off with a murderer. Which surely is more frightening than tunnels. It's because you know Carter isn't guilty, isn't it?"

"Of course he's guilty." All I wanted was to flee. Being in a confined, underground space with someone you now have reason to believe capable of committing that most grievous sin against his fellow man has very little to recommend it. "You saw how angry Walker's relationship with Callie made him, and how violently he reacted to Jeremy. His anger gets the better of him, with disastrous results."

"Come now, Lady Emily, we both know Carter is not the man you seek."

46
AD 79

My face streaked with tears, I ran home. Melas, coming out of the house, stopped me, asking what had caused me to be so upset. Finding myself incapable of restraint, I told him everything: about Silvanus and the poem and Lepida's curse.

"You don't know then," he said. "Silvanus did, indeed, recite the opening of your epic to his guests at a dinner party, but he also claimed authorship of it. He never intended to give you credit, Kassandra. He saw your talent and knew he could exploit it for his own glory. I've seen eight new graffiti quoting it — and naming him as the poet — today. Paid for, no doubt, by the man himself. He's already rich, now he wants to be admired and respected for an intellect he does not possess."

"There's nothing I can do to prevent him from getting whatever he wants," I said. "No one would believe me over him. I'm little better than a hopelessly naïve slave." How could I have been so stupid, so gullible? Never had it occurred to me that he might want my poetry for his own. Instead, I had let myself believe, because I wanted it to be so, that part of the need for secrecy stemmed from his attraction to me.

"You can prove that you wrote the poem," Melas said.

"How?" I asked. "He knows the verse almost as well as I do."

"You have a copy of the entire work, I assume?"

"Of course. Two, in fact, as Silvanus did not come to collect his from me."

Melas nodded, his eyes pensive. "In the end, do you care about what his useless friends think? Or do you want to be remembered as a worthy successor to Virgil?"

"My poem isn't that good."

"This is not the time for modesty," Melas said. "I have a friend who lives in Herculaneum. He's a devoted Epicurean in possession of a magnificent library. Tomorrow, we will take your epic to him and ask him to put it in his library, with you named as the author. I'll persuade him to have copies made and distributed to his acquaintances in Rome, those who appreciate fine verse. Silvanus may get credit in Pompeii, but the rest of the world will know the work was yours. It is, perhaps, a slim consolation, but I hope better than nothing."

"Silvanus will get credit in Rome as well as in Pompeii. He won't limit himself to the provinces."

I did want to be known for my work, but even if no one recognized my authorship, in the future, perhaps, my work would be mentioned along with that of Homer and Virgil — though never with the same awed respect. For the rest of the day and all of the night, I read through the scrolls that would become the exemplar of my epic, from which, I hoped, hundreds more copies would be made. When Melas collected me the next day, we told my father we were going to his friend's so that I might peruse the library at his villa. By midday, we were close to Herculaneum.

Much though I longed for a way to ensure my name would be connected to my poem, at least I knew that copies would be distributed and that it would be read. What more could I desire than that? Glory? No, let Silvanus have that. I did not need it. At least I tried to convince myself of this, but I brooded as we walked, thinking of nothing but my poem until the sound of a massive crash assaulted us. Melas and I turned to look in the direction from whence it came. There, hanging above Vesuvius, far up in the sky, was an enormous dark cloud shaped like a pine tree. The mountain no longer looked as it had only a few minutes ago — the top section of its great cone had vanished, thrown by angry Vulcan. The ground trembled violently, Neptune's fury as great as his fellow god's, and an acrid, vile smell filled the air.

Melas and I flung ourselves down, and I clutched to my chest the wooden case that held my scrolls. We remained there, watching the sky until the earth stopped moving beneath us.

"We should press on," Melas said. "The earthquake is over, but I'd prefer to reach the house before anything else happens." He looked at the mountain and murmured quick prayers to Vulcan and Neptune.

More earthquakes came as we walked the last mile to his friend's house, and when we arrived, we found only the steward in residence. The family, he explained, had fled to the port, where they would seek passage on one of the boats there. They wanted to get as far from Vesuvius as possible. "You're welcome to shelter here with me until it's all over," he said. "The house is well built."

What choice did we have? We were not

about to return to Pompeii with that dreadful cloud hanging over Vesuvius. The steward gave us beakers of cool water and we sat in the long garden, away from any sculptures that might tumble over should the earth shake again. And shake again it did. The hours crawled by as the black cloud above the mountain grew more and more ominous, parts of it dark, parts of it bright. Ash had started to fall, but we could not decide if we were safer inside, shielded from it, or whether the threat of additional earthquakes made remaining where we were the better choice. The sun had disappeared behind the cloud of ash, plunging us into a gloomy darkness, punctuated by an occasional burst of flame shooting from the top of the mountain. I could no longer tell what time it was. Eventually, the steward went back inside to gather his belongings. He was tired of waiting, worried about the mountain, and had decided to flee the city.

"To go where?" Melas asked. "It's unlikely there are any boats still lingering in the harbor."

"I'll risk it," he said. "I don't feel good staying here. You should come, too — even if there are no boats, there's nothing better built than the storage areas for the port. We can take shelter there. It's bound to be safer than staying here."

"You said the house is well built," I reminded him.

"I'd feel better at the port."

Melas and I did not go with him.

"I shouldn't have brought you here," the painter said.

"Pompeii would've been no safer. Besides, we've survived plenty of earthquakes. Why should this be any different?"

"It's not the earthquakes that concern me." He kicked at the ash piling around us. "Aren't you scared?"

"Terrified," I said. I'd pulled my veil over my nose and mouth to make it easier to breathe. He stood in front of me and took my hands.

"I'm sorry, Kassandra."

"It's not your fault." I wished I could infuse my voice with a lightness of tone, but it was impossible. So I met his eyes and saw in them what I'd hoped — and almost believed — I'd seen in Silvanus's. And then I remembered my favorite line of Ovid's, *Let love be introduced in friendship's dress.* "Why did you paint Venus's face as my own?"

"Is it not obvious?" He took half a step forward, and I thought he might kiss me, but then he looked away from me, back at the book box I'd carried with us. A thick layer of ash covered it. "We should put your scrolls in the library with a message explaining the situation in which you have found yourself."

"Now?"

He nodded. "The ash is coming harder and I fear we're in for worse. Let's make sure your legacy is preserved."

"And then?"

"Then we shall discuss my painting of Venus." Something stirred in me, unexpected but welcome. Melas squeezed my hands and then dropped them. "There's papyrus in the tablinum. I would name Silvanus if I were you — let history decide what to make of his deception."

"And what deception is that, painter?" The steward must not have bothered to lock the door behind him. I recognized Silvanus's voice before I could make out his form in the darkness. "I will take the scrolls and that will be the end of it. I had never intended to hurt you, Kassandra, but my wife tells me that you are not to be trusted, and, indeed, the conversation I have overheard shows she speaks the truth."

"How did you know I was here?" I asked, backing away from him.

"I had gone to your house looking for you,

wanting to get the rest of the poem you owe me," Silvanus said. "I told your father I'd come to order a volume of Horace's poetry and then asked after you. He told me about your excursion to visit this library. I found it odd. You cannot be acquainted with the villa's owner, and would have no reason to be admitted to the house. But then I remembered Melas did work for him. And then your father told me you were carrying a book box with you. It took no leap of imagination to deduce what scrolls it contained and what you intended to do with them. I will not have some upstart former slave smear my reputation, so I came after you. Neither Vulcan's anger nor Neptune's will stop me, for I am not the object of it. You are."

"I have done nothing to anger the gods and you have nothing to fear from me," I said. "Who would believe my word over yours?"

"I prefer to be above suspicion," Silvanus said.

"Like Caesar's wife?" Melas asked. Silvanus charged toward him and struck him hard in the face.

"I mean to go to Rome and become a senator, but my ambitions do not stop there. We have had enough degenerate emperors,

417

have we not? I am cultured and educated and will be adored by all. And I will not have idle rumors about a cheeky slave girl follow me there."

Melas spat blood and a tooth onto the ground and wiped his mouth with the back of his hand. "You've now ensured that it will be more than idle rumors."

"No, not when I've finished with you."

What would have happened next, had the gods not interfered, I know not. Silvanus started for Melas again, but my friend sprung to his feet and ran toward me, slipping me a dagger and urging me to make my escape.

"You can't protect her, painter," Silvanus said. "I will start on her when I finish you." With that he lunged at Melas again.

"Run!" my friend ordered.

I obeyed without thinking and charged into the house. The ground was rumbling again, and the rain of ash even more relentless. I could hear screams and crying coming from the city streets as the rest of the population that had not fled during the afternoon desperately searched for shelter or safety or rescue.

I found the library, but before I could deposit my scrolls there, I heard footsteps and Silvanus was upon me.

"Your friend is dead," he said, standing close. Once again, I could feel his breath against my cheek, but it no longer warmed me. Now, it brought only a dark chill. "I have always admired you, Kassandra, so I will give you a few moments to say whatever you must to your favored gods, but then, you, too, must fall."

My heart ached for Melas, but now was not the time to mourn. I plunged the dagger my friend had given to me — had he kept it, he might have saved himself — into Silvanus's gut. It took all my strength, but I managed to drag it upward and twist it hard. He collapsed. The wound would kill him, but not immediately, and I had no time to sit and watch him die. Once he was unconscious, I tugged the bloody weapon free and retreated to a small room near the tablinum, where I have sat for all these hours since, writing my story and waiting for the fall of ash to stop. I believe Silvanus is dead by now, but will not go look until the morning, when it is light again. And then I will find Melas and prepare his body for honorable burial.

His knife is still at my side, for until I see Silvanus's corpse, I will remain on guard. I cannot free myself from the image of his face as I twisted the knife in him, but the air is becoming hotter and hotter, and I am finding it increasingly difficult to breathe. My limbs have grown weak and the heat is unbearable, so here I will stop my account, having given the full story, written on this scroll that accompanies the poem of which I am so proud. But, now, on this awful night, all I can think of are the words of Virgil, not my own.

His limbs went slack and chill, and his life fled with a cry, indignant, below to the shades.

47
1902

"I've never been the sort of man who would wantonly harm another human being," Mr. Taylor said, the lamp casting ghastly shadows on his face. "It's not in my nature, as you've had ample time to observe. I'm generous and intelligent and a man capable of doing great things for the world. Not many surpass my philanthropy, and the work I am funding at Pompeii will not only bring delight to tourists, but will expand our knowledge of ancient Rome. It will also improve the science of archaeological method. Consider how I am supporting Callie's career and forwarding a cause dear to your own heart, that of the advancement of women's rights."

"Your achievements are to be lauded," I said. I had no doubt now that he was our murderer, but was not about to confront him while alone with him, a hundred feet underground. I would keep him talking —

distract him — and convince him I harbored no suspicions about him. "Finding myself here with you in an ancient villa with a magnificent library prompts me to ask if you have ever considered funding its modern equivalent."

"I'm happy to leave that to Carnegie."

"I appreciate your devotion to science, Mr. Taylor. I realize you are passionate about history — ancient Rome in particular — but not many of your colleagues are content to support efforts that don't bring them public recognition. Your method is more honorable, seeking neither fame nor glory. It is a rare man who is content keeping to the background."

"You do understand me, don't you, Lady Emily?" His eyes darkened as he stared into mine.

"I believe so," I said. All this time, I had been surreptitiously evaluating our surroundings, trying to determine how I might best get away from him. We were in a small room not far from the peristyle, but I was not confident I could easily retrace our steps. The maze of corridors through the villa would be confusing even if flooded with light.

He stepped toward me. "And now you're happy to sit and chat about libraries when, moments ago, you were overwhelmed by claustrophobia and wanted to flee. I see what you're doing. You know I can't let you leave these tunnels, not now that you understand me and why I shun recognition. I've given you opportunity after opportunity to stop this futile investigation — how many warnings did I send? — in how many ways did I appeal to your better judgment? I knew that as a student of ancient Greece you'd understand the ostraca, but they had no effect. I followed you to Naples with the curse tablet and slipped it into your parcels without you ever suspecting I had done it. Benjamin had to tell me he was taking the day off, so I knew of your plans. And the paintings of Alexander's omens. You didn't believe me capable of producing them, because I've hidden from you my artistic talent. Art was my first love. That's why I wanted to make sure Carter had time for his paintings. I never meant for your husband to be injured when I threw the marble into the Temple of Isis. I don't want to hurt anyone. All I was trying to do was put you off. But now, here we are, both of us aware of my guilt."

"I know nothing about the specific circumstances of Mr. Walker's death," I said. "If he attacked you — or threatened you —

you were acting in self-defense, and —"

He laughed, a hideous, inhuman sound. "Come now, it is beneath you to try to wriggle out of your fate. We're all governed by our natures, and yours compels your dedication to the pursuit of justice, no matter the cost. Mine drives me to live a good life, to make the world better. You've threatened my ability to do that, and I can't stand by and accept what we both know you'll do if I let you go back to the surface."

"A good man would let me return to my friends."

He shook his head. "There are times when we are faced with situations, terrible situations that force us to act against our natures. You've tricked me into one of those situations now."

"Like Clarence Walker did before?" I would get every ounce of information I could from him while I figured out a way to escape. "Is that how this all started? Or was it earlier, in the mines of Montana?"

"The mines are worse than hell, not because of their diabolical working conditions, but because of what they do to the minds of men."

"Was that what led to the bar fight that resulted in the death of Mr. Walker's brother, Fergus?"

"I never meant that man any harm," Mr. Taylor said, clenching his fist. "I don't drink to excess and avoided the saloons because I knew all too well how ugly things got in them. But my business partner did not share my scruples. There was trouble that night, over some girl, and he and Fergus started arguing. It was Fergus who landed the first blow, Fergus who is to blame. Things got bad, and the girl came to me, begging me to help. By the time I arrived, my partner was a bloody heap, half-dead. I tried to reason with Fergus, but he was in no state for listening, and started in on me. Gave me a terrible beating. I fought back, as hard as I could, and everything around me went red. I didn't know what I was doing until I realized I was on top of him, battering him. Someone pulled me off. I could see then that Fergus was not long for the world, and I was not about to let my entire life be derailed by trying to defend an innocent man from the brutal attack of a ne'er-do-well."

"So you left Montana?" I asked. "Who could blame you for that? You're not a violent man, Mr. Taylor. You were acting in self-defense."

"I wasn't willing to run the risk of being branded a murderer. I made my way east, to New York, and traded work for passage on a ship. I deserved another shot. I changed my name from Felix Morgan to Balthazar Taylor during the crossing and, when I landed in Southampton, determined to make a fresh start."

"That's why you had Morgan's cuff links," I said. "They had always been yours."

"Yes, they were a gift from my mother. I kept them as a reminder of that former life. I constructed the remains of the camp hoping it would inflame your interest in finding the elusive Felix Morgan. I knew you planned to meet Carter that morning at the House of Marco Lucretius Fronto, and I knew he always returned from that area to my dig via a little-traveled route. I set up the site and left the red fabric where you could not miss it."

He was standing too close to me. I inched back and tried to get him talking about his life rather than his attempts to elude justice for his crimes. "After you reached Southampton, did you go to Vienna and meet Herr Baeder?" I asked.

"Yes. As soon as I adopted my new persona, my fortunes changed. What better confirmation that I was following the correct course of action? Herr Baeder knew I had no experience, but he took me under

426

his wing. By the end of three years, I had acquired an unimaginable amount of money. Soon, I owned a house in Vienna and a mansion on Fifth Avenue in New York and had the respect of all those people who before would have refused my acquaintance. From then on, I have made it my mission to do what I can for those less fortunate than myself."

"How did Mr. Walker find you?"

"Because I had the misfortune to wind up in a picture that accompanied an article in *National Geographic,*" he said.

"The article Mr. Walker brought with him when he returned to Pompeii," I said. "But why was that significant? He knew you were here when he came to research his article. You told me you met him."

"I lied. I saw him from a distance the day he arrived. He'd been milling around in search of someone to give him a basic understanding of archaeological technique. I panicked. If he saw me, he'd recognize me. You don't forget the face of the man who killed your brother. I fled to Rome and stayed there until he'd left."

"He never saw you?" I asked.

"No. I thought I was free and clear of him. But I got careless a couple of years later and let my guard down. I ought have been

427

more careful to stay clear of that magazine photographer. I didn't know he was taking the picture, let alone that he would bother to identify every individual in it, even those of us in the background. Such irony. It's not as if I was unaware of the risk. I had counseled Stirling to avoid being photographed, because he didn't want his old Harvard friends to know where he was."

"You let Kat photograph you."

"She's little more than a child. What would she have ever done with her pictures that might have exposed me? If I'd refused to cooperate with her, that might have drawn your attention. I decided that was a greater risk than letting a girl pursue a harmless hobby."

"But you attacked her. Did she say something that made you believe she might publish her photos?"

"I never laid a hand on the girl. I would not harm one so innocent."

I believed him, partly because I had never quite accepted Kat's story, and partly because it fit with his character. Convinced he was a good man, he would not have struck out in violence unless he felt she posed a threat. "So Mr. Walker recognized you in *National Geographic*?"

"He read the magazine religiously, not

that I knew that until he told me. As soon as he saw it, the jig was up. He knew exactly where to find me. He didn't announce his arrival. Hid in the shadows until he found me alone. And then, he confronted me, saying he would give me the opportunity to explain my side of the story."

"The bar fight was not murder," I said. "You could've defended yourself against any charges made regarding it."

"Not without destroying my reputation. And what does a man have without that? He said he'd write a piece illustrating how much good a man could do even after having committed so vile a crime. He pretended to believe I deserved rehabilitation, but I knew he was bent on nothing but revenge. I had to stop him, or my life's work would've been for naught. I didn't consciously choose to kill him, but again my nature deserted me, and again I saw red. The next thing I knew, my hands were around his throat, and he was as dead as his brother, all those years ago."

"So you covered the body in plaster and hid it in plain sight?" I asked.

"Yes. An inspired plan, you must agree."

"When did Mr. Jackson figure out what you'd done?"

"Jackson? He had no idea. He was a

competent archaeologist, but never showed any interest outside of the field."

"Some might consider his employer committing murder as the sort of thing that might have drawn his attention."

"I had nothing to do with his death. I would never take a life unless absolutely necessary. I do everything in my power to avoid such situations, but unfortunately did not have the foresight to anticipate coming up against someone whose own nature would compel her to destroy me. You should've left well enough alone. I have no desire to harm you, yet you leave me with no choice." The veins in his temples pulsed. "Why, why do people keep doing this to me? Forcing me to act in a manner that goes completely against the kind of man I am?"

Now was not the time to point out the deep flaws in Mr. Taylor's understanding of his own nature. I was terrified, trapped with a murderer, and could think of only one thing to do. I lifted my skirts and kicked him as hard as I could — in a part of his anatomy no respectable lady should so much as consider, but a part Colin had assured me would bring a man to his knees — knocking him to the ground. He dropped his lamp as he fell. I grabbed it, kicked him again, and ran toward the peristyle.

But I turned in the wrong direction, and instead of finding myself in the remains of the ancient garden, I was in another room, slightly bigger than the one in which I'd left Mr. Taylor. I could hear him following me. My only advantage was the lamp, but I knew he had carried candles as well. He must have paused long enough to light one of them, and was now coming, hard on my heels.

I couldn't go back without running into him, so I would instead have to find some other route to the peristyle. Knowing the general layout of Roman houses, I was confident this would not prove impossible, but at the same time, I was not certain where I was relative to the garden. There was nothing to do but press on. The room I was in had two doors; I exited through the one I had not entered.

Columns! I was in the peristyle! Relief flooded over me. But, no, the feeling was short-lived. The space was too small and its columns much closer together than those in the peristyle — later, I learned it was a first century BC atrium, but then, all I knew was that I was not heading in the right direction. I retraced my steps to the edge of the colonnade and turned to the right. A few feet further along was another passage, which I ducked into, praying it would take me in the general direction of a tunnel that would lead me back to the garden. From there, I knew I could find my way to the ladder.

I heard footsteps and extinguished the lamp — I had matches and could relight it — as I could not risk giving away my location. He must be in the atrium now, but instead of turning, as I had, it sounded as if he were going straight across it. I held my breath, waiting as the echo of his boots grew more distant. I started to move again, slowly, as I could not see, feeling my way along the wall.

The wall opened into a tiny room — a cubiculum, as I discovered when I paused to relight my lamp. My hands were shaking so violently that I had to sit down in order to compose myself before I could strike a match. When I did, and light pulsed against the darkness around me, I saw that I was not the only occupant of the space. Not more than a foot away from me was a skeleton lying on the mosaic floor. Whoever it was must have taken shelter here during the eruption, curling up in a fetal position. I had a deep affinity for this fallen soul and prayed that I would not meet death here as well.

I could hear the sound of footsteps again, coming closer and closer. I examined my surroundings. I had entered the room not through a door, but through a hole in the wall made by the Bourbon explorers. The actual door, opposite where I sat, was completely blocked by debris. I was trapped. If he found me here, I would have no hope for escape. In vain I looked around, searching for anything I could use as a weapon — a heavy rock, perhaps — but there was nothing suitable. All I could do was turn off the lamp and pray that he chose to follow a different tunnel. But then, I caught sight of something glint beneath the sad pile of bones next to me.

It was metal. I grabbed for it and cut my hand on the blade of an ancient dagger, still surprisingly sharp. Offering a silent apology to the skeleton for having disturbed it, I clutched the knife and extinguished the lamp. Then, moving silently, I rose to my feet and crept along the perimeter of the room until I reached the opening on the other side. There I stopped, pressed myself against the wall, and waited. If Mr. Taylor did not enter the room, but only looked in, he would not see me. If he did enter, I would be able to catch him unaware and use the knife to incapacitate him.

I have been involved in enough murder investigations to have learned that wielding a knife is not so easy as writers of sensational detective stories would have us believe. I had no illusions about the difficulties I would face, but what choice did I have? I held the weapon firmly above my head and wrapped both my hands around its handle. He was close now, very close. Through the corner of my eye, I could see the flicker of his candle through the opening in the wall. I took a deep breath, held it, and waited.

If only he had glanced in and gone back the other way! But Fortuna was not smiling on me that day. He stepped inside, leaving me only an instant to act. With one swift movement, I lowered the dagger and plunged it into his neck. He cried out and fell to the ground, his candle still burning after he dropped it. I did not wait to see if he was alive or dead. I pulled out the knife, retrieved the lantern from where I'd left it, stepped over his body, and fled from the room.

In the relative safety of the tunnel beyond, I lit the lamp and somehow made my way back to the atrium. Now, I could retrace my steps. If I could remember them. The darkness pressed in. Even with the light I could only see a few feet in front of me. Twice I took wrong turns, but I pushed on, trying to stop the forward march of the panic surging through me. When, after an eternity, I reached the peristyle, I paused and stood very still, listening for any hint of footsteps. I heard nothing.

I can barely recall the rest of my race to the ladder at the end of that first tunnel, but, somehow, I reached it and managed to get to the top. I flung myself from the last rung onto the ground in the little garden, where Ivy, Kat, and Mr. Stirling were sitting, waiting.

"Dear Lord, what happened? You're covered with blood!" Ivy rushed to me.

"Covered must surely be an exaggeration," I said, barely able to catch my breath.

"Has there been an accident?" Mr. Stirling asked. "Where's Taylor?"

I gulped in air. "I stabbed him. He — he is our murderer. I don't know if he's alive or dead. I don't know if he tried to follow me. I don't —"

"Don't say anything more." Kat was wiping my face with her handkerchief. "Mr. Stirling, we need the police, a doctor, and my father."

The doctor was the first to arrive, summoned, on Mr. Stirling's order, by the owner of the house. I started to explain that I was not certain of Mr. Taylor's condition, nor of how long it would take us to reach him, but Ivy stopped me.

"Your hand is sliced open, Emily," she said.

"But Mr. Taylor may be —"

"We will see to him in good time." She wrapped a blanket around me while the doctor tended to my hand. I could not stop shaking. When he was finished, Kat approached me.

"Did he — did Mr. Taylor mention anything about me?" she asked, whispering, her eyes focused on the ground.

"I know he did not attack you."

"No, he didn't." Her voice was a whisper. "I fell and made up the story of being attacked. I don't know what I was thinking. I'm so sorry. I don't know what I was thinking. I —"

I touched her arm. "It doesn't matter anymore."

She fell silent as Mr. Stirling, who had been making a careful examination of the knife I had carried out of the tunnel, started to speak. "It's a prime example of a first century pugio, the same type of weapon wielded by Caesar's assassins. Wherever did you find it?"

"Beneath an ancient skeleton," I said. "I'm fortunate that the Bourbon excavators were more interested in treasure than human remains. I don't know how they missed the dagger. Perhaps they didn't want to disturb the bones, perhaps they —"

"It doesn't matter," Ivy said. "It was there, and for that, I am grateful."

Colin was at my side impossibly soon. He hadn't come because of our message; he hadn't received it. Half an hour after he'd started questioning Benjamin, he'd determined the young man was not our murderer. "I wish I could say I suspected Taylor, but I flew back here, worrying that I'd left you with Stirling."

When the police arrived, I once again descended the ladder into that awful tunnel, for although they were confident they could find Mr. Taylor without me, I knew it would take longer than if I led them. He might be a nefarious murderer, but I was responsible for his injury and would not stand in the way of him getting medical attention without further delay.

Kat tried to insist on coming, too, but her father forbade it in a tone that no one can disobey. She was not happy, but she didn't argue. With Colin in front of me, gripping my hand, and Mr. Stirling behind, I was able to keep from panicking. We had many more lamps with us now — the police had brought them — but, even so, the darkness was overwhelming. I was somehow able to retrace my steps, surprised at how familiar the buried rooms of the villa had already become, but when we came to the opening in the wall beyond which Mr. Taylor lay, I tasted bile and stopped short.

Mr. Stirling stayed with me, but Colin and three of the policemen went into the room. When my husband returned, I was standing in the tunnel, my back pressed hard against the wall. "He's unconscious, but not dead," he said. We waited until the police had removed the injured man. When they had gone, I forced myself back into the room, wincing at the puddle of blood staining the mosaic floor.

"I don't know how you managed to overcome him," Colin said. "Were you holding the knife over your head?"

I nodded. "It was the only reliable way to ensure I struck him with enough force to incapacitate him. I aimed for his neck. You've told me countless times how vulnerable that area of the anatomy is."

Mr. Stirling was crouching next to the skeleton. "She's female," he said. "That much is clear from the pelvis. The Bourbon

438

excavators would have taken any jewelry she was wearing, but they must have missed this." Gently, he retrieved a charred clump from beneath the woman's rib cage. "Papyrus." He cradled it in his hands and held it out to me.

"If only we could read it," I said. "Perhaps she wrote her story while she took shelter here, waiting for the eruption to end."

"Unlikely," Mr. Stirling said, "but it would make for gripping fiction. Perhaps you should write it, Lady Emily. I'll go through the excavation records and see what else, if anything, was found in this room."

"Why would they have left her here?" I asked.

"They were searching for treasure," Colin said, "not a pile of old bones."

"You're more cynical than I," Mr. Stirling said. "I think they left her here, where she fell, to remind us of her humanity. As Horace tells us, *we are but dust and shadow.*"

"You're giving them far too much credit," Colin replied. "Such optimism would be better suited to that fiction you suggested Emily write. Perhaps you can be her archaeological consultant. Now, though, there's nothing more to be done here. Let's remove ourselves from this subterranean nightmare."

48
1902

The carriage took us back to Pompeii. This time, Kat plopped down next to Ivy and insisted that I sit next to her father, to whom she refused to speak. She did, however, make a point of loudly telling me that she would never forgive him for forbidding her to go into the tunnels with us. It proved, she explained, that he did not consider women as capable as men.

"That's patently untrue," I said. "I was with him, wasn't I? And he never doubted your mother's abilities. It is your youth, not your gender that concerns him." She frowned and stared out the window, not looking at either of us again for the rest of the journey. Colin did his best to engage her in conversation, but eventually abandoned the cause. He never did like a futile endeavor.

When we arrived at the villa, Jeremy and Callie were having an epic row, shouting at each other across the sitting room. He wasn't angry about whatever her relationship had been with Mr. Walker, but he was furious to learn she had ordered the attack on Mario. She insisted the man she had hired took matters further than she had instructed him to, that she had only wanted to scare the guide into keeping silent, because he had discovered — after observing them in an unguarded moment (she declined to tell anyone but Jeremy what, exactly, Mario saw) — that she and Benjamin were not brother and sister. That catalyzed their meeting atop Mt. Vesuvius. She eventually convinced Jeremy to forgive her. How, I would rather not know.

Ivy, her face a mask of discontent, only just managed to keep from interfering, in the end limiting herself to suggesting that Callie compensate Mario for his injuries. Callie agreed to this at once, while Benjamin, bruised and silent, brooded in the corner. Jeremy went to him and held out his hand.

"Beastly of me to attack you when I didn't know the whole story," he said. "I realize now you were trying to save me from the heartbreak you suffered, but sharing private details of a lady's life is never appropriate. I didn't need to know about Walker."

441

"I need to know," I said. "I believed you, Callie, when you said he was beneath your interest."

"I wasn't lying," she said. "Not about that, anyway. I did speak to him on the ship, but nothing of import transpired between us. He was unexpectedly charming and took my teasing about his sideburns in good humor. I didn't have the heart to rebuff him altogether. We walked together the last three mornings of our voyage. Benjamin drew an erroneous conclusion when he claimed anything more happened between us."

"The less said about that the better." Ivy scowled. "You ought to give more consideration to how your behavior affects those around you."

"You've every right to scold me," Callie said.

"Did you see Walker in Pompeii?" Colin asked.

"No. He never mentioned it as his destination, only told me that he was going abroad to see an old friend. When I saw Emily's sketch of him, I panicked, knowing what Benjamin suspected me of having done. I was afraid he'd killed him in a jealous rage and that it was all my fault. I didn't dare deny having seen him on the ship — you could easily have got the passenger manifest

— so I pretended never to have spoken to him."

"You needn't have tried to protect me." Benjamin pulled himself up to his full height. "I never saw Walker in Pompeii, and even if I had, I wouldn't have interfered with him. I'm not quite the lovesick puppy you think."

"But what about Mr. Jackson?" Ivy asked. "Who killed him?"

"We have no evidence to prove that his death was anything but accidental," Colin said. "Taylor confessed to killing two men. I agree with Emily that he was telling the truth about Jackson."

"And Kat?" Ivy asked. "Did he admit to attacking her in an attempt to put us off our investigation?"

I hesitated, but only for an instant. "He did." Kat opened her mouth, but closed it when I almost imperceptibly shook my head. She might not like me, but she could not deny I could be an ally.

Soon thereafter, a message arrived, informing us that Mr. Taylor's condition had stabilized; he would live to face justice, and for that, I was relieved. I might not yet be able to free myself from the sickening sound of the knife sinking into his neck, but at least I had not killed him.

"You would have been totally justified in doing so," Jeremy said. "I'd like to see him dead, and I'm certain Hargreaves feels the same."

"I would have done anything to escape," I said, "but all in all, I'm glad not to have his demise on my conscience, no matter how awful his crimes. I prefer official justice to vigilante."

Three days later, we all gathered on the terrace, at Mr. Stirling's request.

"I should have spoken about this earlier," he said. "But I was ashamed of myself. Hargreaves, you were correct to question my relationship with Michele Fabbrocino. I was short of money, once again having fallen into the habit of living beyond my means. I'd tried — in vain — to write a novel about the life of Alexander the Great, hoping it might provide an income, but couldn't find a publisher interested in working with me. Soon thereafter, I met Fabbrocino in the ruins and we fell into easy conversation. I believed we were friends, and I swear I knew nothing about his connection to the Camorra. Not at first. He offered me a small loan, at low interest, and I took it. And then another after that, and another, larger one, at the end of last season. The payments I owed him made it impossible to cover my rent, which is why I turned to Jackson for a loan. I've returned what I borrowed to his estate and settled my debt with Fabbrocino, all thanks to Callie's generosity."

"It's the least I could do, given how much trouble I've caused," Callie said. "Perhaps it will go a small way in rehabilitating my reputation with the rest of you."

"You're not the only one of us who requires large measures of rehabilitation," Benjamin said. "I'm ashamed of my own behavior."

Mr. Stirling looked uncomfortable. "Allow me to turn our attention to a more gratifying topic. I have something to share with you all that I hope will bring a happy sort of closure to the events in Herculaneum. I've read through all the excavation reports and learned that the room in which Lady Emily found the skeleton — and the knife that saved her life — was tunneled into in 1753. A pair of snake bracelets, gold drop earrings, a ring, and a wooden box, the sort used by the Romans to store books, were with the bones. The jewelry was removed to a private collection, a gift from the king. There was no mention of the dagger or the scroll. It's possible that neither was immediately visible beneath her, buried in dust, but that, over the ensuing centuries, the ground shifted — there have been numerous earthquakes, after all — and exposed enough for you to see the knife when you most needed it."

"Why was her skeleton left in situ?" I asked.

"An earthquake halted work in the room in which she died, and no later explorers ever went back to it. The men digging grabbed the jewelry but left her behind. The remains of two other people were also found in the villa, one in the peristyle — a male, approximately twenty-five years old, missing a front tooth — and one in the library, another male, in his mid-thirties. His skeleton showed signs that he had been stabbed. Both sets of bones were put in storage. Our girl was no more than twenty and in the wooden box found with her were thirteen scrolls, now in the museum in Naples, but not on display."

"Have they been unrolled?" I asked.

"No, not yet. Perhaps, someday," he replied. "I had a word with the current owner of the jewelry, and he agreed you should have these." He handed me a velvet-covered box. Inside, were the twin snake bracelets.

"I couldn't," I said. "They belong in a museum."

Mr. Stirling folded his arms across his chest and shot me a look so full of authority it made him all but unrecognizable. "They're not going to wind up in a museum, regardless of whether you accept them. As I said, they went into a private collection and have changed hands several times since then. I'm of the opinion that the original owner would prefer you to have them."

"You can't argue with that theory, Emily," Colin said. "After all, in a way, she saved your life."

I touched the polished surface of the thick gold. I could picture them adorning the slim wrists of an elegant Roman girl — her most treasured possessions, the things she chose to keep with her on that horrible day when Vesuvius exploded. The emeralds in the serpents' eyes gleamed.

Mr. Stirling continued. "The earrings are not in wearable condition, and the owner's wife, while rather fond of the ring, has an aversion to snakes."

"The Romans considered snakes a symbol of abundance," I said. "I shall be honored to have them."

"There's one other thing," Callie said.

447

"We've arranged for you to take possession of the scroll we found. Someday, I hope, the techniques for unrolling and reading them will have improved, but until then, I know you will keep it safe."

"However did you manage that?" I asked.

"Much though I regret to admit it, it appears dukes can, on occasion, achieve remarkable ends," Callie said.

Jeremy grinned. "She still won't marry me."

"No, I won't." She leaned against his side. "Isn't it enough to know I adore you?"

Ivy's eyebrows arched, but she said nothing.

"What's going to happen to Mr. Taylor's excavation?" Kat asked. She'd been hanging back from the rest of us, keen to continue avoiding her father — she had not spoken to him since we'd returned from Herculaneum — but was having trouble keeping away. The bracelets, if nothing else, were hard to ignore. "Has anything been decided?"

"Unfortunately, as a result of his crime, we've been shut down," Callie said. "Pais rescinded our permit. Through some incomprehensible loophole, the property is going to revert to the previous owner — the man who runs the Hôtel Suisse. I am hoping to persuade him to continue our work, but at the moment he does not have the funds to do so."

"What a loss," I said. "Is there nothing else that can be done?"

"Not at present," she said. "We are going to rebury what we've already excavated, so that it's protected from the elements and give him copies of all of our records so that when, eventually, work recommences, he won't start with nothing."

"And what will you do in the meantime?" Kat asked.

"Perhaps you should find a wealthy aristocrat in possession of more money than sense who could fund a dig of his own," Jeremy said.

"I appreciate the gesture, but must refuse," Callie said. "I'll find another position on my own merits. I don't deserve more than that."

Benjamin, who had sat quietly through all this, finally spoke. "I'm afraid I don't share Callie's scruples. I'm accepting the duke's patronage."

"He wasn't easy to convince," Jeremy said, "but you know how relentless I can be. Won't it be a jolly good lark, my being a patron of the arts? Carter can traipse about the Continent painting whatever he wants and I will happily foot the bill — no matter how expensive it proves to be — showing myself, once again, utterly profligate."

"I'm not convinced *profligate* is the correct word," Colin said. "Regardless, I suspect your association with Carter will prove fruitful. If nothing else, you could announce that you plan to get rid of all those Old Masters covering the walls of Bainbridge House in favor of controversial modern landscapes."

"Now, that, Hargreaves would make a pretty scandal," Jeremy said. "I'm indebted to you for the suggestion."

Before we said good-bye to Pompeii, I made one more trip to the tunnels beneath Herculaneum. With Colin by my side, I returned to that fateful room in the Villa dei Papiri. He cleaned the bloodstains from the mosaic while I wrapped the skeletal remains in a simple silk shroud before transferring them to an archival box. Someday, I hoped, we would be able to read the contents of the scroll she had died holding, but for now, I slipped into the box a new one, on which I had written the story of how I came to find her, how the dagger she had possessed nearly two thousand years ago had saved my life, and where her scrolls and jewelry could now be found. Perhaps, someday, far in the future, new excavators will come to Herculaneum and uncover the city buried deep beneath solid volcanic rock. No doubt they will despise us for having taken the jewelry and the scrolls from their original resting place, but sometimes, the human connection transcends the quest for information. The Kings of Naples likely justified their own thefts in a similar manner.

The next morning, Kat asked to speak with me privately.

"I should thank you for not telling anyone that I lied about being attacked," she said.

"Your father ought to know the truth, but it needs to come from you."

"I'm sorry. I shouldn't have lied, but I am grateful that you did not feed me to the wolves. Thank you. I've done nothing to deserve your kindness."

"Part of belonging to a family is being treated with love even when we're at our worst," I said. "Sometimes that takes the form of kindness."

"Oh, Lady Emily, I can be much, much worse." Her tone revealed a mixture of pride and just a bit of shame.

"I hope I never see it."

Soon thereafter, she decided to stop pouting and asked if we might take a short pleasure cruise on the bay. Colin agreed so readily it was obvious to me that she would soon realize she could manipulate him into almost anything. But she did confess to her lie and he showed no leniency in his reaction. Nonetheless, by the time the sun was setting and our boat approached the shore, she had agreed to come to England.

"I know it won't be easy," Colin said, after we'd retired to our room that evening. "Don't think, Emily, that I'm unaware of how she's treated you. It won't be tolerated at home."

"Why was it tolerated at all?" I asked.

He was pacing while I sat on the bed, propped up against a mountain of pillows. "Guilt, cowardice, general incompetence."

"None of those words could ever apply to you."

He stopped pacing and leaned against the wall, crossing his arms. "I've behaved abominably. She took me by surprise and disturbed emotions I'd thought buried forever. I didn't want to drive her away. Can you forgive me?"

"You might be able to persuade me. Cleopatra forgave Antony of worse, but, then, he did have that Roman general's kit. Irresistible, I imagine."

"If I have to don leather skirts and a

cuirass and grovel before you, I shall."

"Is that so?" A delicious tingling warmth made its way from the tips of my toes to the top of my head. "I just happen to have a costume of that description ready and waiting for you. I had it made in Naples before Ivy's banquet. I never much liked the idea of a synthesis. Shall I fetch it?"

"Not now. If you're to be my Cleopatra, I'm going to fill our room with rose petals and get you an obscenely large pearl that I won't allow you to dissolve in wine. Tonight, you'll have to content yourself with a disappointing Englishman rather than a Roman general."

"That Englishman has never disappointed me." I held my hand out to him and he came to me, kissing it, relief relaxing his handsome features. Forgiving him was never difficult, but even as he lowered himself on top of me, whispering words of love, I felt the tug of distraction. I heard footsteps. Was someone outside our room?

"Father?" Kat was knocking and called through the door. "I'm having trouble fitting all my photography supplies in my trunks. Could you help?"

"I'm asleep, Katarina," Colin said. "Tomorrow. We will sort it out tomorrow."

"If you could just come now —"

"Tomorrow."

Perhaps the lot of us ensconced en famille wouldn't be so bad as I had feared.

AUTHOR'S NOTE

Pompeii and Herculaneum have fascinated me since I read an article about the city in *National Geographic* when I was a child. There's no better window into the daily life of ancient Romans than the ruins at these sites. As I researched the history and the archaeology of the site — a process that took years, and would merit a lifetime — I was surprised by how much our understanding of the eruption has changed over the centuries. Until groups of skeletons were discovered in Herculaneum in the 1980s, very few human remains had been found there. These people, who sought shelter in boat chambers near the port, gave us a significant insight into how different the impact of Vesuvius's eruption was on the two cities. While Pompeii was buried in pumice and ash, Herculaneum was destroyed by pyroclastic flow (a fast-moving mass of ash, rock particles, and gas), after a long day during which ash — but very little pumice — fell. Hot gas, reaching temperatures above 900 degrees Fahrenheit, instantly killed the population. Examination of their skeletons showed that they did not even have time to pull themselves into protective postures. Until these discoveries, the common belief was that most of the people in Herculaneum had fled in time to escape death. Now, however, we know better.

Pliny the Younger (nephew of Pliny the Elder, admiral and naturalist, who died on that fateful day in AD 79 — some say in the process of trying to rescue people from the beaches) left an astonishing account of the eruption, which he watched from a villa in Misenum, across the Bay of Naples from Vesuvius. He wrote two letters to his friend Tacitus, the historian, describing the events so vividly that scientists named that type of eruption after him: Plinian. When Mt. St. Helens in Washington State erupted in 1980, witnesses saw a Plinian eruption that confirmed how accurate Pliny's description had been nearly two thousand years earlier. Before then, most had assumed the account was not precise.

Pliny's letters also gave us a date for the eruption: 24 August AD 79. Recent research suggests this is a mistake, not on Pliny's part, but on that of later scribes making copies of his work. While some manuscripts include the August date, printed fifteenth-century editions say November, and some mention no date at all. The historian Dio Cassius, writing a hundred years after Pliny, says it occurred "at the end of autumn."

Archaeologists in 2006 presented key evidence to support Dio Cassius. Grete Stefani and Michele Borgongino analyzed the food found in Pompeii, Herculaneum, and Oplontis. The cities were full of newly harvested autumn and late summer fruits (pomegranates and walnuts) and what summer produce remained had been dried (figs, dates, and prunes). In Boscoreale, Stefani found wine fermenting — a process that could not have started before the grape harvest, typically in September.

Controversy abounds, with no clear agreement as to the precise date, but most scholars now believe it occurred in October AD 79. Emily, however, wouldn't have known any of this. In the early twentieth century, the August date was accepted as fact.

The locations in my novel are all taken from specific places in the ruins. Plautus's house is the Villa of the Mysteries, outside the city walls. Although the site was not excavated until 1909, I gave it to Balthazar Taylor before then. His staff, unfortunately, did not make much progress.

Silvanus's house is modeled on the elegant, luxurious, and immense House of the Dioscuri in Region VI, first excavated in 1826. Kassandra's house is based on that of Fabius Amandius, an example of a small, middle-class dwelling. Located in Region I, its atrium was originally part of the much larger House of Paquius Proculus. It was excavated beginning in 1911.

Galen's thermopolium is borrowed from the Thermopolium of Asellina, across the street from the House of Fabius Amandius. The election graffito Kassandra reads is what still remains on the walls there. We don't know whether Maria was, in fact, politically active. Lots of political graffiti in Pompeii was sponsored by women, despite the fact that they could not vote.

The graffito Emily finds in the basilica is not fictional.

The astonishingly well-preserved caupona that Emily and Colin visit with Mr. Stirling in Herculaneum stands next to the House of Neptune and Amphitrite. In fact, neither it nor the house was excavated until the early 1930s, but I couldn't bear for them not to see it. Thank goodness for fiction.

I have depicted the tunnels in Herculaneum as more accessible than they actually are. The Bourbon excavators filled many of them in after they'd finished plundering their treasure. Today, visitors to the site don't have to navigate tunnels at all, but most of the ruins still lie undisturbed beneath the modern city of Ercolano. Excavation there is difficult, because the residents do not want their homes impacted. The mayor made the unpopular decision to have the town purchase several buildings on the edge of the site, beneath which archaeologists found a section of the Forum, untouched since antiquity. Even the promise of treasure has not changed the current population's feelings about the work, and it is unlikely that much new ground will be broken in the immediate future. The Camorra, still a force to be reckoned with in Campania, isn't eager for more excavation either. A few weeks before I visited, archaeologists uncovered a cache of weapons the Camorra had buried within the ruins.

There is, however, new hope for the contents of the library at Herculaneum's Villa dei Papyri. American researcher Brent Seales has recently developed a technique that uses medical imaging technology to reconstruct the text of the scrolls without unrolling them. He's proved the concept, and in 2019 after receiving grants from the National Endowment for the Humanties and the Andrew W. Mellon Foundation, now has the funding to continue his work. He's managed to gain access to the scrolls, and we may, at last, be able to read a treasure trove of previously lost ancient works.

Region V, largely unexcavated in Emily's day, is the site of new work at Pompeii today. Current digging has revealed extraordinary frescoes, skeletons that offer new glimpses into the human reaction to the eruption, an inscription that supports the theory that the event took place in the autumn, and stunning mosaics. The area is not yet open to the public, but the photographs released offer a tantalizing glimpse of what's been found.

I could not have written this book without the abundance of scholarly work done on Pompeii. My story is fiction, but I wanted to get the historical details correct. I particularly relied on Mary Beard's keen insights into Roman life found in *Pompeii: The Life of a Roman Town*. Jeremy Hartnett's phenomenal *The Roman Street: Urban Life and*

460

Society in Pompeii, Herculaneum, and Rome made the cities come alive — how they looked, how they sounded, and how it would have felt to live in them. Robert Knapp's *Invisible Romans,* an enormously important book about ordinary Romans, gives an unparalleled analysis of slaves. Robert Fagles's excellent translation of Virgil's *Aeneid* was never far from my side while I was writing. All errors are my own.

I would be remiss not to cite my sources.

Baedeker, Karl. *Southern Italy and Sicily.* Vol. 3. Italy: Handbook for Travellers. Leipzig: Karl Baedeker, 1903.

Barker, Ethel Ross. *Buried Herculaneum.* London: Adam and Charles Black, 1908.

Bayardi, Ottavio Antonio. *The Antiquities of Herculaneum.* Translated by Thomas Martyn and John Lettice. London: Printed for S. Leacroft, 1773.

Beard, Mary. *Pompeii: The Life of a Roman Town.* London: Profile Books, 2008.

Blix, Göran. *From Paris to Pompeii: French Romanticism and the Cultural Politics of Archaeology.* Philadelphia, PA: University of Pennsylvania Press, 2009.

Butterworth, Alex, and Ray Laurence. *Pompeii: The Living City.* New York: St. Martin's Press, 2006.

Ciarallo, Annamaria. *Gardens of Pompeii.* Translated by Lori-Ann Touchette. Los Angeles, CA: J. Paul Getty Museum, 2001.

Croom, Alexandra. *Roman Clothing and Fashion.* Stroud: Amberley, 2010.

———. *Running the Roman Home.* Stroud: History Press, 2011.

D'Ambra, Eve. *Roman Women.* Cambridge: Cambridge University Press, 2007.

De Caro, Stefano. "Excavation and Conservation at Pompeii: A Conflicted History." *The Journal of Fasti Online: Archaeological Conservation Series,* 2014.

Dobbins, John J., and Pedar W. Foss, eds. *The World of Pompeii.* London: Routledge, 2008.

Epicurus. *The Art of Happiness.* Translated by George K. Strodach. London: Penguin Classics, 2013.

Giacosa, Ilaria Gozzini. *A Taste of Ancient Rome.* Translated by Anna Herklotz. Chicago, IL: University of Chicago Press, 1992.

Grant, Michael. *Cities of Vesuvius: Pompeii & Herculaneum.* London: Folio Society, 2005.

Hales, Shelley, and Joanna Paul. *Pompeii in the Public Imagination from its Rediscovery to Today.* Oxford: Oxford University Press, 2011.

Hamilton, Edith. *The Roman Way.* New York: W. W. Norton & Company, 2017.

———. *The Greek Way.* New York: W. W. Norton & Company, 2017.

Hartnett, Jeremy. *The Roman Street: Urban Life in Pompeii, Herculaneum, and Rome.* Cambridge: Cambridge University Press, 2017.

Houston, George W. *Inside Roman Libraries: Book Collections and Their Management in Antiquity.* Chapel Hill, NC: University of North Carolina Press, 2017.

Janko, R. "The Herculaneum Library: Some Recent Developments." *Estudios Clásicos* 44, no. 121 (2002): 25–42.

Knapp, Robert C. *Invisible Romans.* Cambridge, MA: Harvard University Press, 2011.

Lefkowitz, Mary R., and Maureen B. Fant. *Women's Life in Greece and Rome: A Source Book in Translation.* 4th ed. Baltimore, MD: John Hopkins University Press, 2016.

Lobell, Jarrett A. "Saving the Villa of the Mysteries." *Archaeology* 67, no. 2 (March 2014).

MacLachlan, Bonnie. *Women in Ancient Rome: A Sourcebook.* London: Bloomsbury, 2013.

Mastrolorenzo, Giuseppe, Pier P. Petrone, Mario Pagano, Alberto Incoronato, Peter J. Baxter, Antonio Canzanella, and Luciano Fattore. "Herculaneum Victims of Vesuvius in AD 79." *Nature* 410, no. 6830 (2001): 769–70.

Mattusch, Carol C. *Pompeii and the Roman Villa: Art and Culture Around the Bay of Naples.* London: Thames & Hudson, 2009.

Mau, August. *Pompeii: Its Life and Art.* London: Macmillan, 1902.

Niccolini, Fausto, and Felice Niccolini. *Houses and Monuments of Pompeii.* Taschen, 2016.

Ovid. *The Love Poems.* Translated by A. D. Melville. Oxford World's Classics. Oxford: Oxford University Press, 2008.

Panetta, Marisa Ranieri, ed. *Pompeii: The History, Life and Art of the Buried City.* Vercelli: White Star Publishers, 2012.

Petronius. *The Satyricon.* Translated by J. P. Sullivan. New York, NY: Penguin Books, 2011.

Pirozzi, Maria Emma Antonietta. *Herculaneum: The Excavations, Local History and Surroundings.* Napoli: Electa Napoli, 2003.

Pomeroy, Sarah B. *Goddesses, Whores,*

Wives and Slaves: Women in Classical Antiquity. New York: Schocken Books, 2015.

Rowland, Ingrid D. *From Pompeii: The Afterlife of a Roman Town.* Cambridge, MA: Belknap Press of Harvard University Press, 2014.

Shelton, Jo-Ann. *As the Romans Did: A Sourcebook in Roman Social History.* Oxford: Oxford University Press, 1988.

Sider, David. *The Library of the Villa Dei Papiri at Herculaneum.* Los Angeles: J. Paul Getty Museum, 2005.

Virgil. *The Aeneid.* Translated by Robert Fagles. New York, NY: Penguin Books, 2008.

von Goethe, Johann Wolfgang. *The Collected Works: Italian Journey.* Edited by Thomas P. Saine and Jeffrey L. Sammons. Translated by Robert R. Heitner. Vol. 6. Princeton, NJ: Princeton University Press.

Waldstein, Charles, and Leonard Shoobridge. *Herculaneum Past Present & Future.* London: Macmillan, 1908.

Wollner, Jennifer L. "Planning Preservation in Pompeii: Revising Wall Painting Conservation Method and Management." *Studies in Mediterranean Antiquity and Classics* 3, no. 1 (September 5, 2013).

ABOUT THE AUTHOR

Tasha Alexander, the daughter of two philosophy professors, studied English Literature and Medieval History at the University of Notre Dame. She and her husband, novelist Andrew Grant, live on a ranch in southeastern Wyoming.

The employees of Thorndike Press hope you have enjoyed this Large Print book. All our Thorndike, Wheeler, and Kennebec Large Print titles are designed for easy reading, and all our books are made to last. Other Thorndike Press Large Print books are available at your library, through selected bookstores, or directly from us.

For information about titles, please call:
  (800) 223-1244

or visit our website at:
  gale.com/thorndike

To share your comments, please write:
  Publisher
  Thorndike Press
  10 Water St., Suite 310
  Waterville, ME 04901

8320